Hard Bit Men

A Heck & Early Western

Robert Peecher

For information the author may be contacted at

PO Box 967; Watkinsville GA; 30677

or at mooncalfpress.com

This is a work of fiction. Any similarities to actual events in whole or in part are purely accidental. None of the characters or events depicted in this novel are intended to represent actual people.

FOR JEAN

XO

José Tejada tossed a rolled newspaper into Hector Espinoza's lap and grumbled angrily, "You find jobs in there."

"Find what?" Heck asked, picking up the newspaper.

Heck was sitting in one of the rocking chairs on the front porch of José Tejada's boarding house where Heck and his partner Early Bascomb both rented rooms. Early occupied the other rocking chair. Early had his hat down over his face, but the gentle back and forth motion of the rocking chair suggested he was not yet entirely asleep.

"Open it," José said in his thick accent. "Is for you. And for him. Jobs for the both of you."

Heck opened up the newspaper and scanned the page in front of him. The newspaper was out of the territorial capital of Santa Fe.

"What am I supposed to see here, Señor Tejada?"

"You owe me for two months, and Señor Early, he owe me for one month. Today is Tuesday. Friday is the first of the month, and then it will be three months for you, and two months for him."

Heck shifted uncomfortably.

"Yes, sir. I talked to Mrs. Tejada, and I explained –"

"You always explain," José Tejada said. "You go to Maria, you explain to her. She tell me, you no have rent money but you full of explaining. I no want explaining any more, Señor Espinoza. I want rent money."

José Tejada pounded his index finger into his open palm to emphasize his anger, but the gesture was unnecessary. The man's face had turned beet red. Heck looked back at the newspaper.

"And what's this?" he asked.

"There is job. Job for both of you. You go and take the job, and then you pay your rent."

Heck scanned the paper, but he didn't see anything about a job.

"Right here," José Tejada said, and he jabbed a finger at the paper.

Early Bascomb, hearing the conversation, had lifted up his hat and was watching Heck through one eye.

"'Town marshal wanted,'" Heck read from the boxed advertisement at the bottom of the page. It was just a small, single column advertisement. "'Good man wanted to clean up rough town. Apply in person.'"

Heck chuckled.

"Señor Tejada, if I didn't know better, I'd say you was trying to get rid of us," Heck said. "Why, this is a job up in the mountains."

"I know where job is," Tejada said. "I trying to get

rent paid."

Heck glanced over at Early, and Early gave him a small shrug. Heck turned back to the newspaper and continued to read. "'Twenty dollars a month for a marshal and his deputy. Marshal must provide his own deputy, and his own guns. Ammunition, room and board will be provided by the town council. One hundred dollar signing bonus.'"

"Si!" Tejada exclaimed. "One hundred dollars! You go and take jobs, and you pay rent."

"We ain't lawmen," Early Bascomb said, and he dropped the hat back over his face and resumed the gentle rocking.

"You pay rent Friday morning – all of what you owe – or you move out Friday afternoon."

José Tejada slammed the front door of the boarding house behind him as he stormed inside, leaving the newspaper in Heck's hands.

"You got three months' rent?" Heck said.

"I only owe two months," Early said, his voice muffled from behind his hat.

"No, hombre, that ain't what I'm asking," Heck said. "I'm asking if you've got three months' rent I can borrow from you."

Early chuckled.

"I don't have two months' rent I can pay for myself," Early said.

"Huh," Heck grunted. He sat for a moment looking at the advertisement. "You ever considered hiring on as a deputy marshal?"

Now Early sat up, plucking the hat from his face and propping it on his head. He leaned forward on the edge of the chair, looking directly at Heck Espinoza.

"Look here, Heck Pinoza," Early said, his voice full of Southern drawl. "I ain't never once considered pinning a badge on my chest, and I ain't going to consider it now. But if I was to entertain a career in the constabulary, I can tell you for a fact I ain't going to be no deputy to nobody."

Heck chuckled.

"So you'll apply for the marshal's job, and I'll be your deputy?" he said.

Early shrugged his shoulders.

"If we were going to be lawmen, that's how it would have to be. I'm the marshal and you're the deputy, amigo."

Heck looked at the newspaper again and read through the advertisement.

"So is that what you want to do? You want to ride out west and be a town marshal?"

Early squinted at the thoroughfare running in front of the boarding house.

"I don't think so, partner. What we need to do is put our minds to scaring up some money around here."

Heck took off his hat and hung it from his knee. He ran the sleeve of his shirt over his forehead and then rubbed his eyes.

"I hear they're hiring hands at the Hixon place to drive cattle into Kansas," Heck said. "How's that suit you?"

Early grunted.

"I'll pin on a badge before I drive cattle."

"All I know for sure is we'd better come up with some rent money from somewhere, or we'll be sleeping in the stable."

"I've slept in worse places," Early said.

"What's your opposition to wearing a badge?"

Early rapped out a drumbeat on his knee and then stood up and paced some along the boards of the porch, his boots sounding heavy on the planks.

"I'm a free man, Heck Pinoza. I have a philosophical aversion to the white man's laws."

"The white man's laws?" Heck chuckled.

"All of them – white men, Mexican men, red men – I have a philosophical aversion to laws, generally. I don't like to be corralled by laws, and it would be the height of hypocrisy for me to pin on a badge and start enforcing the laws of the white man."

"And yet, your primary way of earning a living is bringing in people who are wanted for breaking the white man's laws," Heck said.

Early shrugged. "Everybody's got to earn a living."

Heck shook his head.

"It sounds to me like you'd better be the deputy, white man, and I'll be the marshal."

"Ha! And then I'll have you telling me what to do. That don't set no better."

Heck sighed and returned his hat to his head.

"Well, partner, I'll tell you what – we need jobs. We

owe Señor Tejada and his wife money, and not paying the man what we owe is what doesn't set right with me. So unless you've got a better idea of how we can get money in a hurry to pay the man what we owe him, I think we should ride up to the mountains and have a look around this town. Marshalling is just exactly the sort of job that suits our skills, and this here newspaper says there's a hundred-dollar bonus just for showing up and taking the badge. We could pay off Señor Tejada and work for a couple of months, and if we don't like it, we can move on."

Early frowned at Heck.

"A hundred-dollar bonus just for showing up? That alone should be enough to warn us away from it. They're not paying that kind of money as a bonus unless they've got some serious problems up there, Hector."

Heck shrugged.

"Maybe that's right. So it's back to the Hixon ranch to drive cattle."

"We need a way to come up with a way to get some money that don't involve any sort of difficult labor," Early said. "Driving cattle is back breaking work. You're talking about saddle sores and early mornings and hard riding and pulling cattle out of mud and all manner of unpleasantness. I need a hundred dollar signing bonus for holding down this rocking chair right here."

Heck shook his head.

"Okay. No marshal job. And we won't sign on with Hixon to be drovers. But if the sheriff don't hang a wanted poster before Friday, we're going to be sleeping on the straw at the livery."

About an hour later, Sheriff Frank Calvo and two of

his deputies rode up and dragged reins there in front of the boarding house.

"Hola, boys," Calvo said. Like a lot of the locals, Calvo was born to parents who were citizens of Mexico in '53, and after la Venta de la Mesilla suddenly found themselves citizens of a territory of the United States. His English was peppered with Spanish words, and his seldom-practiced Spanish was just what he remembered his parents speaking at him when he was young. Heck was no different. His grandparents had been citizens of Spain. His parents, Mexican. And he'd never known anything other than the United States territorial government.

"How do you do, Sheriff," Early said convivially. "Heck and I was just talking about whether or not we ought to pin on badges and become lawmen."

"Were you?" Calvo said.

"What are your thoughts, Sheriff? Do you think we'd do all right?"

Calvo frowned and shook his head doubtfully.

"I don't know, boys. But I ain't hiring, if that's what you're thinking."

"We're thinking about going west, taking a job as marshals in some mountain town," Early said.

Calvo eyed Heck Espinoza.

"He'd do all right as a marshal," Calvo said to Early. "But I don't think you'd make a very good lawman."

"Why's that?" Early asked with a laugh.

"You don't got the right disposition for law work, Early. You're too casual."

"You hear that, Heck?" Early said. "Too casual."

"But I like the idea of you boys leaving town for a while," Calvo said, and he said it without a hint of mirth, drawing the attention of both men in their rocking chairs.

"Why is that?" Heck asked.

"You remember when you brought Johnny Thorpe in?"

Of course Heck remembered. Johnny Thorpe was a local bad man. He held up stagecoaches and stole horses and anything else he could get his hands on. Mostly, Heck and Early made their money recovering wanted men. They'd traveled all over the territory doing their work, but Sheriff Calvo was their most common customer. He was always glad to pay the two of them twenty dollars to bring in a wanted man. A few weeks back, they'd collected the bounty on Johnny Thorpe. In the process, Heck had to shoot and kill Johnny's brother Ben.

"Johnny went to trial today, and the jury said he was not guilty. Half of the men on the jury was his cousins, but never mind that. What's important for you boys to know is that Johnny's loose and feeling emboldened. The word is he's planning to come looking for the two of you for what you done to his brother."

"Hell, I wasn't even there when Heck shot his brother," Early said. "Why's he looking for me?"

"Everybody knows the two of you are partners," Calvo said. "What one of you does, the other one does."

"Dadgumit," Early complained, staring hard at Heck. "Why'd you have to shoot Ben? He was the only one of those Thorpes that was worth anything."

"He was pointing a scattergun at me when I shot

him," Heck said.

Calvo's horse, a big white gelding, started getting restless and danced a jig there in the street. Calvo swung the reins to get him straightened back out.

"Do what you want," the sheriff said. "I'm just giving you a warning. There's a good chance Johnny's going to come looking for you the next time he puts on a drunk, and I expect – knowing the Thorpes – he'll be along with some number of his cousins. If you're thinking of leaving town for a while, I wouldn't try to talk you out of it."

"Huh," Early grunted, and he folded his arms and leaned back in the rocking chair.

"Obliged for the warning, Sheriff," Heck said. "We'll watch our backs."

"That's the direction he'll come from," Calvo said, and his tone betrayed his disgust for Johnny Thorpe.

***

Junior Thorpe staggered along the boardwalk across from the boarding house. By the sway of his walk, Heck and Early both judged he was drunk, which was Junior's usual state.

"You see this?" Early muttered.

"Uh-huh," Heck grunted.

"Johnny Thorpe's cousin, Junior," Early said unnecessarily.

"Can you tell if he's heeled?" Heck asked.

From under the brim of his hat, Early squinted at

Junior's hip. His gun hand was away from them, but Early thought he could see a strap across his thigh where a holster might be.

"I believe so," Early said.

"Hell, if Junior Thorpe is across the street, that probably means that Johnny is –"

But Heck didn't have an opportunity to finish the sentence. A clattering at the side of the boarding house had both Heck and Early spinning in their chairs, and there was Johnny Thorpe, coming around the side of the boarding house right behind the two barrels of a scattergun.

"Hell on you, Heck Pinoza!" Johnny Thorpe shouted.

"Get down!" Heck yelled as he threw himself off the porch and into the dirt of the thoroughfare. Early spun himself out of the rocking chair into a crouch and then grabbed the thing and swung it in front of him like a breastwork just as Johnny Thorpe let loose with both barrels.

The shot tore hell out of Early's rocking chair, and a splinter shot across his cheek and tore a gash that commenced to bleeding right away.

"Carajo!" Heck cursed as he scrambled to his feet and reached for the Colt Peacemaker on his hip.

Johnny disappeared around the side of the boarding house, and Heck started to give chase, but across the street Junior Thorpe had given up his swaying and drawn out a six-shooter from his holster. He fired off four or five shots. One busted out a window on the boarding house, the others lodged harmlessly into the boards of the front of the building.

Early drew his Colt and took aim at Junior, but the man was fast to start running, and even as Early watched, Justin Thorpe came riding up with a spare horse. Junior mounted, and the two rode off. Heck rounded the side of the boarding house but immediately holstered his gun. He turned back to Early.

"Riding off," Heck reported. "Had a horse waiting on him."

He narrowed his eyes at the blood on Early's cheek. "Are you shot?"

Early reached up to his face and wiped away blood. His cheek stung, but he knew he wasn't hit bad.

"I'm all right," he said. "What about you?"

Heck now bent down and looked at his leg. He drew out his knife and plucked a lead shot that had embedded in the leather of his boot.

"That's going to bruise," Heck said. But then he examined his boot closer and let loose a string of oaths. Early stepped nearer to see what had angered him so and watched as Heck plucked the loose heel off his boot. "Ruined a good pair of boots."

"Be glad that's the worst he did," Early said. "That was Ben's boy, Justin that rode up with the horse for Junior."

"Was it?" Heck said. "Well, I'm glad that boy's able to ride. Last I saw him, his mama shot him in the hip with a big ol' Colt Dragoon when she was trying to shoot me."

"He appears to be recovered," Early said.

Just then, a commotion from inside the house announced the appearance of José Tejada, the landlord. Tejada was in a rage, pointing at the broken window.

"Who did this?" he demanded. "Who shoot my house? That is it! You two are out. Get your things and go! Right now!"

Maria Tejada appeared at her husband's side, placing calming hands on him, but he would not be calmed.

"Out! Out of my house!"

Heck and Early exchanged a resigned glance. They weren't in much position to argue with the man, considering they owed him back rent.

"We'll get you the money we owe you, Señor Tejada," Heck said, stepping past the older couple and into the boarding house.

"You just get out!" Tejada shouted in his face.

On the stairs leading up to their rooms, Heck and Early could still hear the man complaining – in Spanish now – to his wife about the broken window and the damage to the front of the boarding house.

"Hey, partner," Early said.

"Yeah?"

"What did you say was the name of that town that's looking for a marshal?"

"Mogollon. It's a mining town in the Sierra Diablo."

"Sierra Diablo? The Devil's Mountains?"

"That's right," Heck said.

"How long do you reckon it would take for us to get there?"

Heck shrugged. "Maybe a week."

"Huh," Early said. "We'd probably better get started

if we're going to be the first ones applying for those jobs. If we're lucky, Johnny Thorpe will shoot us before we hire on."

"You really don't want to be a lawman. Do you, Early?"

- 2 -

"Pronounce it for me again," Early said.

The buckskin stallion Early called Tim Buck Too was now at an easy walk, his hooves falling with a rhythmic clop-clop that nearly lulled Early to sleep. Heck was just behind him on Poco a Poco, his pinto gelding.

"Muggyown."

"But it's spelled m-o-g-o-l-l-o-n?"

"That's how it's spelled."

"Muggyown," Early said. "Is it an Apache word? What's it mean?"

"Spanish," Heck said. "The town is named for a territorial governor when this was part of Spain."

"They should call it Lew Wallace Town," Early said. "Why name it for a Spanish governor?"

"Sheldon Town," Heck corrected him. "Lew Wallace ain't the governor any more. Lionel Sheldon is the governor of the territory now."

"When did that happen?" Early asked.

"A few months ago, hombre. You really should pay more attention."

"Everybody in Santa Fe is corrupt anyway," Early said. "What difference does it make to me if it's Lew Wallace or Lionel Sheldon?"

They were twelve days on the trail now, riding through a dramatically changing landscape in the southern part of the territory, and they'd run out of things to talk about. They'd made the Black Range a couple of days ago and had spent all of this and the previous day riding a precipitous trail through the mountains. Ruts in the road suggested wagon trains and a stagecoach passed this way with some regularity, but it seemed an unlikely place to try to drive a thing on wheels. Above them, a steep slope rose off their right shoulders, covered in a thick forest of ponderosa pines that stood like thousands of masts, replaced only by the occasional rock cliff. Below them, to their left, the mountain dropped away, but the abrupt drop was masked by the tops of the big pines rising up from the slope. But then they came to a place where the trail ran above a rock face, and the pines no longer blocked the view. Early edged the stallion to the left a touch more to get a look down the sheer drop, but Heck gave Poco a touch with his left knee to get the horse to step closer to the solid ground rising off his right shoulder. When Heck was satisfied that they were not too close to the ledge, he pulled back on Poco's reins.

Early gave a tug to Tim's reins and brought the buckskin to a stop.

"What's up, amigo?" Early said.

"Have you ever seen a more glorious sight?" Heck asked, his eyes sweeping the rolling mountains that spread out before them, far into the distance.

Early frowned at the view. Brown mountains layered in a carpet of ponderosa pine and juniper, with scattered hardwoods dotting the darker greens of the pines. The air here smelled of pine. It was a clean, fresh air here in the mountains. The only reliable trees at home were down in the bosque where the river and the cattle gave the trees a thick, wet odor. Otherwise, at home, everything was dry and dusty. Even the grass seemed to have a layer of dust, and there was certainly no smell of pine. Early liked this air. He liked it even better than the air back in Mississippi where he grew up. Everything there was constantly wet – rivers and summer thunderstorms and winter downpours and humidity that made even the air wet.

But for a mountain vista, Early had seen the Ozarks and the high Rockies – places that Heck Espinoza had never visited – and Early knew the Black Range of the Gila Mountains offered a poor comparison to some of those views.

"I've seen better," Early said.

"Huh," Heck grunted. "Well, I haven't. It's beautiful here. I could live here."

"It's a good thing, considering you're going to be a

deputy marshal."

"I thought we decided you'd be the deputy," Heck joked.

Early took in the view a moment longer before he gave Tim a touch with his knee and got the stallion moving again, but Heck sat a while longer. He'd been to the foothills, and seen the mountains over Las Vegas, but he'd never before been deep within a mountain range and seen views as spectacular as this. He was enchanted by the trees, the rock faces and the formations. A creek bed snaked in the valley below, and in a wide clearing, there was small camp of tents. Heck could see how the road ahead wound its way along the mountainside, descending lower until it dropped out near the camp.

"Timber camp down below," Heck called to Early, who was almost around a bend on the road. "Might be a good place to camp for the night."

"Get some supper," Early suggested.

"That's my thinking."

Heck gave Poco a tap on his rump with the long tail of the reins. The pinto gelding was as calm a horse as Heck had ever encountered. He didn't spook much, didn't rile much, and he preferred an easy walk to just about everything except for standing still. When called upon, Poco a Poco could lope for days, even if he didn't like it. There was no pointing in a lope now, and the horses had been on the trail for the better part of a week. So both riders took it easy to spare the horses. As such, it was coming onto dusk when they at last rode down into the valley.

Their appearance immediately caught the attention of several men working the timber claim, and one man, shirtless and covered in a sweat, stepped forward from what appeared to be a hastily-constructed sawmill.

"Evening," the man called out.

"Howdy," Early said, raising up a hand in greeting. "You wouldn't mind if we bedded down here for the night, would you?"

"Be glad to have you," the man said, plucking a shirt from a pile of lumber and pulling it over his head. "You boys riding up to Muggyown?"

"How'd you know that?" Early asked.

"Nowhere else up here for you to be going," the man laughed. "Unless you're looking to help us fell timber, here."

Heck and Early dismounted and tied their horses to a tree branch. Those men standing nearby introduced themselves, as did the one who'd come forward to greet them, but nobody much paid any attention as the introductions were made. Heck and Early did catch the name of the man who seemed to be in charge – Stan Davis – and it was Davis who called to the cook and told him they'd have guests for supper.

"He won't make it any better just because we're having guests, but maybe there'll be more of it."

The beans lacked much flavor, and the bacon was cut too thick and cooked too little. Heck Espinoza cleaned his plate, and Early took a second helping of the beans but didn't touch the bacon.

"Our cook ain't much of a cook," Davis confided as the men sat around the campfire in the last remnants of dusk. "He worked the saw before he cut off two more fingers, and now all he can do is stir a pot of beans."

"We're grateful for it, all the same," Heck said. "It's been mighty meager eatin' on the trail."

"So, you boys is headin' up to Muggyown, huh?" Davis asked.

"That's our plan," Early said. "Is it hard to find from here?"

"This canyon we're in is Silver Creek Canyon," Davis said. "You can't miss Muggyown if you keep riding west through the canyon. It gets mighty narrow, and the town sets down on the floor of the canyon right alongside the creek."

"How far?" Heck asked.

"If you're a bird, it ain't far a'tall. But if you're following the trail, you'll have to twist and turn with the creek, and it's about five or six miles, but them's some twisty and turny miles. Might take the better part of two hours to get there from here."

"You sell most of your timber to the town?" Heck asked.

"The town or the mines. We do most of our business with the Little Fannie Mine or the Three Sweethearts Mine. Those are the big ones. There's probably five or six other mines within about eight or nine miles of Muggyown, but the Little Fannie and Three Sweethearts are the big uns. We sell a little bit of timber to the folks in Muggyown, but they come here to buy. Personally, I don't go into Muggyown. Where you boys from?"

"Down southeast of here, a little town not far from the Rio Grande," Heck said.

"It's called Mesilla," Early said.

"I've heard of Mesilla, but I ain't never been there."

"You haven't missed much," Early said. "If you've seen one little town in this territory, you've just about seen them all."

"You ain't seen none like Muggyown," Davis said.

"Is that right?" Heck asked, prompting him to share more information.

"I don't see no pans or shovels among your gear, so I don't reckon the two of you for miners," Davis said. "And if you ain't miners and you're bound for Muggyown, that means either you're gamblers or road agents or hired killers or some combination thereof."

Early gave Heck a glance, and the two men frowned at each other.

"We ain't none of those things," Heck said.

Davis chuckled.

"Well, you'd better figure out which you want to be if you're determined to stay for any length of time in Muggyown. I won't let anyone from crew go to town. Not for anything other than supplies. And I'd rather they head the eighty miles to Silver City than to step foot in Muggyown."

"It's that rough a place, is it?"

"It's a rough place, all right," Davis said with a knowing grin. "Let me tell you how bad it is in Muggyown. If you walk away from a card game with just the holes the good Lord put in you, then you can count yourself a winner no matter how much money you lost. When the stagecoach leaves out of there, the driver throws on a mask and holds it up his own self."

Davis drew a laugh from a couple of the other timber men.

"They ain't got no law there, but that's just fine cause they ain't got no lawmen, neither. I'm joking around about the place, but in I'd bet it's a fact that they have at least one stabbing a week."

"Huh," Early grunted. "I hear they're hiring a marshal."

Now the timber men acted like it was Early who told the joke as several of them started to chuckle.

"They already done that," Davis said.

"They hired a marshal?" Heck asked.

"About two weeks ago they hired a couple of men who come to answer a newspaper advertisement. The new marshal was the stabbing that week."

"They killed him?" Early said.

"Didn't kill him," Davis said. "But his deputy stitched him up and put him on a horse, and the two of them rode through here the next day. Hired on a Monday, quit on a Tuesday."

Heck and Early exchanged another glance, and in the firelight, Heck could see the disgust on Early's face. He could almost read Early's mind, and right now Early Bascomb was more than a little frustrated.

"Hang on, now," Davis said. "You two boys ain't looking to hire on as the town marshal, are you?"

"Well," Heck said.

"Oh my Lord," Davis said, and he gave an incredulous look to the men of his crew. "No you boys ain't! I feel obliged to try to warn you off of that notion. You don't want to pin on a badge in Muggyown. Not if you boys like being topside of the ground."

"We've come a long way to take the jobs at the marshal's office," Heck said.

"Then I hope you're a couple of hard bit men, harder than you look anyhow, 'cause a man with a badge in Muggyown is going to have to be hard bit."

- 3 -

Silver Creek flowed year round, cutting a narrow ditch with tall banks down through the floor of the canyon. In places, the canyon floor spread wide enough for Heck Espinoza to imagine a little cabin, a kitchen garden, and maybe a few cattle.

"I could see settling down here," he said off-handedly to Early.

"It's a pretty place, but this ain't nowhere to settle down," Early said. "Not unless you reach down in that creek and find a handful of gold in the bottom."

"Why not?" Heck asked. "It's pleasant here."

"Snow in the winter, floods in the spring. Besides, you ain't close to nothing up here. Silver City's a two day ride, it's probably eight or nine days to Santa Fe, and it's almost a week back to Mesilla. And remember what Stan Davis said about the Apache."

After warning Heck and Early away from the marshal job, Stan Davis spent the rest of the evening talking about the Apache raids at Mogollon and the times a band of Apache attacked the timber camp. Victorio. Davis spoke the name like a curse. Heck and Early both knew of Victorio and the war he was waging against those he considered to be intruders on his people's land, but neither of them realized that these were the mountains where Victorio made his raids.

The canyon narrowed as they approached the little town of Mogollon, and in places it became difficult to believe that a single cabin could occupy the narrow canyon, much less a town.

The first indication that they were nearing the town came from the sound of music, muffled by distance and the trees and the hills, but growing louder as they approached. The two riders rounded a curve in the canyon, and up ahead they could see the source of the music. Outside a large walled structure with a canvas roof, a half-dozen men were playing fiddles and guitars, and one man was blowing into a jug, and they were singing some sort of lively tune. Around them, standing or seated on logs or boxes or crates, there must have been a score of men and women. Two women, hardly wearing more than the dresses they were born in, kicked up their heels – maybe for the enjoyment of the men around, but they seemed to be enjoying themselves plenty. Every soul outside the place had a tin cup or a bottle from which they were drinking heartily, and the merry bunch paid no heed at all to the two new arrivals.

The structure, which they assumed was some sort of cantina, sat on a wide ledge overlooking Silver Creek and the trail that ran beside it, and the festivities were taking part in the side yard of the tent saloon.

"Is this Muggyown?" Early called up to the crowd.

A couple of men turned and gave him a hard stare but did not respond. One of the dancing women, a red-head with pale skin who wore only her underclothes, and barely kept everything within, stopped her dancing and laughed gleefully.

"What else would it be?" she asked.

"Fair point," Early said, and he touched the brim of his hat.

Early twisted in his saddle and grinned at Heck.

"I take back everything I've said, amigo," Early said. "I've got a feeling I'm going to like this place just fine."

Heck chuckled.

"Nobody's too friendly," he said.

"I'm sure they'll warm up just as soon as we pin on a couple of badges."

Now the narrow canyon started to open up a bit, and up ahead they could see where another canyon intersected this one as a second stream flowed into and joined Silver Creek. And as the canyon opened up, the two riders could now see more of the town.

Most all of the buildings sat on the north side of the creek, where the two canyons joined, though a few were tucked in against the southern canyon wall. There was a large, two-story building made of plank boards, and a sign hanging from the second-story balcony declared it to be a hotel. Another plank-board house a couple of lots down had the word "theater" painted on the front. There were a couple of other stick-built structures, and a couple under construction, but most every building in the town was made of canvas. A few had board walls with canvas tops.

They passed by a line of steel tracks leading up the steep slope to the north, and they could see that the tracks led to a mine up the hill. Early had to wonder how they'd managed to get the steel tracks here. A load that heavy would have had to come in on a whole train of wagons. But where there was gold and silver, men's ingenuity to get at it proved excessive.

At the junction of the two canyons, dozens of tents stretched up into the canyon that came in from the north. They were scattered pell-mell into the canyon, facing any old way, some near to the creek and others tucked in among the trees, some arranged in circles near to each other, and some scattered up the hill and sitting all alone. Among the tents there were a couple of sturdier abodes, like the other buildings made of rough-hewn board walls and covered over with canvas.

Not many people were out, it still being the middle of the day. Most of the men went about in just their shirtsleeves and britches, covered in dust and sweat. Here and there, a man wore a suit, or at least a vest, and Early reckoned them to be the professional gamblers. Over near the hotel and the theater a couple of men were erecting a new wooden building on the same lot where there was currently a large tent serving as the camp store. The tent was erected over a frame of raw timber beams, long ponderosa pines cut right from the hillside and erected in an A-frame, canvas strewn over it like a ball dress with plenty of ruffles and frills. All manner of items stood on display out front of the tent – pans and shovels and picks and even a couple of cradles intended for shaking the gold from the dirt – but the store also displayed for sale cans of beans and canned fruits and blankets.

"Outside of the whores and the saloon owners, the storekeeper will be the wealthiest man in town," Early said.

"No doubt about that," Heck agreed.

"Where do you reckon a man would go to apply for the job of local constable?" Early said.

"Maybe we should start at the hotel," Heck suggested.

Mogollon gave the impression of the sort of town where a man didn't leave his rifle unattended on his saddle, so Heck and Early looked like a couple of gunfighters when they stepped into the doorway of the hotel.

The hotel lobby was a small affair, not that the hotel itself was any impressive, grand place. The lobby ended in a wide hallway that stretched to the back. The front doors stood open wide, as did the door at the back, to let a breeze through. Though with the hotel backing up to the rocky incline of the hill overlooking the town, not much breeze made its way through the back door. The breeze through the open windows at the sides of the lobby was tolerable, though.

A narrow staircase occupied a fair portion of the lobby to the right of the door, turning at a landing and then ascending behind a wall the rest of the way up to the second story. A counter stood over by the left wall, and a sofa and two chairs occupied the rest of the lobby. Down the hallway to the right, several doors led into rooms. On the left of the hallway, Heck and Early could see that there was some sort of large room and assumed it was a dining hall.

A man in a dark suit sat on the sofa, bent over a coffee table where he was flipping playing cards from a deck in his hand. He seemed intent on his purpose and did not bother to look up. Another man, balding and wearing a pair of spectacles, stood at the counter perusing a newspaper that he had in front of him. He did not look up at the two men as they entered the hotel.

"Good afternoon, gentlemen," he said. "If you're looking for a room, we're full up. If you're looking for supper, the dining room opens at five o'clock."

"Actually, we're looking for work," Heck said.

Now the bald man glanced at them over the rim of his glasses.

"Little Fannie mine is always hiring," he said. "You follow the road up Coffee Gulch down yonder, and that'll take you right to the main office, and you can apply there."

"We ain't looking for a job as miners," Heck said.

The bald man looked up at them now and started to chuckle.

"Then you boys have come to the wrong place. This here is a mining town. That's the kind of job we offer."

Heck reached into his vest and withdrew a torn square of newspaper that he handed over to the man.

"We've come to see about that."

The bald man narrowed his eyes, looking at the

advertisement seeking a marshal and deputy.

"Well, then, that's different. Ain't it? You need to go down to the theater and see Captain Beaumont."

Heck knocked his knuckles against the counter.

"Obliged to you," he said.

"Better let your friend do the talking to the Captain if you want to get hired on," the bald man said.

***

If they weren't leaving their guns on their horses, they also weren't leaving their horses tied out front of the hotel while they walked down the street, so they took Tim Buck Too and Poco a Poco by the reins and led them along the thoroughfare, past the store and the lot where they were building a more permanent structure and down to the next stick-built building that had the word "theater" painted on the front.

The door to the theater stood open, and Heck and Early invited themselves in. Against the front wall stood a long bar, behind which there were plenty of bottles and a couple of casks. To the left of the door was a cage just large enough for a man to sit inside. This was the ticket office, caged off to protect the money from what were likely raucous crowds by the end of the night. It was currently unoccupied.

The theater was just a big box of a building with a false front, and when they got inside, they saw that the facade hid the fact that the roof was just stretched canvas. A large mast in the center of the open room held up the tent top and gave it an angle. The theater housed a stage at the back and judging from the number of seats it could only host about thirty people in the audience, but the ample floor space suggested that patrons stood through many a show.

In the back of the theater, a door on either side of the stage presumably lead backstage to changing rooms or prop rooms. The side walls had two large windows apiece, and all of them now stood open, allowing in the light and a breeze, making the theater immensely comfortable.

There at the stage, two men stood talking. One of them was an older gentlemen, gray-haired and dressed in a pair of black trousers and matching vest. He had a chain leading to his pocket, and his shirt was clean, his gray hair and beard were trimmed, and he looked like wealth. He also had an air of ownership, leaning casually against the stage.

The other man was wearing just his trousers and shirt, with the sleeves rolled up to above the elbows. He had on a black town hat that appeared gray from all the dust. He was a much younger man with jet black hair that fetched out every way from under his hat, but his face was clean shaven, revealing a strong, square jaw. He had shoulders that would not have been out of place on a buffalo and forearms bigger around than most men's thighs.

"You talk," Heck muttered to Early.

"How come?"

"The man at the hotel suggested it."

Early held his Henry rifle in his hand. It was tucked inside its scabbard. He banged the butt of it against the floor to catch the attention of the two men, who now looked up at the two newcomers.

"Can I help you boys?" the gray-haired man asked, and his accent sounded like home to Early Bascomb.

"I'm hoping you can. We're looking for Captain Beaumont," Early said, laying on a thick Southern accent of his own.

The gray-haired man's ears perked up.

"Well, sir, you have found him. And to whom do I have the pleasure of addressing?"

"My name's Early Bascomb, and this here is my partner, Hector Espinoza."

"Mr. Bascomb, do I detect a fellow Southerner?" Beaumont asked, walking up the aisle.

"Indeed you do, sir," Early said. "I come from the Mississippi Delta."

"I'll be," Beaumont said. "Why, we're practically neighbors, Mr. Bascomb. I come from Tuscaloosa, the onetime capital of the great state of Alabama."

"Is that right?" Early said. "It's like old home days."

"It is indeed," Beaumont said, now reaching Early and extending a hand. The two men shook hands, but Beaumont didn't offer a hand to Heck. "And how can I be of service to you and Mr. Espinoza?"

Early turned to Heck and held out his hand, and Heck gave him the newspaper clipping.

"We've come about this."

Beaumont narrowed his eyes at the piece of paper, and then he looked up at Early, studying him silently for some moments. He gave a glance to Heck, as well, and his survey of both men took in their rifles.

"You boys gunfighters?"

"Not exactly," Early said. "Though we've used our guns before."

"Have you? Do you have experience as lawmen?"

"We've brought men in on warrants."

"Bounty hunters!" Beaumont exclaimed, though not in any kind of disapproving way.

"We don't like to think of ourselves as bounty hunters," Early said. "We prefer to think of ourselves as problem solvers. Sometimes a problem looks like a fugitive, sometimes a problem looks like a cattle rustler or a horse thief. We don't always work for the courts."

"I see," Beaumont said with a nod. "And now you want to be my marshal."

"I thought I'd apply for the marshal position, and Heck here could be the deputy marshal," Early said, throwing back a grin at Heck.

"That goes without saying," Beaumont said. "No offense, Señor Espinoza, but Muggyown is a white man's town, and it certainly wouldn't do for a Mexican to be hired on as the marshal."

Heck chuckled.

"No offense taken, Señor Beaumont."

Beaumont grinned at him, a wry grin clearly showing that he'd taken the use of the Spanish word as an intended insult.

"Mister Beaumont will work just fine," Beaumont said.

Heck nodded his head.

"Mister Beaumont," Heck repeated.

Beaumont turned back to Early.

"Do you have references, Mr. Bascomb?"

"In fact, we do," Early said. Just before they left town, they asked Sheriff Calvo to write them up a letter, which he did. Early now handed that over to Beaumont. "That there is a letter of recommendation from Sheriff Calvo back in Mesilla."

Beaumont took the letter and read over it, picking out specific words to say out loud, "Trustworthy ... brave ... dependable ... judicious. It says here you've never caused him more trouble than you were worth. I suppose that's high praise."

"We take it as such," Early said with a prideful grin.

"You ever killed a man, Mr. Bascomb?"

Early gave a small shrug.

"Only those that deserved it."

"How about your partner? Mr. Espinoza?"

"Only when I had to."

"Are you drunks?" Beaumont asked. "I can't have drunk lawmen waving their badges and guns around."

"We ain't teetotalers, if that's what you mean, but we can hold our liquor," Early said.

Beaumont took a heavy, audible breath through his nose, rustling the whiskers of his mustache.

"It doesn't encourage me that you've never had experience as lawmen before," Beaumont said. "But Sheriff Calvo's letter says he's known you both for some time and that he wouldn't hesitate to hire you on as deputies. That recommendation is not nothing, I suppose. And clearly you're men who know how to use your guns – unfortunately a job as a lawman in Muggyown is going to require such knowledge."

Beaumont folded the letter from Calvo and slid it back into its envelope. He handed the letter and the newspaper clipping back to Early.

"Well, Mr. Bascomb, I hate to inform you, but that advertisement there is a bit outdated."

"Y'all have already filled the position?" Early asked.

"The position is open," Beaumont said. "Unfortunately, two men have already collected the bonus. The town's coffers aren't extensive, and we can only offer you fifty dollars to sign on as our town marshal. We'll give you room and board as part of your pay, and we'll pay you twenty dollars a month."

"What's the deputy marshal get?" Early asked.

"As the advertisement says, the marshal must provide his own deputy."

Early glanced back at Heck.

"So, the fifty-dollar bonus and the twenty dollars a month – that's to be split between us? Ten dollars apiece?"

"If we hire you on as the marshal, you'll obviously decide how to split the pay. Personally, I would take thirteen and pay my deputy seven. But that's up to you."

Early cast a smirk toward Heck, but turned quickly back to Beaumont to try a little negotiating.

"I reckon we misunderstood the advertisement," Early said. "We were thinking it was a hundred dollars to sign on for both of us, and then twenty dollars a month for both."

Beaumont laughed.

"Not in a town this size," he said. "But we'll pay you two dollars for every outlaw you kill. Of course, the undertaker will expect a dollar of that as a burial charge. I'll also tell you that the mining companies put up rewards for bandits who hold up the stagecoach – if they have gold or silver ore on the coach. You boys having experience as bounty hunters, I reckon you understand how that might make the job more lucrative."

Early sighed heavily and chewed his lip. He gave a glance to Heck who was now leaning against the bars of the ticket office. Neither of them had come here to work as bounty hunters. They were looking for that bonus, and the monthly wages.

Heck shrugged.

"We've come a long way looking for work," Heck said.

"So you're still interested in the position, Mr. Bascomb?"

"I reckon I am," Early said. "A mite disappointed with the compensation, though."

"Well, don't forget, room and board at the hotel, and the city will pay for your ammunition. I expect you'll find that's worth quite a bit."

"We're still interested," Early said.

Beaumont nodded. He gave both men another long, appraising look.

"Then I think we've got ourselves a new marshal. And, unless I'm mistaken, a new deputy marshal. Congratulations boys, glad to have you aboard."

Beaumont shook hands with Early, but again did not extend a hand in Heck's direction.

"Come on now, and I'll take you over to the hotel."

"What about our horses?" Heck asked.

"What about them?"

"We'll need to get them stalled at the livery. Is the town paying for that?"

Beaumont frowned.

"I suppose that's only reasonable," he said. "Our previous marshal and deputy rode the stagecoach in, but I never did know how they thought they'd catch bandits on foot, so I reckon we'll accommodate your horses at the livery."

Beaumont waved a hand to the man still standing at the stage.

"Mr. Suttles, come and meet the new marshal," Beaumont called. The dark haired man strode up the aisle between the theater seats.

"I'm Curtis Suttles," the man said with a handshake for both Heck and Early.

Beaumont busied himself at the desk inside the ticket office, and then he emerged from behind the brass bars with two badges in his hand. He gave both of them to Early, who handed the deputy badge over to Heck.

"Mr. Suttles is my manager here at the theater."

"Is there a town council? A mayor? Who exactly are we working for?" Early asked, a little concerned at the propriety of Beaumont hiring them on the spot.

Beaumont offered a wry smile.

"Understand something. You boys are wearing badges, but nowhere is there a law or a government body of any sort that is placing any authority behind those badges, neither is there a law or a government body giving me the authority to hand you badges. You're being paid by a consortium of business owners here in Muggyown, largely backed by the Little Fannie Mining Company. Your job ain't to worry with the laws of the territory or the laws of the Yankee government in Washington, D.C. Your job is to protect the property of the business owners who are paying your salaries. Half of the miners in this town are dumb Mexicans, and the other half are dumb white men. Neither half will question the legitimacy of your badges."

"You going to tell them about Saturday nights?" Suttles asked.

"What happens on Saturday nights?" Early said.

Beaumont chuckled.

"Saturday night is when the boys from the Three Sweethearts Mine come to town," Beaumont said. "They are the reason we're hiring a marshal and a deputy. They show up here, get drunk, fight, steal, beat on the women, bully the gamblers, and make a general raucous in the town. It's bad for business."

"We heard the Three Sweethearts Mine was one of the bigger ones around here," Heck said.

"And that's true enough," Beaumont said. "They employ more men than any other single mine, other than the Little Fannie. But the owners are up there at the mine, brothers by the name of Gabe and Jubal Rathbone. They're a couple of prospectors who struck it rich, and instead of selling their claim – like any self-respecting prospector should do – they decided to hire hands and work it themselves. The trouble with the Three Sweethearts is that ain't no adults in charge up there. The Rathbones come down to town with their outfit and raise hell like the rest of them. They're nothing but trouble, the lot of them. The crew is a bunch of gutter trash and saddle tramps, and that's all the Rathbones are, too. Now I'm not saying we don't have plenty of trouble without the Three Sweethearts outfit, but they're the worst of it."

"They don't sound like the sorts who are going to respect our badges," Heck said, casting an ominous glance at Early.

Beaumont reached down and tapped the scabbard that held Early's Henry rifle.

"You boys are being paid to make them respect."

- 4 -

"Captain Beaumont owns the theater and the Two Forks Saloon – that's the saloon that sits down at the confluence of the two creeks."

Ronald Beatty, the bald hotelier, invited himself to sit with Heck and Early while they took their first meal on the town's tab in the hotel dining room. Captain Beaumont brought them to the hotel and introduced them to Beatty, essentially passing off the new marshal and his deputy to another business owner. Beaumont said the hotel was part of the consortium hiring the lawmen, and clearly Beatty now intended to add his counsel to their understanding of their new jobs.

"Captain Beaumont is a good businessman. He's also a veteran of the war. He served in the Confederacy, of course. An artilleryman, as I understand it. And he has a certain martial view of the world. For my part, I want things calmed down, but not by compounding violence with violence, if you understand. We're building a town here, not trying to get a reputation as a place where men go to get shot – either by ruffians or by the lawmen. You understand?"

"Sure," Early said. "You don't want us shooting down every hotel guest before they've settled their bill."

"That's true, but we also don't want you to rial the Rathbones. They're the owners of the Sweethearts Mine. I'm sure Captain Beaumont mentioned them?"

"He did."

"They're troublemakers, and they need to be made to behave when they come into town. But we don't want you gunning them all down, regardless of what Captain Beaumont might have said to you."

Beatty struck them as a nervous man, generally, and he seemed particularly worried about what instructions Captain Beaumont might have given them.

"He didn't say that," Early said.

"Well, maybe not to you, but three months ago he was recommending a course of action that involved putting together a posse and riding up to the Three Sweethearts and murdering every man we could find. My point is simply to stress to you that the other business owners in town unanimously voted him down on that recommendation. If he even hints at that, you need to know that murdering people is not what we're about. Could you imagine how quickly my hotel would empty if word got out beyond this gulch that Muggyown is the sort of place where the legal owners of a mine and their employees might get gunned down by an angry mob? No sir! I'd be ruined."

"I can see how that might deter travelers," Early agreed.

"Captain Beaumon said we'd be paid two dollars for every outlaw we kill," Heck interjected.

Beatty went apoplectic at the suggestion.

"Oh, my Lord, no," Beatty said. "It's two dollars for every outlaw you arrest. Nobody said anything about killing. We'll convene a jury and hang a bandit legally if it comes to that, but nobody wants you going out and assassinating bandits. It's two dollars to cover the prisoner's meals until such time as a trail can be held. That's what we agreed on. If there's anything left over, of course, that goes to the marshal."

"Is there a jail?" Heck asked.

"Not exactly," Beatty said. "We built a small shack that we used once before as a jail to hold – well, we built a shack to use as a jail once before. You can detain people there, but only for a short while."

"Where is that?" Heck asked.

"It's just down the main thoroughfare here, just beyond the last building in town. You cannot miss it – it's just a small log building with a door and no windows."

Early gladly let Heck ask the questions, enthusiastically eating what remained of his meal. The hotel's cook wouldn't be able to find work in a proper eating establishment – he cooked the chicken too long and didn't cook the potatoes long enough, but it was something other than jerky and beans, and it delighted Early to eat a meal he didn't have to cook himself over a fire he also had to make.

"I hear you've had a problem with stagecoach holdups," Heck said. "What do you expect us to do about that?"

Beatty shrugged.

"No coach has been held up in Muggyown," Beatty said. "If a stagecoach is held up somewhere along the road, that's an issue for the sheriff in Socorro or for the Wells Fargo Company. The only time you boys need to concern yourselves with a stagecoach holdup is if it happens within the boundaries of this town."

"That makes it easier for us," Heck said.

"If you got concerned about stagecoach holdups, all you'd ever do is chase shadows in the mountains," Beatty said. "Now, as to your accommodations. We've got a room here in the hotel set aside for the marshal. If you choose to share the room with your deputy, that's your business, but I'm happy to provide a bundling board."

Early looked up and gave Heck a wink.

"I expect my deputy will be fine sleeping on the floor," Early said.

"We'll take the bundling board," Heck interjected.

"In addition to the room, you get two meals a day in the hotel dining room, provided by the city. I'll be watching to make certain that you're not abusing the privilege."

"How do you mean?" Early asked.

"A meal is a plate," Beatty said, casting a look at Early's empty plate. "It's not two or three or four plates."

"I find that the definition of a meal is in the appetite of the beholder," Early said. "What might suffice as a meal to one man might only be a morsel to another."

"A meal is a plate," Beatty said again, ending the conversation.

That was about the time Curtis Suttles walked into the dining room. Beaumont had said he'd send Suttles over to give the marshal and his deputy a tour of the town. Beatty took them to their room in the hotel, a room in the back corner on the second floor. The room's only amenity to recommend it was a window on the back and at the side that gave a decent cross breeze. The view from both windows was nothing more than the rocky wall of the canyon.

When they'd stashed their saddlebags and other gear in the room, Heck and Early went with Suttles out collect the horses. The three men walked the horses down to the livery, nothing more than a crudely built barn made of logs and canvas. The livery had a corral off to the side with a score or more of horses. Suttles talked to the hostler, and the man reluctantly agreed to board the horses at the price of just ten cents a day – a sum that he complained wouldn't even cover the cost of feeding them.

"We'll check in on these horses daily to be certain they're being fed and cared for properly," Early warned the man.

The hostler, a broad-chested man who stood taller than most with a thick beard and angry eyes, threw back his shoulders and hefted up his full weight so that he stood at his extremity, making him just slightly taller than Early, took a step forward, putting him very near to Early's face.

"I take care of the horses in my charge," he said, and the words came out like a threat.

"Huh," Early grunted. "Then I guess we won't have no problems."

Heck grinned, and he and Early followed Suttles away from the livery.

Suttles gave Early a key.

"That's for the lock on the jail. Don't lose it. We ain't got another key."

The three men walked down the thoroughfare, which beyond the livery was largely abandoned. There were a few tents down this way, a couple of scattered log cabins with canvas roofs, and then they came to a tiny log cabin with a stick-built roof and no windows, just a single door, currently chained closed.

"That's your jail," Suttles said.

Early stepped forward with the key and opened the lock, removed the chain and swung open the door.

It was dark inside the cabin, though gaps in the log walls allowed in some light. The air inside was hot and stale and smelled foul. Not much breeze got into the cabin.

"I'd hate to be locked in here overnight," Early said.

"Or during the day," Heck commented, sticking his head inside and looking around.

"You don't know the half of it," Suttles said.

Suttles stood a moment, looking at the inside of the jail and chewing his lip.

"Listen to me now, that jail is only for the worst folks. You get a man for murder, you put him in there. A drunk causing a raucous, you just sit on him until he calms down, or knock him unconscious and tote him to his tent for the night. You don't throw a drunk in there just for getting carried away with his good time."

Early locked the door to the jail, and the three men started back up the trail toward the town.

"That's about the extent of it," Suttles said. "If you follow that other canyon up about a mile, you'll get to the Little Fannie Mine. They're kicking in on your wages, so you should probably pay them a visit. Most of the men who work at the Little Fannie are decent sorts, but you'll find if you're here for more than a few months, that the folks here is pretty transient. Whenever word reaches that there's been a new gold or silver strike, about half of our population disappears overnight. But new folks come in all the time."

"You don't notice this slope walking down it," Early said, sweat beading on his forehead and his breath coming with more difficulty.

"It's a gentle slope, but it don't quit," Suttles agreed.

Just then, the three men heard the report of a pistol from up in the town somewhere – a single gunshot echoing through the canyon. Heck and Early both cocked their heads, listening for a second shot. The bark of a gun out on a ranch or in the empty spaces of the desert seldom caused any alarm, but in the confines of a crowded town, a gunshot often portended trouble.

"Better pin on them badges," Suttles remarked. "It sounds to me like you boys have an early opportunity to start earning your wages."

- 5 -

A crowd of two dozen men or more stood around a tent on the opposite side of Silver Creek. The creek in places ran on the north side of the thoroughfare, and in other places on the south, and through the town the pioneers had erected several footbridges, allowing for easy access to both sides of the creek.

The new marshal and his deputy crossed one of those footbridges now, with Suttles hanging back a few steps to watch.

"What's happened here?" Early asked, stepping into the crowd and looking around.

A couple of men had pulled back the flaps on the tent and were peering inside, and between them, Early caught a glimpse of a pair of bare feet resting on the ground, toes up.

"Deadwood Sam killed hisself," one of the men pronounced, turning to face Early. "Who the hell are you?"

"I'm the new marshal," Early said, indicating the badge he'd pinned to his vest.

The man started to laugh.

"We'll see if you last longer than the previous marshal," he said, and then he let the tent flap fall closed and walked away through the crowd.

Early stepped forward and pulled the tent flap away. One look told him all he needed to know. A pistol, an old cap-and-ball six-shooter, was on the ground. Deadwood Sam was also on the ground, a sizable hole in his head leaking fluid, and there was an overturned chair leaning against the cot. The cot was made up, the heavy wool blanket tucked in under a saggy, straw mattress from the foot to the head. On the blanket was a piece of paper.

Early stepped into the tent far enough to reach the paper, and then stepped back out. The words on the note were few, but they told a complete story.

"Gon bust. Ow to many to much. Ant got no prospeks."

Early handed the letter to Heck who glanced over it and handed it back.

"I guess this a job for the undertaker now," the other man at the tent flap said to Early.

"I reckon so," Early agreed.

Just then, a pot-bellied man with long beard and a ragged looking hat came thundering over the footbridge.

"Is that Deadwood Sam!" he demanded from the back of the crowd. "Did that no-good so-and-so off and kilt hisself? Dadgummit! He owed me ten dollars from Wednesday's gambling. Said he'd pay me next week."

"You won't be gettin' paid now!" someone shouted at him.

Several people from the crowd pushed forward to get a morbid look at death. Satisfied, they then dispersed. Early didn't hold the tent flap open for them, but he did step back far enough that the procession had room to pass.

"He owed me money, too," one man muttered.

"Had a powerful credit at the saloon, too. I reckon Captain Beaumont'll get his before you get yourn."

Early stepped away from the tent and walked back to Suttles.

"Do we need to send for the undertaker?" Early asked.

"Naw," Suttles said dismissively. "That man can sniff out a dead body. He knows the city'll pay him for an indigent burial, and he'll be along presently."

"You get many of those here?" Heck asked.

"A fair few," Suttles said. "Some of these fellers get to missin' their mamas or the sweethearts, or they run up the debts too big. My guess is Deadwood Sam's debts got to him."

"That's what the note says," Early said, handing it to Suttles.

The three men made their way back to the hotel.

"We passed a saloon when we first came into town, back up the canyon. They had some folks on banjos and some women dancing in the side yard. Whose place is that?" Early asked.

"That's Admiral Moe's place," Suttles said.

"He a veteran, too?"

"Ha! Not hardly. The Admiral got his nickname on account of last spring during the flood he climbed aboard a door and rode it all the way through the canyon. He bet the owner of the place that he could do it without drowning himself, and his prize was the saloon."

"I'm excited to meet the Admiral," Early said. "Sounds like my sort."

Suttles nodded his head.

"He's a decent man. Enjoys his fun. I expect you'll meet him soon. His saloon gets out of hand early in the evening."

"Is he part of the consortium?" Heck asked.

Suttles chuckled.

"You pick up quick, don't you?"

"How so?" Early asked.

"Well, marshal, your deputy seems to understand that the order you enforce only applies to the members of the consortium. Yep. The Admiral is a member. Things get out of hand in his saloon, you boys need to go up there and calm them down. But remember, don't you cause serious harm to the paying customers."

"We'll remember," Early said.

"I suggest you boys go and rest up. You'll find most of the work you have to do comes after the sun sets. My advice is that round about supper time, you post up somewhere in the middle of town and make yourselves available for when you're needed. And if you hear a gunshot, you'd best come running."

***

Early Bascomb blew into his coffee mug, and the bitter scent rose in tendrils of fog to his nostrils.

Six men sat around a green-clothed table in the Two Forks Saloon, smoke rising into the halo of light cast by the oil lamp hanging from one of several rafters over which stretched the canvas roof. They'd been at it for the last hour, betting on the cards as they flipped them over on the table in front of them. Their table had been placed at the front of the saloon, near the door. Except when he went to refresh his coffee, Early stood leaning against the wall just beside the door frame, the table easily within his view.

He watched the play closely, reading the signs and discovering early which man at the table held cards up his sleeve.

As a boy, Early fled a murder warrant back in Mississippi, and he ended up under the wing of a riverboat gambler on the Mississippi River. He knew the signs to watch for, he could read the faces of the men, and he was a pretty fair judge of knowing when the losses were too much, the drink was too much, the cheating was too far, and a table was about to turn hot.

He'd picked these boys out early in the evening and

decided someone at this table would be the first to get out of hand tonight.

"We don't need to walk far from where we are," Early muttered to Heck, who'd occupied a bench on the front porch of Captain Beaumont's saloon.

As a rule, professional gamblers preferred to play against unsuspecting tenderfoots. It didn't do for two men at a table to be toting extra cards or arguing about which marked deck they would play with. Around this table, three men wore their clothes still dirty from the mines, hats tattered, hands raw and cut and thick with callouses, beards matted with three-days of sweat and dirt. That was three of them, triplets from the mines. One of the men, wearing a black suit and a thin mustache, would make one believe that Silver Creek flowed as wide and deep at the Mississippi and he'd just stepped off a riverboat. A fifth man looked as much like a professional gambler as the other, though it was all in his eyes and his cut-from-marble face that revealed nothing of the cards in his hand. He was dressed more like the miners, a pair of britches held up by his suspenders and a worn coat, though conspicuously absent was the layer of grime. The sixth man at the table was just sober enough to keep his eyes open, but he was working hard to alleviate that burden. He sat out every other hand or so in favor of returning to the bar for another drink.

They went through several hands, and the riverboat gambler was on the losing side of professional with the stone face.

"Three aces!" one of the triplets shouted, slapping his cards down on the table and grinning ear-to-ear. The betting around the table had been severe this round, and Early suspected both of the professionals were bluffing. When the cards went face-up, both men revealed losing hands.

"Is it three aces, or is it four?" the riverboat gambler asked, watching as the man swept the pot toward himself.

"What's that supposed to mean?" the miner asked. "Are you accusing me of something?"

The miner with the three aces was sitting directly across the table from the riverboat man, and Early twisted around now. His line of sight went right over the riverboat man's shoulder, down his arm, and to the front of the miner's shirt. The riverboat man stuck his hand into the miner's shirt.

With his hand in the shirt, the gambler snapped the fingers of his other hand and shouted, "Crook!"

With a flick of his wrist, he came out with two additional aces.

The maneuver had been a deft one, a blink of an eye would've missed it. But Early Bascomb saw the entire thing. The riverboat man slid those aces from the cuff of his own sleeve – he planted his own evidence on an innocent man.

"Cheat!" one of the other men at the table shouted.

For the space of a heartbeat, Early thought there would be guns drawn all around as the six men at the table all sprang to their feet.

But the marble-faced man stepped away from the table. His face didn't show his delight at the controversy, but undoubtedly this had taken a good turn for him, for he was as much on the losing end of that last hand as anyone else.

"I ain't no cheat!" the miner said.

"Then pray, tell, sir, where have these extra aces come from?" the riverboat man demanded.

One of the other miners, though, was quick to come to his colleague's defense.

"I've known Jack for four years, worked in mines all over Arizona Territory with him. I say he ain't no cheat."

"Nobody here is saying he's a cheater," the riverboat man said. "I just happen to have found an ace of spades and an ace of hearts in his shirt. And on the table in front of him he has the aces of diamonds and clubs, and another heart. What's the man doing with two aces in his shirt?"

"I ain't no cheat!" the miner repeated his own defense.

"Let's see what the deck says," the riverboat man said confidently, snatching up the deck.

He held it close to him, where Early couldn't see, but it didn't take an imagination to believe the man was sliding two more aces from his own sleeve into the deck.

At the first sound of commotion, Heck had come up off his seat, and now the two men stood in the open doorway watching the proceedings.

They weren't alone. The patrons at the other tables inside the Two Forks had all gone quiet, their eyes fixed upon the table at the front.

"What do we do here, marshal?" Heck asked, a hint of derisiveness in his tone. Early enjoyed the fact that it irked Heck to be his deputy.

Early spoke softly from the side of his mouth.

"We put our stamp of authority on this town right now tonight," Early said.

Just as the riverboat man shouted in triumph and held up an ace of clubs that he supposedly discovered in the deck, Early stepped into the saloon and gave the man a sharp rap on the back of the head with the butt of the Henry rifle. The gambler pitched forward onto the table, knocking bottles and cards and coins to the ground.

"That's enough!" Early shouted. "You boys are finished for the night. Collect up your winnings, or what you've not yet lost, and go on back home. I know who at this table cheated, and I know who didn't. But all of you are going to call it a night and go on home."

The riverboat man spun quickly from the table, and Heck saw that his hand was inside his coat as he came around. Heck struck out with one hand, like a sidewinder, and snatched the man's wrist, turning it up and twisting it around until he dropped the derringer that he'd drawn from inside his coat. The two-shot pistol clattered to the floor. Heck released the man's wrist and then slapped him hard across one cheek and then backhanded him across the other.

Slapping a man in a saloon full of witnesses is the harshest of humiliations, and the gambler felt every bit of the abasement. His face flushed red, hot with anger and disgrace.

The man started to bend over for the gun, but Heck dropped a heavy foot on it.

"I'll be keeping that," he said, and now Heck brought his Winchester rifle up so that both hands gripped it across his body. He could use it as a club or could shoot a hole through the man's head, whatever he decided to do next. "And you'll be going home, like the marshal said."

The word caught all six men by surprise.

"Marshal? Since when?" the gambler demanded.

"Since this afternoon," Early said, and he slid a hand up to his vest and pulled the badge out prominently. "I'm the new marshal of Muggyown, and this here is my deputy. As long as we're in town, everybody is going to be on their best behavior."

From somewhere in the shadows at the back of the saloon, someone called out, "Well, that ain't going to be long if you don't last no longer than the last marshal!"

This brought on a cacophony of laughter from the witnesses, and some men might have paled in response to becoming the butt of the joke. But Early Bascomb grinned his teeth at the crowd, unable to lay eyes on the jokester himself.

"As I understand it, the last marshal didn't last any farther than his first night on the job," Early called out in a loud voice. "I'll now entertain any bets from anyone who thinks I won't be here come morning."

A few men offered an appreciative chuckle, but nobody took the bet.

- 6 -

"The cutest lawman I ever did see is what you are," the lovely red-headed woman said in her soft voice and her lilting Irish brogue, running her fingers delicately over the stubble on Early Bascomb's cheek and chin.

Early sighed contentedly and smiled at the woman.

Late in the evening, the new marshal had decided that the night's potential for trouble had died down enough that he could stroll up to Admiral Moe's saloon at the edge of town hoping to meet the sea commander himself.

A battered and cracked door hung from the outside

wall of the place, and in bold white paint, letters on the door proclaimed: "The Admiral's Ship."

Early addressed his question to a couple of men standing out front engaged in conversation: "Is this the famous craft that Moe rode down the mighty Silver Creek?"

"The very same, friend," one of the men said, casting a drunken, admiring glance at the door.

"Is the Admiral aboard?" Early asked with a nod at the saloon door.

"Probably not now. I saw him rip-roaring drunk earlier, and I expect he turned in early for the night."

The other man reached out and put a shaky index finger on the badge pinned to Early's chest.

"You a lawman?"

"I am," Early said. "They hired me today as the new town marshal."

Both men gave him an appraising look.

"Well, good luck to you," the second man said.

Inside, Early found the liveliest place he'd encountered in some time. A couple of men were perched over near the bar strumming on banjos, and about half the crowd joined in a chorus of an upbeat tune that Early did not recognize. They were all off key and off time, but no one seemed to care too much.

Early ordered a coffee at the bar, and he was set upon pretty fast by the woman with the fiery hair.

"You don't look like a miner," she said, and Early caught a whiff of a foreign accent, though not enough of one to say if it was English or Scottish or Irish. "And I know you're not a sporting man."

"How do you know that?" Early asked.

"I've a notion you'd be at one of the tables if you were one. This is the hour when the gamblers go to work. When I saw you over here drinking a coffee, I asked myself what is this one doing in Muggyown. And then I saw the badge. Tell me you ain't a lawman, now."

"I'm the new town marshal," Early said.

The red-head gave him a skeptical grin.

"No, you're not," she teased.

"I am," Early said, indicating the badge.

"Well, isn't that too bad?" she said.

"Why's that too bad?"

"You won't be around long. The first marshal was killed, and the last marshal was stabbed. He run off after one bloomin' day on the job."

This was something new. Nobody had talked to Early about a marshal who'd been killed.

"What's that about the first marshal?" Early said.

The redhead shrugged her shoulders.

"We don't want to talk about him, now. Let's talk about you. What's your name, love?"

"Love?" Early repeated with a chuckle. "I didn't realize we were that far along."

She laughed at that, and she had a pretty, lilting laugh that went along with her accent. "Love, I don't earn a living by moving slow. Now do I?"

"I suppose not. I'll tell you my name if you tell me

yours," Early said.

"My name is Maybelle O'Malley, but the boys in the camp all call me Maybe."

"Is there a reason for that?"

She laughed her pretty laugh again. "Maybe."

Maybelle O'Malley had a tent set up on a high ledge above Admiral Moe's. The trail to the tent cut through tall ponderosa pines, and at night, not even the light of the moon and stars found its way down to the trail. But she'd taken Early by the hand and led him along the dark trail up to the tent, and there she lit a lantern. The tent wasn't so bad as far as living quarters went. She had a raised, plank floor and a couple of cots pushed together and covered with a single mattress so that she had space to earn her wages. A small stove stood in the back corner of the tent, with a pipe venting through a hole cut in the flap. Maybelle's belongings were locked up in the two trunks pushed against the side of the tent. She set the lantern down on one of the trunks.

"It's cozy," Early said.

"It serves the purpose. I plan to leave before winter sets in."

"Where are you going?"

"I'm bound for San Francisco. Working my way there, I am. But I suppose I'll be going to Silver City or maybe to Santa Fe before I reach me destination."

"You have people in San Francisco?" Early asked.

Maybelle stretched out now on the mattress. She cocked her head seductively and offered an invitation by patting the bed beside her before resting her head on her hand.

"Join me," Maybelle said, and Early obliged her. "Soiled doves don't have people in places, love. If they did, they wouldn't be soiled doves, now, would they?"

Remembering that he'd not yet been paid his bonus or any wages from the town and that his entire purpose for being here boiled down to him being broke, Early said, "Are you going to charge me very much for this?"

"Maybe," Maybelle said with a grin. "I'll let you know in the morning."

Early decided to take his chances.

It was later when Maybelle stroked Early's cheek and chin, hearing the bristly sound of his whiskers under her fingers.

"The cutest lawman I ever did see is what you are," Maybelle said.

Early sighed contentedly and smiled at Maybelle.

"Tell me about the other lawmen you've seen," Early said. "I have a specific one in mind."

Maybelle frowned at him.

"Which one are ye askin' after, then?" she asked.

"The first marshal of Muggyown. I'd like to know what happened to him."

"As it stands right now, Marshal Early, I don't have it in mind to make you pay for spending the night with me. But if you insist on pursuing that topic, I'll change my mind and kindly ask you not to come back here again."

Early nodded and grinned at her.

"Then we won't talk about it," Early said.

He swung his legs over the side of the bed and

started to gather up his wardrobe.

"Won't you be spending the night, then, love?" Maybelle asked.

"I need to get back to work," Early said. "Is it okay if I come around to see you again?"

Maybelle gave him a smile.

"Maybe."

- 7 -

"I'm looking for the new marshal."

From the dining room, Heck and Early heard the man speaking in the lobby, and Heck grinned at Early.

"That's you, hombre. You wanted to be the boss."

Early returned the grin with a grimace and a snarl.

"Watch your tongue, amigo. I still haven't decided how much of my salary I'm going to divide for you."

Beatty stuck his head in through the dining room door and searched the room for Heck and Early. The dining room was crowded at breakfast time, the hotel being one of the few places in Mogollon where a man could get a hot meal, prepared by someone else, at both breakfast and supper time. A line of miners who would soon be going up to the Little Fannie wound its way among the tables, and it took Beatty a moment to see that Heck and Early were sitting right beside the door, beneath his nose.

"Are you in, marshal?" Beatty asked.

Early looked at his plate. They'd only just sat down. The scrambled eggs, dotted with diced red pepper, were still steaming. The cured ham, of which he'd taken two bites, tasted like home.

"Who is it?"

"I believe the gentleman's name is Ace Cleveland," Beatty said. "He was a lodger here some weeks ago."

Early sighed and Heck grinned at him. Quickly, Early shoveled a large spoonful of scrambled eggs into his mouth as he stood up from the table.

Early rounded the corner and immediately dropped his hand to the grip of his Colt.

"What do you want?" Early asked.

Before him stood the riverboat gambler from the night before at the Two Forks, the one who'd pulled the derringer. He raised up his hands now to show empty palms.

"Peace, marshal. I come in peace. I don't mean to interrupt your breakfast, but I'd like to have a word with you."

Early narrowed his eyes and scanned the lobby. There were a couple of people in there, including a man he'd seen the previous day who was sitting on the sofa with his legs crossed, watching the gambler and the marshal with interest. He had packed bags on the floor beside him, and he appeared to be on his way out of town.

"A word about what?" Early said.

"My behavior last night," the man said, dropping his eyes to the floorboards in a show of contrition. "My name is Horace Cleveland, my friends call me Ace. And, marshal, I made a jackass out of myself last night. I blame the combination of the liquor I'd had to drink, my foul mood at having a poor night at the table, and – not to share the blame, but merely to explain myself – the knock I took to the back of the head by way of your rifle butt. I'm embarrassed by my behavior, and I've come to apologize and make amends. I pride myself in always having an amicable relationship with the law wherever I go, and I wouldn't want Muggyown to be the exception."

Early continued to squint at the man, nor did he remove his hand from the grip of his gun.

"Experience has taught me that a man who cheats at cards will keep his fingers crossed behind his back when he expresses his regret."

Ace Cleveland smiled. He again held his hands up, fingers spread wide.

"None are crossed," he said. "I assure you, my regret is genuine."

The gambler had a silver tongue, and Early enjoyed a man gifted with the ability to make a lively discourse. But he also didn't quickly forgive a man who pulled a gun on him.

"If my partner hadn't been there, you'd be speaking your contrition at a tombstone right about now," Early said. "Might I suggest that, in the future, you not be so quick to move to irrevocable actions when you're suffering from a mixture of alcohol, bad luck, and a friendly knock to the head?"

Ace Cleveland chuckled.

"Indeed, marshal. That's a fair enough request. I've had a good run here in Muggyown, and I'd like for it to continue. I'd hate to think that our brief dispute last night might strain my continued presence here."

Early shrugged.

"You can stay on as far as I'm concerned," he said. "But if your aim is to retrieve that little two-shot pistol, I'm afraid my deputy and I are going to continue to hang onto that."

"No such aim was ever my intent," Ace Cleveland said. "So we can part friends?"

"We can part fair foes," Early said. "I'll not hold anything from last night against you."

"That suits me," Cleveland said, and he stretched out a hand.

Early twisted his lips thoughtfully as he considered the hand for several moments. But he then shook the hand.

"Don't cheat in my town," Early said, giving the hand a thorough wringing.

"Never again," Cleveland said.

The gambler spun on his heel and stepped out of the hotel, and Early watched him go.

The man with the luggage on the sofa cleared his throat, as if attempting to catch Early's attention.

"I've run across Ace Cleveland in many a town, marshal, and my advice to you would be not to trust that man any further than you can throw him. First time he sees you with your back turned, he'll shove a blade right betwixt your shoulder bones."

Early nodded his head to the man and returned to his breakfast.

"What was that?" Heck asked. His plate was nearly clean.

Early slid his chair up and fetched his spoon. He tasted his eggs, and wrinkled his nose at them.

"Damn eggs have gone cold already," Early complained. "Listen, if you see that gambler from last night again, especially if that cheating sonuvabitch is at my back, you don't hesitate. Knock him out."

Heck nodded his head.

"Don't you worry, hombre. I'll cover your back."

***

Cold eggs can spoil an appetite, and a spoiled appetite can ruin a day.

Early Bascomb was already feeling three kinds of sour when Suttles found Mogollon's new marshal and his deputy on the street a little after breakfast.

"Morning, Marshal Bascomb," Suttles said. "Big day today."

"Is it?" Early said.

"The men from the Three Sweethearts will be

coming to town this afternoon," Suttles said. "You can count on that. Word will spread pretty quick that we've got a new marshal, and they'll be eager to test you."

"Was it the men of the Three Sweethearts testing your last marshal that got him stabbed?"

"It was," Suttles said.

"I ain't lookin' to get stabbed," Early said.

Heck Espinoza sniffed the air. He liked this mountain air with the scent of pine hovering everywhere. He also liked that almost anywhere he turned, he could find a good spot of shade. Back home, there wasn't shade enough to cover a man and his horse, and in the higher reaches of the mountains, the heat didn't seem so bad, either. When he stepped into a shady spot, Heck could feel the temperature drop.

"What is it about these men from the Three Sweethearts Mine?" Heck asked.

Suttles shrugged and looked away, his eyes moving up along the walls of the gulch.

"They just act like they own the place," he said. "They're prospectors who struck rich, and they stayed here to work their claim. The men who work for them are loyal to the owners because it's the first time they've ever seen owners get in a mine and swing a pickax."

"That doesn't really explain why they'd cause so much trouble in town, though. Does it?"

Suttles shrugged his shoulders.

"They act entitled because they're digging out gold every day and getting rich," Suttles said with a shrug. "I don't know what else to tell you. You'll see it for yourselves, the way they've got the town terrified."

Early took a heavy breath of the morning air. Groups of men were making their way through the gulch leading up to the Little Fannie Mine. They walked in twos and fours or more. Some coughed against the strenuous walk uphill through the gulch – their lungs thick with dust from the mine. Others, who hadn't been around quite as long, outpaced the old timers.

"How long has the Little Fannie been up there?" Early asked.

Suttles shrugged his shoulders and looked to the sky as he tried to remember.

"I guess it's been five or six years now. I haven't been there the entire time since they first struck gold here. Me and Captain Beaumont come up three years ago. We're just coming to the end of our third summer here."

"So you were around when the town had its first marshal – a year ago?"

Heck looked up sharply. Early hadn't mentioned to him what the woman at Admiral Moe's had told him.

Suttles narrowed his eyes, squinting against a sun that hadn't yet come over the top of the eastern slopes. He seemed to be trying to reach a decision in his mind.

"I was here," he said. "Bad business. It's why nobody here wants your job and we have to advertise in the Santa Fe newspaper to try to get a marshal."

"Tell us about it," Early said.

"The town was growing. At the time, we didn't have much trouble other than just general lawlessness. Drunk miners fighting, sporting men shooting each other. A couple of times we even had some trouble with claim jumpers. So we thought we'd hire a marshal. Harvey

Spokes had been a deputy sheriff in Kansas and Arizona Territory before he came here to open a store. So we made him the marshal. He arrested one of the boys from the Three Sweethearts Mine, and they killed him for it."

"Just like that?" Heck asked.

"Pretty much like that," Suttles said. "Like I said, those boys from the Three Sweethearts, they act entitled, like we owe them. You'll see it for yourselves. They drink without paying, they take the women without paying, they bully the gamblers and the shop owners. Most of the men from the other mines stay away on Saturday nights."

"That can't be good for business," Heck said. "Saturday night should be the biggest night in town."

"That's right," Suttles said. "It's bad for business."

Early's foul mood did not improve as he listened to Suttles.

"Do they tote guns?" Early asked.

"They do," Suttles said.

"So did they shoot the first marshal? What was his name? Harvey?"

"Harvey Spokes, that's right. They didn't shoot him, no."

"Stab him, like they done to the other one?"

"No," Suttles said.

"Well, how'd they kill him?" Heck asked.

"They dragged him behind a horse through the town, then hanged him from a branch on that pine tree."

Suttles pointed to a lone pine standing over Silver Creek a little ways downstream of where the three men stood talking.

"They hanged him?" Early asked. "Dadgumit. That's a helluva thing to do to a marshal."

"That was back last summer," Suttles said. "Things didn't get any better after that. In fact, they got worse. Through the fall and winter we thought maybe those boys would cool down with the weather, but they didn't. Like I said, they got worse. I guess they got more bold about stealing whatever they wanted after that. They got more bold with the women. Come spring, a lot of folks just packed up and left town. That's when we started advertising for a new marshal."

"I reckon Captain Beaumont should have mentioned some of this before we agreed to take the job," Early said.

"He don't have to say any of this for you to know a marshal's job is dangerous," Suttles said.

"When do we get our bonuses?" Early asked.

Suttles twisted his lips, again hesitating to answer the question.

"Come around to the Two Forks Saloon tomorrow and Captain Beaumont will pay you."

"Tomorrow," Heck said with a chuckle. "Is that to see if we survive our first Saturday with the Three Sweethearts outfit?"

Suttles shrugged his shoulders.

"I need to get to work," he said, walking off toward Beaumont's saloon.

Heck and Early watched the man leave, and after several moments of silence, Heck turned to Early.

"Hombre, I believe we've been buffaloed."

- 8 -

The men rode down through the gulch, coming in from the east along the same trail that Heck and Early used to reach Mogollon just two days prior. They rode horses with saddles that still appeared new. They walked their horses in a long line stretching back through the canyon. They could have been a company of cavalry for as well-heeled as they were, each man toting a gun on his hip and a rifle on his saddle.

For Heck and Early, the day had progressed painfully slow. It seemed to Early that he'd checked the watch in his pocket a thousand times, and never more than five minutes had passed from the previous time he'd checked it. The air was hot and still all day, and even accounting for the miners who were at work, the town seemed quiet.

The new marshal and his deputy generally stayed in the vicinity of the hotel through most of the day, either rocking on the front porch or pacing the street out front. Around midday, Suttles came out of the theater and called to them.

"I've got something for you," he'd shouted up the street.

Both Heck and Early walked down to the theater, and inside, Suttles called them over to the bar.

"I've seen you boys are toting rifles," Suttles said. "I thought for town work, you might find these to be more effective."

Suttles reached below the bar with both hands and came out with a double-barrel shotgun in each hand. Both guns had been shortened, the barrels removed about a quarter inch beyond the stock.

"They shoot a little high, and anything much beyond six yards is going to be questionable, but for close-in work, these little guns will serve you better than those rifles. I keep four behind the bar here, but I'm happy to share."

About two hours later, and armed now with shotguns instead of the Henry and the Winchester, Heck and Early leaned against the posts of the hotel's front porch and watched the men from the Three Sweethearts Mine ride into town.

They were slow at first, keeping their horses to a walk, but when they got in sight of the Two Forks Saloon, one of the men at the front turned in his saddle and said something to a couple of the men behind. Then those men, five of them, gave their horses some leg and worked them into a fast trot. Only one man was down on the thoroughfare, and the horses skirted so close to him that he spun around and fell over in a panic. Then the five men jerked back on their reins, dancing their horses out in front of the Two Forks, and all five of them drew six-shooters and started firing into the air. Each man fired three or four shots, and the cacophony of noise echoed ominously within the confines of the narrow canyon.

"Good afternoon, Muggyown!" one of the mounted men shouted, and he alone fired off his gun another time. "It's Saturday! Time to open for business!"

Now the other men in the line began to break from their formation. Several of them made for the Two Forks Saloon, a couple of them rode their horses up in front of the store and dismounted. A half dozen men, including the two who'd been riding at the front of the pack, rode directly to the hotel.

The shooting had garnered the town's attention, without a doubt. All along the thoroughfare, folks who'd been holed up in their tents for the afternoon now opened their tent flaps to peer out or walked outside and stood watching. Early had noticed sometime before that from the front of the hotel he could look back over his shoulder and see through the canopy of the pines the little ledge where Maybelle's tent was perched. He glanced up there now and could just see her fiery red hair standing out against the dirty white canvas tent.

The six men who rode up in front of the hotel all dismounted now and hitched their horses to posts near a couple of big water troughs.

Four of the men definitely showed deference to the two who'd been riding up top, and Early paid close attention to those two. Both of them were broad-shouldered, they wore thick but not unkempt beards. They had heavy brows and dark eyes, and their features were distinct enough – and so similar to each other – that it was easy to spot them as brothers. They handed their reins off to the others who hitched their horses for them. They stepped out in front of the four men, and those four stepped in behind and followed a few paces back. And then Early heard one of the other men call one of them "Mr. Rathbone," and that confirmed it. These two men were Caleb and Jubal Rathbone, the owners of the Three Sweethearts Mine.

Heck stood to one side of the hotel's front door, leaning against the post. Early was to the other side. The men from the Three Sweethearts Mine paid no attention to Heck and Early as they walked between them and into the lobby of the hotel.

"Beatty!" one of the Rathbones called angrily. "Tell your cook it's suppertime. Me and my boys have an appetite."

Without drawing attention to himself, Heck turned and watched through the door of the hotel as the six men entered the dining room. Beatty was there behind them, scraping and bowing and begging their pardons and calling for the hotel staff to come and wait on the Rathbones.

When all six men were in the dining room, Heck cast a look at Early who grinned and shrugged his shoulders.

"I reckon this is why we're here, 'ey amigo?" Early said.

Heck grunted.

"Hard to count all those men on horseback, but I

made it at about forty men," Heck said.

"Somewhere about that," Early agreed. "In the forty to fifty range."

Heck shook his head and squinted as he turned back to look around at the men from the Three Sweethearts Mine who were still out on the street.

A crowd of them gathered down at Captain Beaumont's saloon, and several of them had turned their horses to go back up toward Admiral Moe's. Early glanced up at the ledge at Maybelle's tent and still saw the shock of red against the white canvas, and he was satisfied to know she'd not ventured down to the saloon.

Early was just about to say something to Heck when two men came out of the hotel, their boots sounding loud against the plank boards of the porch.

"Jubal Rathbone, I'd like you to meet Muggyown's new marshal."

Early turned to see Ace Cleveland standing before him, a wide grin across the gambler's face. Beside him was one of the broad-shouldered men who Early had picked out as one of the Rathbones. Of the two men, one was clearly older with plenty of gray showing in his dark beard, and this was the one now standing in front of Early.

For a moment, none of the three men moved. Early leaned casually against his post. Jubal Rathbone stood menacingly, his arms bowed a little from his sides, a scowl on his face that did nothing to hide his disdain for the man to whom he was being introduced. Ace Cleveland, meanwhile, stood grinning at Early, showing his teeth like he'd just won some sort of victory.

"Marshal, I just wanted to bring Mr. Rathbone out

here to introduce the two of you," Ace Cleveland said. "This here is Jubal Rathbone, and he and his brother own the Three Sweethearts Mine. You may have heard of it. The Three Sweethearts and the Little Fannie are the two biggest mines in these hills."

"We're bigger," Rathbone grunted. "We're fetching more gold every month out of the ground than the Little Fannie, even though they've got more men than us."

"Congratulations to you, Mr. Rathbone," Early said, and now he smiled broadly and stretched out a hand. "I'm glad to make your acquaintance. My name is Early Bascomb, and that there is my partner, Hector Espinoza."

Rathbone didn't shake hands, nor did he cast anything more than a flick of his eyes at Heck.

"You're the new town marshal?" Rathbone asked, his voice guttural, his manners rude and bordering on hostile.

"I am," Early said pleasantly. "Second day on the job."

"Understand this," Jubal Rathbone said. "My men have the run of this town. No lawman better step in their way."

Early nodded his head in agreement.

"Yes, sir," Early said. "So long as your men behave themselves, they get the run of the town just like any other free man in this territory."

Jubal Rathbone took a step forward, his boots sounding thunderous against the boards.

"You leave my men alone."

Rathbone glared at Early for the space of three or four heartbeats, and then he turned and went back into the hotel, leaving Ace Cleveland standing there smiling.

"The marshal is an important man in town," Cleveland said. "Arbiter of the law and all that. I just thought it was appropriate to introduce you to one of our leading citizens."

"How's your head feel, Mr. Cleveland?" Early asked.

Cleveland's smile faded and he turned and followed Rathbone back into the hotel lobby.

"Huh," Heck said.

"What's that mean?" Early asked.

"Hombre, it means I think we've bit off a world of trouble, and I've got a feeling that's not the last time we're going to be face-to-face with that man."

Early nodded his head.

"It was your idea to come here," Early reminded him.

- 9 -

The ruckus started just inside the store that sat next to the hotel. Two men from the Three Sweethearts Mine were standing in the entryway trying to step outside, one of them holding a rifle he'd not been carrying when he walked in. The owner of the store stood blocking their exit and speaking to them in a loud voice, but something just under a shout.

Tim Kesler was the store owner. Heck and Early had met him briefly the previous day.

One of the men gave Kesler a push, and the storekeeper now turned helplessly toward the thoroughfare. His eyes lit on Heck and Early, who were watching what was going on.

"Marshal!" Kesler shouted at them. "This man's stealing from me!"

Early glanced at Heck.

"That didn't take long," he said. "I reckon it's time to get this over with."

The brief confrontation with Jubal Rathbone was just minutes old. If he'd been served his supper in the hotel dining room, Rathbone hadn't had his first bite yet.

With his new acquired shotgun in hand, Heck crossed the narrow yard between the hotel and the store, standing just at the corner of the big tent. He couldn't really see the entryway where Kesler and the two miners were having their altercation, but he didn't have any interest in that. Early could handle that situation himself. Heck's interest, instead, was the men he expected to shortly be coming out of the hotel.

Early walked around the front of the store and up the steps cut into the side of the slope rising up from the thoroughfare to the little plateau where the tent store had been erected. The entry was wide enough for the two men to push past Kesler without any trouble, but so far, they'd not laid hands on the storekeeper.

"What's going on?" Early asked.

"That's a forty-dollar rifle, and he's refusing to pay for it," Kesler said.

The men who rode into town from the Three Sweethearts outfit ranged in age from teenagers to weathered old miners. While they all were big, strong men accustomed to breaking rock for a living, some looked more eager for a fight than others. Both of the men standing in the entryway of the store were among the latter. They were young men, younger than Heck and Early. One wore a mustache that was just a shadow, and the one with the rifle had clean, rosy cheeks. Boys, but with pinched and angry faces.

"Pay the man for the rifle or give it back to him," Early said.

"Who the hell are you?" Rosy Cheeks asked.

"I'm the town marshal."

Both boys looked at each other and started to laugh.

"Ain't no marshal tell me what to do," Rosy Cheeks said. And then he addressed Kesler. "Get out of the way old man, or I'll beat you like a dog with this rifle."

"Nobody's beating anybody with that rifle," Early said. "But you'll pay for it, or it'll stay here."

Early Bascomb knew that this would be the defining moment of his tenure as a marshal in Mogollon. Whatever happened next would set the boundaries going forward. If he backed down, every man with the Three Sweethearts outfit would know that the marshal would step aside for them. He'd drawn the line – the gun would be paid for or it would stay in the store – and now Early had to hold the line or risk declaring himself and his badge impotent.

Now Mustache reached up a hand and gave Kesler a shove. It didn't seem like such a forceful gesture, but Kesler was off his balance, and he tumbled off the landing in front of the tent and down the slope to the thoroughfare. He went with much howling and dramatic flair, and the two boys from the Three Sweethearts guffawed at the sight of the storekeeper going ass over head.

Mustache's arm was still outstretched from where he'd shoved Kesler, and Early made his move. He grabbed mustache by the wrist and jerked the man forward, at the same time kicking with his right foot and catching Mustache across both shins. Mustache spilled headlong over the side into a heap beside Kesler.

Rosy Cheeks took up the rifle by the barrel, holding it like a club, cocked over his shoulder. He started to swing, but Early was ready, plunging forward and throwing his shoulder into the boy's chest.

Early Bascomb was tall with broad shoulders of his own, and though he hadn't made his living swinging a pick, he was blessed with strong genes. His shoulder hit Rosy Cheeks like a sledgehammer and the boy toppled backwards to the ground – the rifle sliding away from him.

Now Early dropped the shotgun to the ground and reached down with both hands. He grabbed Rosy Cheeks and manhandled him to his feet, twisting him around and shoving him through the open entryway of the tent store. At the precipice of the steps, Early kicked Rosy Cheeks' feet out front under him and threw him into the dirt. Early spun around, snatched the shotgun from the ground and thumbed back one hammer as he faced Mustache, who had drawn his six-shooter.

"Drop that dadburn gun, or I'll shoot a hole through you bigger than this gulch," Early said. "Do it now, boy."

Rosy Cheeks and Mustache may have looked eager for a fight, but they were never ready for one. Mustache dropped the gun to his feet.

There'd been enough commotion by now that several of the men from the Three Sweethearts outfit who were still out on the street had stopped what they

85

were doing to watch the transaction on the steps of the store. Also, those residents of Mogollon who'd lingered outside their tents were all watching. And someone had rushed into the hotel dining room, and Jubal Rathbone and a couple of other men were now making their way from the hotel to the store.

"What's going on here?" Rathbone demanded. "Marshal, why the hell are you pointing that shotgun at boys from my crew?"

"They were trying to steal a rifle, Mr. Rathbone," Early said, easing down the hammer on the shotgun with his thumb. He lowered the gun, but held it ready to go right back up. "Like I told you, if your men behave themselves there won't be a problem."

Rathbone looked from Mustache to Rosy Cheeks.

"Is that true? Were you boys stealing a rifle?"

"I just wanted to test it out before I paid for it," Rosy Cheeks said.

"Is there a law against testing a rifle?" Rathbone said, looking at Early.

By now, Kesler had climbed to his feet and mounted the slope back up to his store, and he'd come around to stand behind Early.

Heck and stepped around the corner of the tent, though he was still several feet away.

"There's a law against taking something without paying for it," Early said.

Rathbone nodded his head, and he looked to be thinking about how to proceed.

"Where's the rifle?" he asked.

Kesler stepped into the store and fetched it from the ground. When he came back out, he continued to stand behind Early.

"This is it," Kesler said.

Rathbone hardly gave it a glance.

"Looks like it's in fine working order," he said to Rosy Cheeks. "Give the boy the rifle and put it on my account."

Kesler hesitated.

"What's the problem?" Rathbone said. "My supper is getting cold. Give him the gun."

"Your account, Mr. Rathbone, is becoming excessive," Kesler said.

Early sighed heavily. Clearly the storekeeper felt a little audacious with the marshal standing in front of him, and he'd decided to test not only his own luck but also Early's. A word from Rathbone would have more than a dozen guns drawn.

Rathbone started to laugh.

"I'm the richest man in this canyon and my credit's no good?"

"That's not what I'm saying," Kesler said. "But I have to pay for my inventory."

"Shut up!" Rathbone barked. He reached back a hand to one of the men walking with him and tapped the man on the chest, holding out his hand. The man reached into his shirt and withdrew a little pouch that he placed in Rathbone's hands. Rathbone tested the weight of the pouch and then tossed it up to Kesler. "That should cover my debts and the cost of the rifle."

Kesler opened the pouch, and Early glanced back. He could see it was full of gold dust.

"Yes, sir," Kesler said. "This should cover your debts."

"Now give the boy the gun, and fetch him a box of cartridges, too," Rathbone said.

Kesler did as he was told, handing Rosy Cheeks the rifle, then he hurried back into the store and came back out with a box of bullets.

"There," Rathbone said. "Everything's square now. Ain't it marshal?"

"Everything's square," Early said.

"You best be careful, though. You humiliate a man by throwing him in the dirt, and you never do know when he might come back with a brand new rifle to square that up, too."

***

From rocking chairs on the front porch of the hotel, Heck and Early spent the remainder of the afternoon watching the men from the Three Sweethearts outfit go about the town.

They came to the hotel for their supper in shifts so as not to overwhelm or anger the chef – even a rough bunch like this Three Sweethearts outfit avoided angering their chef. They went in crowds up the slope to Admiral Moe's and down to the Two Forks Saloon. But the Three Sweethearts men were almost alone in patronizing the establishments. Those who lived and worked in Mogollon stayed out of the thoroughfare.

Around some of the tents there were card games starting. In small groups of two or three, miners cooked their suppers outside of their tents on open fires and passed around bottles. In most all respects, the men who worked for the Rathbone brothers had the town to themselves.

"The band up at Admiral Moe's isn't performing," Heck noted.

"Nope."

"The sporting men aren't even trying to win any money off the Three Sweethearts miners."

"Nope."

"They've got this entire town cowed."

"Uh-huh," Early grunted. "It sure seems that way."

As dusk started to approach, Heck and Early heard a number of whistles and whoops coming from the men of the Three Sweethearts outfit who were up in the direction of Admiral Moe's. At first, they failed to find the source, but then they saw the redheaded woman coming from a trail behind the Admiral's saloon. She wore a bright blue dress that showed her bare shoulders.

"What is this?" Heck groaned.

Though he'd never been in a gold and silver boomtown before, he'd been around enough rough towns dominated by hard working men to know that a woman dressed like this could be the spark that ignites the powder keg.

Early kept his eyes on Maybelle as she sauntered along the thoroughfare. He'd have advised against it, her walking through the town like this with the men of the Three Sweethearts Mine occupying the place like a conquering army, but he also figured that she knew what she was doing.

"Evening, Miss Maybe," Early called out to her as she passed by the hotel.

Maybelle stopped and turned now, as if only just realizing that Early and Heck were sitting on the hotel porch.

"Why, good evening, Marshal Bascomb," she said. "And hello to your deputy, too."

Heck raised his eyebrows.

"You know her?" he asked, glancing at Early.

"We met," Early muttered to Heck. Then to Maybelle, he said, "Just out for a stroll this evening?"

"No, marshal. I'm bound for the theater. In addition to my other assorted vocations, I also do a little bit of singing and dancing. I hope you'll come for tonight's show."

Early grinned at her.

"I wouldn't miss it," Early promised.

Maybelle continued her stroll, to the delight of the men in the thoroughfare and those down farther standing outside the Two Forks Saloon. One man called up to her, "Maybelle! You performing tonight in the dance hall?"

"Of course I am!" she called back, and the man and several of the others all whooped in delight.

A moment later, Maybelle disappeared through the door of the theater.

"A show at the theater tonight probably won't calm things down," Heck said.

"Oh, it'll be fun," Early said. "Besides, Saturday night for a town like this is the big night. Everyone'll go broke if they don't put on their shows and serve their drinks and play their cards."

"It seems to me they're going broke anyway," Heck said. "Look around – nobody is out except for the Three Sweethearts outfit. And if they're not paying or running up credit, it's going to kill all these businesses. No wonder they wanted to hire a marshal."

From inside the hotel there came a shout, and both Heck and Early rose to their feet and started for the door.

Five or six men from the Three Sweethearts were coming from the dining room. A couple from their outfit were on the stairs, coming down into the lobby. Beatty stood behind the front desk, not exactly cowering, but also not involving himself in whatever was going on.

Behind the two men from the mine came a drummer who was staying at the hotel. Early had seen him several times in the lobby and the dining room, and it was the drummer now who was making the ruckus.

"Those are not samples. Those are meant for the druggist!" the drummer shouted. "You cannot just take them."

One of the men from the Three Sweethearts outfit who was on the stairs held in his hand a large, black samples case. He'd stopped on the stairs to face the drummer. The other miner, who was between him and the drummer, had twisted around on the steps and had both hands on the drummer, holding him back.

"I'll take what I want," the man with the case shouted back.

The other one gave the drummer a heavy shove and

knocked him onto the steps.

"What's going on here?" Early asked.

Early made for the steps, blocking the path of the man with the case. Heck stepped in front of the men coming from the hotel dining room.

"They're stealing my case!" the drummer shouted. "It's full of bottles of laudanum meant for the druggist."

The man with the case eyed the shotgun in Early's grip.

"You better step aside, marshal," he said. "These bottles are going up to the Three Sweethearts Mine."

"Did you pay for them?" Early asked.

"He didn't pay for anything!" the drummer said. "These two barged into my room, opened the case and then just took it."

"Step aside," the man said, and he took a step forward.

Early brought the scattergun to his shoulder and leaned forward, jabbing the short barrels towards the man on the steps.

"Set the case down," Early said.

For the second time in just a couple of hours, Early found himself squared off with one of the men from the Three Sweethearts outfit. The man with the case held it in his right hand, and his gun was holstered on his right hip. It wasn't the man with the case who worried Early, but the man behind him. Both hands were free, and he wore a gun on his right hip and a derringer was tucked into his belt. That was the man who most concerned the new marshal.

None of the men in the crowd had moved, from the entry into the lobby, and Heck held his shotgun in both hands with the barrel pointed at the floor. But he was ready to bring it up in a heartbeat. The nice thing about a scattergun is that two shots at close range can cause damage to three or four men all grouped together in a narrow hallway.

For the space of several moments, nobody moved and nobody spoke. Every man in the room sized up his opponent, trying to decide who was more serious about it, trying to decide who might shoot first.

Then Early broke the silence.

"Drummer, I'd suggest you back up those steps and find yourself a safe spot to hide," Early said. "Heck, I'm about to open up these two boys and see what their insides look like. When I do, I'd recommend you start shooting those fellows down there in front of you."

Hector Espinoza swallowed hard. He knew Early as well as anyone, and he knew that Early didn't bluff. This was no idle threat, and Heck wondered if he could let loose with both barrels and get his Colt from its holster fast enough to beat all six of the men in front of him.

The drummer was first to respond, scrambling backwards up the stairs and around the landing.

Then the man with the case reacted.

He held up his left hand and slowly bent to the side to set the case down on one of the steps.

"All right, marshal. You win this hand. The drummer can have back his samples and we'll be on our way."

Early took a couple of steps back to give the men room, and with their hands up and empty, both men from the stairs strolled leisurely out of the hotel. Early kept the barrels of the shotgun pointed at them as they walked past.

The others, those who'd come from the dining room, now turned and walked back to their meals.

"Come fetch your case," Early called up to the drummer, who reappeared immediately from behind the wall beyond the landing. "I'd recommend you lock your door."

"Yes, that seems like a fine suggestion," the drummer said. "Thank you, marshal."

Heck and Early both stepped toward the door now, but Beatty, still standing behind the front desk and now wiping his bald head with a handkerchief, cleared his throat to catch their attention.

"Backing them down is fine," Beatty said. "But they're just testing you right now. Sooner or later they're going to stop testing."

"We know what they're doing," Heck said.

Outside on the hotel porch, Early scanned the thoroughfare until he saw the two men who'd been on the stairs walking down toward the Two Forks Saloon. Then he let out a heavy breath and chuckled.

"That was funny to you?" Heck asked, his jaw clenched.

"That was close, amigo," Early said, grinning. "I thought I was going to have to shoot them two."

"I wasn't sure that you had to, but I thought you were going to," Heck admitted. "You know, the first time you pull a trigger and put down one of these boys, we're going to have the entire outfit on top of us, guns drawn."

"We may want to have a plan for what we're going to do when that happens," Early said. "'Cause I'll tell you, hombre, I think the time is coming."

- 10 -

A few of the seats inside Beaumont's theater were occupied, but not even half of them. A handful of men stood at the bar, and a few stood in pockets around the seating, but Heck and Early didn't have any trouble getting through the thin crowd as they moved from the door toward the bar.

"Evening, Marshal Bascomb," Suttles said, stepping behind the bartender and walking down to the end of the bar where Heck and Early stood. "I understand you had some trouble over at the hotel."

"Not much trouble," Early said casually.

"You see what they're doing for business here," Suttles said. "It's Saturday night and Maybe is singing. We should have them crowding just for a glimpse of her at the door. But the Three Sweethearts outfit here, we can't even fill all the seats."

Two heavy men with clubs had been at the door charging a nickel entry fee, but Heck had noted that everyone coming through the door simply said they were with the Three Sweethearts and declined to pay.

"They're not causing any trouble in here right now," Heck said.

"Just wait," Suttles said, furrowing his brow, his face darkening in the already dim light. "We don't get through a Saturday anymore without some kind of trouble."

Just then, Jubal Rathbone walked up to the bar. His younger brother, Caleb, was with him, as were the two men from the hotel stairway – the men who'd tried to steal the drummer's case of laudanum.

"Evening, marshal," Jubal said pleasantly. "Did you meet my younger brother yet? Caleb, say hello to the marshal."

"Hello, marshal," Caleb said, and Early immediately did not like the man. He wore a mischievous grin and had a cool manner that reminded Early Bascomb of every no-good hustler he'd ever met in his life.

"I understand you had a bit of a Mexican standoff with a couple of my men over at the hotel this afternoon, a misunderstanding about some medicine the boys were bringing up to the mine."

"No misunderstanding," Early said coolly. "Those boys of yours were stealing the drummer's case, and I stopped them."

Jubal Rathbone gave a shrug and tilted his head to the side. Whether intended or not, Early took every gesture and every word from the man as condescending.

"We don't want any trouble, marshal. But if you're going to have a long and fruitful employment in this town, you need to figure out how things work."

"Enlighten me," Early said.

Rathbone grinned at him.

"Ask Mr. Suttles here," he said with a nod at Suttles. "The town steps aside for my men. We have an understanding with the business owners here. They don't want trouble, and as long as they cooperate with me and the other boys from the Three Sweethearts, we won't have any trouble."

Early nodded his head thoughtfully and gave a glance at Heck.

"That sounds like a fine understanding, Mr. Rathbone," Early said. "And I reckon it worked well for you up until yesterday. But yesterday, the folks in Muggyown hired me and my partner to enforce the law here, and so now there's going to be a new understanding."

"What's that?"

"Everyone acts right. You acted right today at the store when you paid for that rifle. And that's how things are going to go now. That's how we're going to avoid trouble. It's not stepping aside and ignoring it when people act wrong – that's not the understanding no more. It's acting right. That's the new understanding."

"Ha!" Jubal Rathbone scoffed, but he did it in a pleasant, friendly sort of way. "I like the original understanding better."

Early took a step forward, bound to make some sort of snide remark that would come off as a challenge, but just then a man walked out onto the stage wearing a suit and a top hat and toting a cane. He banged the cane loudly against the boards of the stage floor and brought the conversation within the theater to an almost immediate stop. Early, like the others, stopped himself from saying anything else.

"Gentlemen!" the man on the stage shouted. "For your entertainment, I have the pleasure tonight to introduce to you the siren of the stage, the red-cockaded songbird, the captivating Miss Maybelle O'Malley!"

A withering applause, complete with whoops and whistles, erupted from the men on the floor of the theater, and a pianist that Early hadn't yet noticed in the shadows of the stage began to play. And then a man strolled out onto the stage with a violin tucked into his neck, and he was already drawing his bow across the strings.

It was a soft, solemn tune, and from off stage a woman's voice filled the theater, and to their credit, the men of the Three Sweethearts Mine stopped their calling and shouting, and the woman's voice rose and fell and filled the theater, in the crescendos she even drowned out the piano and the violin. The lyrics were haunting and the tune seemed designed to give a man chills, and near the end of the song, Maybe O'Malley stepped out into the lights at the front of the stage, and the applause rang out again – thunderous and enthusiastic.

Now a man playing a handheld drum appeared at the back of the stage, and the beat was faster and the violinist's bow moved quicker and the pianist's fingers tinkled across the ivories, and Maybe began to dance a spirited jig, and the applauding continued so that it was hard to even hear her sing until she was a full verse into the song. The pace of the lyrics was fast, and Maybe's tongue maneuvered through it in expert fashion, seamlessly slaying the "whack fo' diddly iddle idy o's" and the "turra lurra lie's."

Through the songs, Maybe clapped her beat with her hands high, she danced her jigs, thundering her heavy shoes against the stage boards, she laughed and joked in some of the choruses, and she put on a show that people would have gladly paid to see in New York or Baltimore or Chicago.

When the performance began, Jubal Rathbone had gone to take a seat at the front of the auditorium, and Heck and Early stood alone now at the bar.

"She's tremendous," Heck said when Maybe took up the fourth song in her set.

"More than you know, amigo," Early said, his eyes wide as he watched the lovely red-headed woman on the stage.

She got through two more songs, and Early was desperately looking forward to seeing her later, but that was when a man came into the theater out of breath, casting his eyes about the place until they lit on Heck and Early. The two lawmen recognized the man from Captain Beaumont's saloon, one of two bartenders who'd been working the previous night. He now dashed over to the bar.

"Marshal," he said, breathing heavy. "Captain Beaumont sent me over here, said you'd best come quick. There's trouble at the Two Forks."

***

Heck and Early were just clearing the door of the theater when they heard the bark of gunshots coming from down near the Two Forks saloon.

"Carajo," Heck muttered as the pair broke into a run.

Already a crowd of about a dozen or so men gathered around the door of the saloon, and when Heck and Early called for them to scatter, not a man moved.

"Out of the way," Early said, shouldering his way past a couple of men.

Heck, though, stopped on the outskirts of the small crowd, deciding it would be better to have a pair of eyes on these men.

As he came through the doorway, Early took a fast inventory of the room.

The smell of stale beer and gunpowder hit Early's nostrils the moment he got through the door.

The place was silent as the grave – the raucous atmosphere dissolved into a tense drama that felt like it was teetering on the edge of enormous violence.

The other bartender from the Two Forks stood behind the bar with a shotgun in his hand. It was a short-barreled job, identical to the ones that Suttles had given to Heck and Early. Early figured that Captain Beaumont must have gotten a deal for buying in bulk. However, the bartender appeared to be in no immediate danger, and the shotgun merely a precaution.

There weren't many people in the place. Maybe a

dozen or so men from the Three Sweethearts and that many more who were men from the town who'd dared to venture out on a Saturday night. Most every man was on his feet, and a fair few of them had their hands on the grips of their guns, but Early didn't see where anyone had yet cleared leather. The few women who were working the room looked frightened, most of them cowering behind a man. The men looked shocked or angry, and a few of them looked amused.

Everyone's focus bore down on a single, overturned table near the bar where a tall, lanky man in a dark suit stood over another man who was slumped in his chair. The slumped man was clutching at his chest and moaning. The lanky man held a six-shooter in his hand and he was moving it about the place, not aiming at anyone in particular but generally threatening everyone to stay back. He wore a scared look.

Early Bascomb never hesitated to make an ill-informed or rash decision. He was a man of action, and in his experience, rushing toward a problem with guns blazing was better than standing around and waiting to get shot.

His quick survey of the room taken, Early deemed the lanky man with the gun in his hand as the immediate threat. The only other man in the room with his finger on a trigger that Early could see was the bartender, and at least for now, Early thought the bartender was probably on his side.

So he rushed the lanky man, coming at him so fast that even as the man swung his gun around in a circle to keep everyone back, he was too slow to fire off a shot at Early.

Using the butt of his scattergun like a battering ram,

Early bashed the lanky man's wrist, knocking the gun clear, and then smacked the man to the ground with the gun's stock.

As soon as the lanky man was disarmed and on the ground, Early sensed the crowd move forward.

He swung around now on his heel, swinging the shotgun around to his hip so that both barrels threatened the men around him, and it was now Early Bascomb who held off the mob.

"Everybody just hold your horses!" Early shouted. "I'm the marshal, and nobody's moving until I figure out what's going on."

The man in the chair who was doubled over and moaning said, "I'm shot, that's what's going on."

Early kept his eyes shifting around the crowd as he took a half step forward to the man in the chair and gently pushed his shoulder back, revealing his chest.

Sure enough, the man had two holes in him, and Early's immediate thought was that he probably wouldn't survive the night.

Early stepped back and looked at two rough men near the front of the crowd who both had their hands on their holstered guns.

"You two help this man to the floor," Early said. "Lie him down and get him a bottle to ease his pain a bit."

The men looked at each other, as if incapable of making up their own minds, and then both of them did as they were told.

"What happened in here?" Early said.

Several people started yammering at once, and Early hushed them. He looked back over his shoulder at the bartender who still had his shotgun against his shoulder.

"You, tell me what you saw."

"Them two was playing cards," the bartender said. "The Three Sweethearts man accused that other one of cheating, and next thing I knowed they was both going for their guns."

Early glanced at the shot man. The other two were just now getting him onto the floor. His holster was empty. Early looked around and saw the six-shooter on the floor up against the overturned table. Early had no question which of the men was the one from the Three Sweethearts outfit. The man bleeding on the ground definitely had the look of a miner, the knees of his britches were patched, his hands were rough and dirty, his shirt yellow with sweat stains. Meanwhile, the lanky man that Early had knocked down wore a dark suit, maybe a little worn in places, but not clothes that had seen the inside of a mine shaft. His hands were clean, or mostly so.

Early kicked the lanky man's gun over next to the other one.

"Who went for their gun first?" Early said, knowing that the order of things would make a difference.

The bartender hesitated, and someone from the crowd spoke up in his place.

"It was that one!" the man called out, stepping forward and pointing at the lanky man. "He reached for his gun."

"I was defending myself," the lanky man said, realizing how this was going to go.

"No, he went for his gun first," the accuser said, still

pointing.

Then a booming voice from the side of the room cut in.

"That's not true!"

Early glanced over and saw that it was Captain Beaumont.

"I saw the entire thing happen, and that man bleeding all over my floor was the first to draw," Beaumont said. "The other man there – he was just defending himself."

A rumble went across the room, muttering and hushed asides, and they bore an ominous, threatening tone.

Early narrowed his eyes as he glanced over at Beaumont. The man was sitting at a table on the far side of the room. Two tables were between him and the table where the shooting took place. The saloon wasn't packed by any stretch of the imagination, but at least two dozen people were in the place, and several of them were standing now between Beaumont and the table where the shooting happened. Likely, though not certainly, some number of those people had been standing there when the shooting happened. The room had a few lamps dangling from the rough-hewn rafters, but it was by no means a brightly lit room.

Standing here now, Early simply could not believe that Captain Beaumont had any sort of view of the proceedings or the order in which they occurred.

The lanky man started to get up from the ground now, and keeping his hand on the grip of the shotgun and the shotgun generally out at the crowd, Early reached down with his other hand and dragged the man up to his feet.

"You're staying right here while I get this sorted," Early said.

The shot man, bleeding on the ground, coughed weakly.

"Is there a doctor in this town?" Early said. "Can someone do something for him?"

"We've got a man who can stitch him up," one of the Three Sweethearts miners at the door said. Early dropped a glance at the bleeding man and thought it was likely he'd need someone other than stitching up. "I'll go and fetch him."

A couple of the men in the room, prompted by someone leaving, made for the door, but the crowd was blocking them. Early correctly guessed that these were locals, not people affiliated with the Three Sweethearts outfit.

"Where are you going?" Early asked one of them.

"I didn't see anything that happened," the man said. "I'm not involved in any of this."

"Me neither," another said.

Both men, and now a couple of others, continued for the door, but the crowd there wouldn't move, and they were blocked from leaving the saloon.

The new marshal had a strong feeling that he was losing the tiny bit of control he had in this situation. The crowd seemed to be getting more hostile.

"They're going to try to let him get away with this," someone said.

"He won't get no further than the end of a rope

before tonight's over," someone responded.

There were other similar mutterings moving among the Three Sweethearts outfit.

"What are you going to do, marshal?" someone asked loudly.

It was a damn good question, Early thought. He felt like his back was against the wall, and the worst of it was that Early had no idea what had happened to Heck. He didn't see him anywhere inside the saloon.

Now a commotion at the door caught his attention, the Three Sweethearts outfit blocking the door spread apart, and there was Jubal Rathbone, almost as if on cue.

"What's happening in here?" Rathbone demanded.

The man on the ground, who'd kept up a constant moaning, now called out, "They shot me Jube! I'm shot bad."

Rathbone strode over to the man and looked down at him. Early noted that the two men from the hotel stairs were with Rathbone, staying close to him like they were his guard of honor.

"Who shot you?" Rathbone asked.

One of the other men, one of them who'd helped the victim to the ground, pointed out the lanky man who had positioned himself behind Early's shoulder.

"It was that one there, Mr. Rathbone," he said. "Shot him down like a dog."

"What are you going to do about this, marshal?" Rathbone asked. "Because from the looks of things in here, I'm going to have a rough time keeping my men from hanging this scoundrel."

Early bristled at the threat.

"If anybody hangs this man before he's been duly tried in front of a jury, I'll charge you with murder, Rathbone," Early said. "Don't think I won't throw your ass in the town jail."

Rathbone's face flushed with fury, and the crowd turned even more angry, and someone rushed at Early from his side. Early was too late to see the man, and a fist collided with his head before he could turn to face the opponent.

***

Heck Espinoza could hear most of what was happening inside the Two Forks Saloon, even if he couldn't see it. But he didn't worry about what was happening inside. He kept his eyes on the crowd around the door. It was pretty evident to Heck that these men at the door had positioned themselves there on purpose to keep others out. There was talk among them, too, whispers of how they intended to handle the present situation, and Heck knew that these men were plotting against the marshal inside the tent saloon.

Heck stepped back, into the shadows, and watched.

Someone from the back of the crowd ran to the theater, and a minute or so later, Jubal Rathbone and his entourage exited the theater and started toward the saloon.

Heck wasn't sure, exactly, who shot whom inside or what started the trouble, but from out here, watching the crowd, the entire thing seemed like a setup. And now that

Jubal Rathbone was coming to involve himself, Heck had a strong feeling things were going to turn south in a hurry.

Like many of the structures in Mogollon – and any other boomtown – the Two Forks Saloon consisted of sheets of canvas tenting stretched over a timber frame, heavy logs making a large box of a structure with rafters and a center beam. The sides of the canvas building were lashed to a plank board platform. Heck moved around to the side of the tent and tried a few places until he found a length of canvas between the tie-downs slack enough for him to crawl inside of the saloon. When he got inside, he found himself back near a back corner, and he quickly took stock of what was going on in front of him.

Jubal Rathbone had just arrived and was standing over a bleeding man on the ground. Early held the crowd at bay with his shotgun, but it was a touch-and-go situation with Early heavily outnumbered and the crowd clearly hostile.

Rathbone and Early exchanged some words, and Heck heard Early say something about tossing Rathbone in the town jail. That's when someone standing just in front of Heck rushed forward and threw a sucker punch into the side of Early's head.

An explosion of cheering went up from the crowd as the fist knocked into the side of Early's head. The new town marshal staggered under the blow, but he did not go down.

Heck stepped out of the shadows now and fired a blast from his shotgun through the canvas roof of the saloon.

He dropped the barrels down and pointed the gun at Rathbone.

"Anybody else moves, and I cut you in half, Rathbone," Heck said. His voice was low and level, and if anyone was looking for a hint of fear or a sign of hesitation, they didn't find it there.

"You shoot me and my men will kill you and that marshal and burn this town to the ground," Rathbone said.

"Maybe they will and maybe they won't," Heck said. "But it won't matter to you, because you'll be dead."

Early recovered. It was going to take a lot more than a punch to face to knock him out of it, and he'd already wrapped up the man who'd punched him and thrown the man to the ground, but it was just the barrel of Heck's gun pointed at Rathbone that kept the others back.

"Clear out!" Heck said, his voice carrying through the room. "Everyone in here, get out the door, except you, Rathbone. You stand where you are."

"You can't hold me here, I've done nothing."

"Clear out!" Heck said again, but this time he shouted it. "I won't say it again. And I promise you, Rathbone, if your men don't clear out of here, you won't live to see how this gets settled."

Several tense moments passed. The men weren't going to be cowed, and Rathbone was giving Heck a harsh, appraising look. Finally he decided that Heck probably meant what he said.

"Go on, boys," Rathbone said. "The marshal and I – and his deputy – we'll settle this. You boys go on and find you a spot to sleep for the night."

The men hesitated, but then they started to move, one-by-one, out the door of the saloon.

Early kept a foot on the man who'd punched him, and he kept a lock-grip on the arm of the lanky man who'd shot the miner from Rathbone's outfit.

Now, with the others moving out, a new man showed up. He went immediately to the bleeding man on the ground, and the two who'd helped the man down stayed put to help. Captain Beaumont also held his position, and the bartender never lowered his shotgun.

When the place was otherwise cleared out, Rathbone was the first to speak.

"What about it, marshal? One of my men was shot in here tonight. What do you intend to do now?"

Early already had his mind made up. He jerked the arm of the lanky man.

"I'm holding this one for trial," Early said. "Your man that punched me can go on with you. In the morning, you and your men clear out of town. If you come back next Saturday, you'd better all come prepared to behave yourselves. I promise you, next week I'm locking up anyone who can't act right."

"Hey, boss, Eddie's dead."

Everyone's attention now turned to the man on the ground. Rathbone's doctor – or at least the one they said could stitch up the man who'd been shot – was kneeling over the body and looking up at Rathbone now.

"He ain't breathing, and I don't feel no heartbeat. He's dead, Mr. Rathbone."

Rathbone's face twisted in anger.

"I want this man hanged for murder!" Rathbone shouted, pointing an accusatory finger at the lanky man whose arm remained in Early's grasp.

"He'll stand for trial," Early said.

Rathbone gave up talking to the marshal, and he turned on Captain Beaumont.

"Does this man speak for you, Beaumont?"

Beaumont pursed his lips thoughtfully.

"He's the town marshal," Beaumont said.

Rathbone looked at the dead man on the floor and nodded his head slowly.

"You'll all pay for this," he said as he started for the door.

- 11 -

"You boys did a fine job of backing down Jubal Rathbone and his outfit of ruffians," Beaumont said.

"Those men are a powder keg," Heck said.

They'd put their prisoner in shackles and had him sitting in a chair inside the Two Forks Saloon. Early was worried about taking the man outside before dawn.

"You think they'll ride out in the morning?" Early asked.

"I expect so," Beaumont said. "They always have in the past."

The Two Forks saloon was entirely empty now except for the two bartenders, who both sat with their short-barrel shotguns across their laps, Beaumont, the two new lawmen, and the lanky prisoner.

Early walked over to the now-closed tent flaps that served as a doorway to the saloon. He pushed one of the flaps aside and looked out at the camp.

Most of the men from the Three Sweethearts Mine had bedded down, scattered in places throughout the town, their horses picketed near them. A few were still awake and drinking or playing cards by a campfire.

Movement over near the theater caught Early's eye, and he saw Maybelle O'Malley walking out of the theater on the arm of a man he recognized as Caleb Rathbone, Jubal's younger brother. They were making their way up the thoroughfare toward Maybelle's tent, and it irked him to see it.

But then Suttles came out of the theater, walking toward the saloon.

Early watched him to see if any of the men from the Three Sweethearts outfit bothered him, but he made it into the saloon without any trouble.

The body was gone now. Rathbone had sent a couple of his men to come and collect the dead man. They said Rathbone intended to bury him up at their mine.

"We should turn in," Heck said. "Just in case tomorrow brings a fresh round of trouble."

"I don't want to put him in the jail," Early said with a nod at their prisoner. "Rathbone could easily go and get him out of there and we'd wake up to a lynching."

The lanky man looked up, shock across his face.

114

"I shot that man in self-defense," he said. "That was justified. You can't leave me where them men can get to me."

"I just said we ain't," Early snapped back at him, his patience thin. He'd been thinking of paying a visit to the tent on the ledge above Admiral Moe's, and now those plans were spoiled. "You keep your mouth shut. We were looking at getting through this night without much trouble if you hadn't gotten promiscuous with your shooting."

"That man was going for his sidearm. I shot him to save my own life."

Still holding open the tent flap, Early now turned on Captain Beaumont.

"You claim you saw it," Early said. "But you were sitting across the room. Tell me the truth, now. What did you see?"

Beaumont didn't flinch.

"That man from the Three Sweethearts Mine, he accused this man of cheating and went for his gun. I was across the room, yes, but I had a clear vantage of the entire incident. Don't doubt me, Mr. Bascomb. I saw the whole thing unfold perfectly well."

The order of things made all the difference. If the Three Sweethearts man went for his gun first, then nobody could say that the lanky man in the suit was guilty of murder. Every man has a right to defend himself.

"Then how do you recommend we proceed?" Early asked. "I won't let them lynch an innocent man."

"Put me on a horse," the lanky man said. "By all that's good and holy, I'll be out of this territory before dawn."

Beaumont pursed his lips and looked up at the stars through the hole Heck Espinoza shot through the canvas roof of the saloon.

"Keep him alive through the night," Beaumont said. "Rathbone and his men will leave town in the morning to head back to the Sweethearts Mine. When they're gone, I'll convene a miner's court. I'll swear to what I've seen, and none of the men from the Three Sweethearts Mine will be here to contradict my testimony. When he's cleared of murder charges, we'll turn the man loose, and – as he says – we'll put him on a horse and may God go with him."

Early gave a severe look at his partner.

"What do you say to that Heck Pinoza?"

Heck nodded his head.

"I don't object to it, but I think we'll have hell to pay when Rathbone and his men come into the camp next Saturday and find out this man has left town."

"We will indeed have hell to pay," Beaumont said. "But we'll be prepared for them. You men backed them down today. They sized you up and found themselves wanting. And that's what we needed. By next Saturday, the entire town will be with you. We'll arm the men from the Little Fannie Mine, if necessary. Mr. Suttles and these other men who work for me can all pull a trigger if needed. We'll get some damn order in this town."

Heck saw that Beatty's estimation of Beaumont was correct – the man was itching for a fight.

"All right," Early said. "Then that's how we'll do it. We'll spend the night here tonight with the prisoner. If your men there would stay with us and help us keep a watch, I'd be obliged."

Just then, Suttles walked into the saloon.

"We'll all stay," Beaumont declared. "The two of you, my bartenders, and Mr. Suttles. If there's trouble tonight, we'll handle it."

- 12 -

In the early morning hours before sunup, Hector Espinoza went quietly from the Two Forks Saloon to the hotel where he fetched his Winchester rifle and Early's Henry rifle, deciding that if the men of the Three Sweethearts outfit decided to attack the saloon, they would be glad to have the rifles in addition to the shotguns and their six-shooters. But in the end, no shots had to be fired.

The morning had a bite of chill in the air. Back home in Mesilla, it'd be hot as blazes, Early decided. But it was late enough in the year that up high in the mountains, the nights and early mornings carried just a hint of autumn.

Typically, Early would have liked it. Being from the Mississippi Delta, he wasn't a man who cared much for cold weather, but he could appreciate a crisp morning. But this morning, nothing was going to improve Early's mood.

Early stood against a pine trunk and watched Jubal Rathbone step into his saddle and start up the trail to the northeast, out of town the way they'd come. Most of his men followed, but Early couldn't help but notice that so far, Caleb Rathbone had not yet come down from Maybelle O'Malley's tent.

"Don't be in such a foul mood, hombre," Heck said, sipping from a cup of coffee and squinting against the sun as he watched the Three Sweethearts men ride away.

"Huh," Early grunted.

They left as they'd come. Riding more or less single file up through the canyon floor.

The last two men riding out toted riderless horses behind them. On the first horse was the body of the man killed in the Two Forks Saloon. The last horse in the line was saddled, but no one was riding it. And then Early saw the explanation when he noticed through the stand of ponderosa pine Caleb Rathbone winding his way down the path from Maybelle O'Malley's tent.

Early took a heavy breath and walked into the saloon to fetch a cup of coffee.

When he returned to join Heck in front of the saloon, the Three Sweethearts outfit was gone, but a lone rider was coming down the other slope, the one that led up to the Little Fannie Mine. The horse was a fine looking palomino, and the man riding the horse carried himself with a style that immediately caught Heck's attention.

There was a swagger in the sway of the shoulders as the horse walked down the slope. Even from a distance, the man's suit looked like wealth in a place where most folks wore a layer of dirt and grime over their clothes.

"This is somebody," Heck said.

Early squinted at the man.

"Looks like the sort who's full of himself. Who do you think he is?"

"Mine manager from the Little Fannie," Heck said. "That would be my guess."

Neither Heck nor Early had any doubt about this new man's destination. As the horse stepped carefully along the gulch, the man's eyes stayed on the Two Forks Saloon and the two new lawmen standing outside.

They watched him all the way in, and after about ten minutes or so, he dropped down out of his saddle in front of them and hitched the palomino to a post in front of the Two Forks.

"You must be the new marshal," the man said, glancing at Early.

The man was not particularly big, but his shoulders stretched the fabric of his coat, and there was obvious strength in his arms. He had a fresh-shaven, square jaw and bright, lively eyes. He wore a town hat that seemed too small for his head, but his suit didn't show the dust from the mine.

"I am," Early said. "Name is Early Bascomb and this is my partner, Heck Espinoza."

The man nodded to Heck.

"My name is Randy Everson. I'm the manager up at the Little Fannie Mine. I figured since I'm just about paying your salaries, I'd come down and introduce myself. I hear talk that you had some trouble with the men from the Three Sweethearts Mine yesterday."

"No trouble," Early said. "A couple of minor misunderstandings. Nothing in it."

"A man's dead?"

"Not by my hand," Early said.

"A dead man is more than a minor misunderstanding, marshal, regardless of whose hand is responsible. Let's go inside, I'd like some coffee."

Everson led the way into the Two Forks, and immediately, Captain Beaumont was on his feet.

"Morning, Mr. Everson," Beaumont said. "I didn't expect to see you on a Sunday morning."

Everson found the coffee pot on top of the stove and poured himself a mug.

Captain Beaumont made fresh introductions and then went through the events of the previous day – the attempted theft of the rifle, the attempted theft of the laudanum, and finally the shooting in the saloon. He pointed out the man who'd done the shooting who now slept on the floor of the saloon in a corner well away from the light streaming in through the front flaps.

"What do you intend to do with the shooter?"

"Convene a court and try him," Beaumont said. "As soon as possible. Tomorrow if we can. I'll give testimony to what I saw."

Everson sniffed thoughtfully and nodded his head.

"I think that's fine. Get it over and done with."

Now Everson twisted his lips and leaned against the

bar and gave Heck and Early a long, appraising look.

"I know that the business owners here in the town are eager to see the new marshal and his deputy deal with the problems created by the men from the Three Sweethearts Mine, and, of course, I have no objections to that. Commerce must be allowed to take place. But as the man who represents the interest of the party paying the bulk of your wages, I'd like to make it clear that my primary interest is in seeing an end to these constant stagecoach robberies."

Early gave a glance in Beaumont's direction.

"I was under the impression that's not a priority for us. I thought that protecting the property of the folks here in town was our job."

Everson shrugged.

"A man can have more than one priority," Everson said. "Of course, you've got to protect the property owners in town. But that should be an easy enough job. It sounds as if you've already established your authority. A few arrests here and there over the next few weeks, and you should have most of the problems quieted down without much trouble. If you really want to get control over the situation here, Captain Beaumont should testify that the shooting last night was murder and hang that rascal instead of protecting him. But that's none of my concern."

Heck glanced over at the rascal in question to see if he was awake yet, but the man hadn't stirred after staying up most the night in fear that a mob might still come for him.

Beaumont raised no objection, but Early believed the man would prefer to force the issue with Jubal Rathbone and his outfit.

Everson rapped his knuckles against the wood top of the bar.

"On Tuesday, the Little Fannie Mine is putting fifteen pounds of gold ore in the treasure box of the Silver City stagecoach. That is not information that I am sharing widely. I'll tell all of you gentlemen right now that if that gold doesn't reach Silver City, my employers are going to start questioning their relationship with the people of this town. They're going to look at what options they have to sever the mine from the town entirely. I'm talking about not allowing the men to drink in the saloons. I'm talking about freighting in all of our own supplies so that we're no longer buying through the local merchants. We'll bring in our own butcher and baker if necessary."

Beaumont blanched at the suggestion. He'd not said it in so many words, but it was plain to see from his reaction to Everson's threat that the town depended on the men from the Little Fannie mine.

"If there is any question, that also means withholding our portion of your wages, marshal," Everson said. "Did you know that over the course of two years, the same man held up the stagecoach between here and Silver City twenty-three times before he was caught?"

"I didn't know that," Early said.

"It's a fact. We hanged that man, but that was back in the days when justice was swift. In the last year, the owners of the Little Fannie have lost something between fifteen and twenty-thousand dollars in holdups. We hired men to ride along with the stagecoach, and one of those men was killed and two others were shot. Your priority, Marshal Bascomb, must align with my priority. And my priority is seeing an end to these constant stagecoach robberies. Surely, you agree, Mr. Beaumont?"

Beaumont nodded.

"I wholeheartedly agree. I'm sure that Marshal Bascomb and Deputy Espinoza fully understand the importance of ending these stagecoach robberies."

***

Heck Espinoza couldn't sleep. Too much daylight worked its way around and through the threadbare curtains blocking the windows, and Heck never could sleep with much light in the room. Early, though, had no such trouble. He was sound asleep, and all appearances suggested he would stay that way through the early afternoon.

After a couple of hours of dozing, and feeling rough from his sleepless night, Heck ventured out of the hotel room on his own, leaving Early to whatever dreams he could conjure.

Heck had not yet made his way to Admiral Moe's, and he thought now would be a good time to go and try to meet the man.

He wasn't sure what he expected from Admiral Moe. For a man of such distinguished rank, even if it was achieved on a door, Heck expected someone older. But Admiral Moe turned out to be a young man, maybe in his late twenties. He wore long hair and mutton chop whiskers, and as land-locked as Mogollon was, he'd procured from somewhere a very formal looking naval officer's cap that he pushed back on his head and cocked sideways. In addition, Admiral Moe wore a mischievous grin that never seemed to leave his face, and his eyes were bright and friendly and seemed to be amused at everything.

"I'd heard we had a new marshal and deputy, and I regret that I've not yet made your acquaintance," Admiral Moe said when Heck walked in and asked for him. "My name is Moe Foster, but everyone here calls me Admiral."

"It's nice to meet you, Admiral," Heck said. "Marshal Bascomb is resting up after the excitement last night."

"A shooting down at the Two Forks," Admiral Moe said. "I heard about that. It seems that unfortunate events always have a way of trailing behind those men from the Three Sweethearts Mine."

Admiral Moe turned out to be an engaging individual. Right away, he started asking Heck questions about himself and about Early, and he showed a genuine interest in the answers.

Heck, whose nature tended toward the reserved, offered as little information as he could without appearing rude.

Through the course of the conversation, Heck also managed to learn a little about Admiral Moe.

"I came here as a prospector, but I never was particularly lucky at hunting for gold. Not that I haven't given a fair shot. I did some prospecting in Arizona and California, as well. I suppose because my luck was so bad at prospecting, I started brewing beer for myself, and I soon found that if I couldn't pan gold dust out of the river, I could trade my beer for it. So I built a brewery and opened the saloon here."

Moe gave a nod toward the side of his saloon.

"I've got a little brewery set up in a shed over there and pull my water straight from Silver Creek. I tell everyone to be sure to piss in a strainer because there's probably silver in the beer."

The Admiral laughed at his own joke, but Heck only offered a wry smile.

"I'm curious, Admiral, what you think of the men from the Three Sweethearts Mine."

Admiral Moe gave an indifferent shrug.

"They don't bother me quite the way they bother Captain Beaumont. I've got a friendly place here, less gambling and more singing. The folks that come into my saloon are here for a good time."

"Nothing wrong with that," Heck said.

"We've got a few faro tables that we set up – everyone has to earn a living, and even beer made from the cool, clear waters of Silver Creek won't make your rich. But we don't get into the heavy gambling the way they do down at the Two Forks. And that keeps everything friendly between me and Captain Beaumont. I'm not cutting in on whatever action the house gets, if you catch my meaning."

"Sure," Heck said.

"And the Rathbones, they understand not to start trouble with me."

"Why is that?" Heck asked.

"All the faro dealers in here work for me, none of them are independent sporting men like they are over at Captain Beaumont's. I've got five bartenders, all living right here in the saloon or in tents right around the saloon, and I've got another six men who are – what do you call them? – strong men. I've got six strong men who make sure we don't have trouble in here. If it came to a shooting match with the men from the Three Sweethearts, I could bring twenty guns. Captain Beaumont has Suttles and four or five bartenders, and that's not much against the forty or fifty men that the Three Sweethearts outfit has."

"They've still got you out-gunned," Heck said.

"They do, but the odds aren't quite so deep. Just because they could get me in the end doesn't mean we wouldn't take half their outfit or better. So they keep the peace with me more than they do with some of the others."

Heck swept the room with his eyes. At the moment, he saw one man behind the bar and one "strong man" over near the door. Two men had faro tables set up. He wondered where the rest were.

"But you asked my opinion about the Three Sweethearts outfit. They don't pay for their beer, I'll say that. They drink for free in here, because – as you say – even with all my people, they've still got me outgunned. And my other opinion about them is that those Rathbones must be about the luckiest men you'll ever find."

"How so?" Heck asked.

"I prospected all around the hills up there where the Three Sweethearts Mine is at, and I never found much more than some flakes. How they found a deep vein is beyond me. I may not have been particularly successful in my prospecting, but I can recognize gold in quartz when I see it. Anyhow, I must have walked past it a hundred times, and those Rathbones from the Three Sweethearts must have found it. So good for them, and bad for me, but I'm having more fun selling beer than I would digging in dirt, so I reckon everything works out in the end."

Admiral Moe took a long drink of his beer, finishing it off before it got too warm to drink. Mogollon had an ice house dug into the side of the slope behind Admiral Moe's Saloon, but the beer only stayed chilled for so long.

"Of course, Jeremiah wasn't lucky, was he?" Admiral Moe said with a heavy sigh.

"Jeremiah?" Heck asked, not knowing to whom the Admiral referred.

"Ha. You don't know about Jeremiah?"

"I don't."

"Well, I imagine you'll find out soon enough." Now he took another drink to drain his glass. "Send your partner over when he's awake. I'd like to meet him. The rumor is that he maybe didn't pay, if you know what I mean, and that would make him a rarity around here."

"Maybe didn't pay?" Heck repeated, thinking that Early might have had some free beers in the Admiral's place. Heck liked the Admiral and his saloon and didn't want Early to cause trouble with the man. "Does he owe you some money?"

"Ha!" Admiral Moe scoffed. "Not exactly."

Admiral Moe grinned at Heck, but did not have an opportunity to let him in on the joke because Curtis Suttles walked into the saloon at that moment.

"Deputy marshal," Suttles called from the door. "Go and fetch Mr. Bascomb. We're fixing to have a trial."

***

Early Bascomb never did learn the name of the defendant.

The trial was a quick affair. Everson and five other men from the Little Fannie Mine sat as jurors. Suttles acted as the judge. The entirety of the testimony consisted of a single statement from Captain Beaumont. As marshal, Early acted as prosecutor, though he wasn't sure how he could prosecute a defendant who he didn't think was guilty of anything beyond defending himself.

"I saw the defendant playing cards in my saloon. He'd been at the table for some time, and I knew that he was playing against some of the boys from the Three Sweethearts outfit. Through the course of the evening I saw that the defendant was winning at the table, and I remember thinking at some point that if fortunes didn't change those men from the Three Sweethearts were going to get fed up. So I was surprised when I saw a man at the table stand up and go for his gun."

"This is the man who was killed?" Early asked.

"Yes. He stood first. He went for his gun. And the defendant, still seated, pulled a gun from his belt, a little derringer, and fired twice."

"You saw all that?" Early said.

"I did, sir."

Early looked around the saloon. Probably twenty-five or thirty men had come to the saloon to see the trial.

"Does anyone else want to give testimony?" Early asked.

A few men muttered among themselves, but no one

stepped up to speak. Early suspected if the Rathbones and their men were here it would likely be a different situation. Probably every man from the outfit – whether present at the time of the shooting or not – would have stood up to say the killing was murder.

Early looked at the defendant.

"You have anything to add to that?" Early said.

"I wasn't cheating," the man said. "And I shot to keep that man from killing me. I had to do it, or he'd have shot me."

Early shrugged and looked over at Suttles.

"That's all I've got," Early said.

Suttles shrugged and looked around at one of the bartenders.

"Give everyone on the jury a glass of mescal or a beer, whatever they want, and we'll leave them to confer."

A quarter of an hour later, Everson announced that the jury had reached its conclusion. The court reconvened, which simply meant that Suttles stood up on a box where everyone could see him and read the results of the juror's ballots. Each man had been given a slip of paper with the words "justifiable defense" and "guilty" written on them, and the men were to circle their conclusion.

"One for defense," Suttles read out, flipping through to the next ballot. "Two for defense."

They all went like that.

"The jury is anonymous that the defendant killed in defense of himself," Suttles called out in a strong voice. "The defendant is free to go, and the court thanks the jury for their service to their community."

"Unanimous," Early said. "They all agree."

"Exactly," Suttles said.

Another quarter of an hour later, the Two Forks Saloon was re-opened for business, the jury was dispersed, and Heck and Early stood outside the livery watching the defendant ride away on a horse gifted to him by the town of Mogollon.

"I never got his name," Early said.

"You didn't?" Heck asked, surprised.

"I never thought about it until just now."

"Well, he's gone, and that's one problem settled. Though I suspect it'll start a new problem."

"Yep. It makes you wonder who Jubal Rathbone is going to want to hang when he gets to town and finds out that fellow is gone."

***

"Don't look so sad, Early," Maybe O'Malley said, snuggling against Early's side as they stood at the bar inside Admiral Moe's saloon.

"I'm not sad," Early said. "I just didn't care to see Caleb Rathbone walking you up to your tent last night and then leaving out of there this morning."

Maybe laughed, her pretty, lyrical laugh.

"I have to earn a living, don't I now? And on what you're paying me, starving to death in a week I would be."

"I just don't like those Rathbones," Early said.

"You make your judgments on people a mite fast, don't you, marshal?"

"I'm a quick study of human nature," Early said, and then he offered the Irish woman a challenge. "Tell me I'm wrong about him."

Maybelle O'Malley eyed the marshal. It was hard to see in here, in the dim light of Admiral Moe's saloon, but Early had caught a good look of her bright blue eyes in the lantern light in her tent the other night, and his memory filled in the details of what he couldn't now see. Those searching eyes, blue like a cloudless sky on a crisp November day. They moved about, searching out his own eyes.

"I'm particular about who I invite into my bed, marshal," Maybelle said. "A man's either got to be rich or else he'd better be handsome and charming."

"Well, I'm skint," Early said. "My debts outweigh my wages by quite a bit."

"Ain't I the lucky one that you're handsome and charming," Maybelle said with a wry grin.

"What about Caleb Rathbone?" Early asked. "Does he pay you in the morning."

Maybelle grinned.

"Maybe," she said. "Now, I don't want to talk about Caleb Rathbone or any other man. We can talk about you or we can talk about me, or we can end the conversation now, and I'll go on about my business."

Early Bascomb wasn't the sort of man who let a good thing slip away if he could help it, and he knew better than to test Maybelle's patience.

"Why didn't you tell me that you're a singer?" he asked.

Maybe smiled wide, her face lit up, evidently pleased that Early had chosen to talk about her favorite subject.

"Didn't I tell you I was trying to work my way to San Francisco?"

"Because you want to sing there," Early said.

"That's right. Real, honest to goodness theaters, and traveling troupes. My dream, that is. To sing in San Francisco and to travel to places like Denver and St. Louis and Chicago – maybe even Baltimore and New York. To see my name printed on the bills and to know that when they come to stand in the theater, it's the name of Maybelle O'Malley what's brought them there. Maybe I could even be famous enough to tour to London and to Dublin. Now wouldn't that be a real treat? Me, going back to the old country and starring in a Dublin theater."

"And the other, up in the tent?"

"I still have to eat. It's a pittance that I'm paid at the Muggyown Theater, isn't it? But I'm saving my money to get a ticket on the stagecoach. I may winter in Silver City or, if I can make it, in Santa Fe. But San Francisco is where I'll be this time next year, whatever it takes to get there."

"I admire your determination," Early said. "I wouldn't bet against you. I had the pleasure to listen to you sign, and there's no doubt that you've the talent. You're quite the songbird."

Maybe laughed and put on a demonstration of humility by dipping her head and putting a hand to Early's lips, but then she grinned brilliantly at him and said, "Tell me more."

"How often do you perform at the theater?"

"Wednesday nights and Saturday nights," she said. "It was just on Saturdays, but the Three Sweethearts men have chased so much business away that Captain Beaumont added Wednesday nights. If not for the lack of an audience, I'd be happy to be in the theater every night."

Maybe emptied the sip that remained in her glass.

"Buy me another drink," she said.

Early knew that girls in saloons often earned a nickel when they could get some tenderfoot to buy them a twenty-cent drink. He also knew that the liquor he bought for her wouldn't be much more than pure water.

Maybe held her glass up until she got the bartender's attention.

"You want a drink, love?" she asked.

"I'll stay with my Arbuckle's," Early said.

"So what about you, Marshal Early? Ever since you were a wee boy you wanted to be a town marshal in a gold town? Is that it?"

"Ha!" Early scoffed. "I'm doing the last thing I ever wanted to do."

"What would you prefer to be doing, then?"

Early shrugged.

"I just like working with my partner, Heck. He's been a good friend to me ever since I come to Mesilla, and we watch out for each other. As long as I'm working with Heck, I reckon I can do just about anything. But one day, I'd like to go back to Mississippi and get my daddy's place."

"What was your daddy's place?"

"My people, going back to my great-grandfather, grew cotton in the Mississippi Delta. We lost the plantation after the war. I reckon some carpetbagger has it now, but I think sometimes about maybe going home and getting it back. If I had the money."

"One day," Maybe said.

Early nodded wistfully.

"It's the hope that'll get you, if you let it. The hope you have when you dream dreams, hoping that they'll come true."

"Huh," Early grunted dismissively. "With your voice, I've got to believe that your dreams are really plans. You've got it all worked out."

"From your lips to God's ears," Maybe said, taking a big swallow from her fresh drink.

She turned and cast a lingering look over the saloon, as if she was trying to find someone who was there. Then she turned back to Early.

"Let's go up to my tent, if you're game."

"I'm always game."

***

"You're going to have to do what Everson wants," Curtis Suttles said.

Heck Espinoza, sitting in the light coming from the hotel window, whittled a branch he'd cut from a little scrub oak, feeling the smooth, cool cambium.

"He's the big boss?" Heck said.

"All the bosses in this town are on equal footing," Suttles said. "Captain Beaumont, Beatty here at the hotel, Everson up at the Little Fanny. I suppose even the Admiral. But Everson's footing is a little more equal than the others. If Everson decides that the Little Fanny is going to open its own store and its own saloon, everyone else in this town goes broke."

"I understand that," Heck said.

"So what he says carries a little more weight – from that respect."

"Who do you think it holding up the stagecoaches?"

Suttles took a heavy sigh.

"I don't know for sure, but I would guess it's someone with close ties to the town here. Not many stagecoaches get held up that don't have gold on them."

"So somebody knows which ones to stop."

"That's how I see it."

Heck pursed his lips and admired the point he'd worked on the little branch. He touched the tip of his index finger against the point to feel how sharp it was, but the green wood bent easily.

"What do you do for Captain Beaumont, besides running the theater?" Heck asked.

His thoughts were on that stagecoach. He'd preferred not to have the burden of the stagecoach robberies on his head. He liked this job better when it was mostly just breaking up arguments in the saloons. He didn't even mind the problem of the Three Sweethearts outfit. Heck figured that was something that could be worked out over the course of a few weeks. But stagecoach robbery was a different matter altogether. He envisioned organizing a posse and giving chase – probably to Arizona Territory. He knew border bandits liked to hide out in one territory and do their banditry in another, that kept them from worrying much about the law showing up at the door while they were asleep.

Twenty dollars a month, split between Heck and Early, wasn't a lot of money to be chasing men across the border.

"I've been with Captain Beaumont for years now," Suttles said. "And I do whatever he needs to have done. Here, I run the theater. In other places I've handled the faro table or looked after the girls or drove a freight wagon to bring liquor to the saloon. Whatever Captain Beaumont needs."

"So Captain Beaumont's always owned saloons?"

"As long as I've worked for him," Suttles said. "It's a good way to make money. Whether it's cowpunchers or sporting men or miners or trappers, men always need a drink."

"How long were you a lawman?" Heck asked.

Suttles grinned.

"You figured me out?"

"From the moment we met, I've been wondering why you didn't take the job here."

"Ha," Suttles said. "I worked as a deputy marshal in Independence, Missouri, for year or two. That's where I first met Captain Beaumont. He was coming west with a wagon train – a whole menagerie of refugees from the South. Entertainers – women, if you know what I mean – and some of the soldiers who'd been in his company.

None of them had anything to stay for or anywhere to go, so they followed Captain Beaumont west. We had some good years with that outfit. Mostly worked in cowtowns. But everyone drifted off in one direction or the other. Now it's just me and Captain Beaumont and whoever we hire along the way."

"And why not pin on a badge again?" Heck pressed.

"I make a good living working for Captain Beaumont."

"So it's just the wages?" Heck asked.

Suttles shrugged.

"I'm Captain Beaumont's lieutenant, you understand? The man still thinks like the old artilleryman from the war, and he likes to have a lieutenant. So, I reckon some of it is loyalty to him. I don't want to abandon him. And, truthfully, I don't get excited about pinning on a badge. Some folks see those badges as a target."

Heck nodded. He wasn't particularly fond of getting shot at, himself.

"As a former lawman, I expect you probably have some ideas about who's been holding up the stagecoaches."

"Sure I do," Suttles said. He looked over his shoulder to be sure no one inside the lobby of the hotel was listening. "Like I said, it's got to be someone who knows when there's gold on the stagecoach. And it's got to be someone who's been around for a long time. In the last couple of years, the stagecoach has been held up maybe fifteen or twenty times – I've lost count. But the descriptions of the men are always similar. They cover their faces, but dark hair or light hair or bald or a black hat or a visible scar. It's not the same people every time, but the same descriptions come out. For instance, I know for a fact a man missing a finger on his left hand has been involved in at least three of the stagecoach robberies."

"That's a useful detail," Heck said. "Do you know anyone missing a finger on his left hand?"

"Ha! In a mining town? About ten men, at least, are missing a finger on their left. More'n that are missing a finger on their right."

Heck made a tisking sound with his tongue.

"That doesn't help to narrow it down enough."

"No. But it tells me that whoever is holding up the stagecoach is living somewhere nearby. But what bothers me most is how they always know."

Heck pursed his lips thoughtfully and made a long stroke on the branch with his blade.

"So who knows when there will be gold on the stagecoach?" Heck asked.

Suttles nodded his head.

"That's a good question, deputy marshal."

Suttles had been in a rocking chair, but now he stood up and paced across the boards on the front porch.

"Everson, obviously. He always knows, and he knows ahead of time."

"Everson didn't strike me as the sort who would hold up a stagecoach carrying his employer's gold."

Suttles gave him a scoffing laugh.

"Everyone is the sort, deputy marshal. Every man has it in him to go bad. How many lawmen have you known in your life?"

"Lots of them," Heck said. "Dozens, I suppose."

"And how many of those were outlaws before they became lawmen? Or the other way 'round? Lawmen who became outlaws, took off the badge when the opportunity came along for a big payout."

"It happens," Heck acknowledged.

"Well, Everson is no different from them. He's a man just like they are. Every man can go bad."

"Could you?" Heck asked.

Again, Suttles chuckled.

"Nobody ever said I ain't already gone bad."

Suttles leaned against one of the posts now.

"Everyone who works up at the mine probably knows when they've got a box full of gold or silver ready to ship to Silver City," Suttles said. "So it could be anyone who works for the Little Fannie. We've got a fair few number of saddle tramps living in town who've been around for a while. They do odd jobs here and there and they gamble, of course. But I always wonder how some of them earn a living."

"Any of them missing a finger on his left hand?" Heck asked.

"One of them is missing two fingers on his right hand. But that don't mean, necessarily, that he isn't involved."

"Do saddle tramps know when there's gold on the stagecoach?"

"Anyone who is within sight of the stagecoach when it's being loaded would know. There's always an armed guard from the mine when they're loading a shipment of gold or silver."

"If you had to guess right now, who would you point to?"

Suttles shrugged.

"I couldn't name anyone," Suttles said. "But you might do well to look for someone who's got at least ten or fifteen men working for him and who knows what's going on in the town."

Heck immediately thought of Admiral Moe and his boast about the number of men working for him.

"I need to turn in," Suttles said. "Sunday night is the only chance I get for a decent sleep.

Heck nodded his reply and watched the man walk down to the Two Forks Saloon where he had a tent out back.

- 13 -

"I'm the marshal, and you're the deputy, so you've got to do what I say," Early told Heck.

Heck shook his head angrily.

"No, sir, hombre. This here is partners. We've always been partners. We'll draw for straws. Short straw goes, long straw stays."

Early chuckled, amused at Heck's obstinacy.

"Deputy," Early said. "Do as you're told."

Heck took a heavy breath. He found some tall grass on the side of the road and he broke off two long pieces,

He evened those out, and then broke one of them in half. He mixed them up in his hand and gripped them so that they appeared to be the same length.

"Draw, partner," Heck said. "It's the only way to do this and be fair about it."

"I'll not draw, because I'm riding in the stagecoach," Early said. "That's all there is to it."

Both men knew that whoever went in the stagecoach was going to be alone. There was no way the other man would keep up. But they had to have horses, too, if this turned into a pursuit. So between them, they'd come up with a plan that one man would ride in the stagecoach and the other would trail along behind with the horses."

If there was a holdup, one of them would be in the stagecoach, and maybe could stop the holdup. If not, the other would come along with the horses a short while later, and they could give chase.

Early intended to be the man in the stagecoach. He knew that if he was there and the coach was held up, he wouldn't let it come to a chase. Early Bascomb never hesitated to let lead fly.

Heck also intended to be the man in the stagecoach. He knew that if there was a holdup and Early was in the coach, it would be a gunfight. He didn't want Early making some foolish decision and getting himself killed.

"I ain't interested in drawing straws, amigo."

Heck shook his head.

"Early, there ain't no other way. We'll draw for straws, and the short straw rides the coach."

Heck held his fist out in front of Early, the two pieces of grass looking to be about the same length.

"You know you can't try to boss me around like this," Heck said. "That's not the sort of friendship we have."

Early sighed, exasperated.

They didn't intend to go the full eighty miles to Silver City. There was a trading post about fifteen miles from Mogollon down on the San Francisco River. That trading post acted as the first stagecoach stop, and everyone from Captain Beaumont to Suttles to Randy Everson agreed that most of the holdups took place in that first leg of the journey. The coach even had two routes to get to the trading post, and the drivers frequently alternated routes – never even telling anyone which route they intended to take.

Standing in the shade of a rocky overhang on the narrow road, waiting for the stagecoach at a place about a mile outside Mogollon where they'd agreed with the driver that he would stop to pick one of them up, Early shook his head and snatched one of the pieces of grass from Heck's hand.

Heck smiled at him, and held his out. Clearly, Heck's grass was about two inches longer than Early's.

"Dadburnit," Early said, agitated by this turn of events. He couldn't hardly go back on it now, not after taking one of the pieces of grass.

"Drawing for straws is about the fairest way I know for settling a dispute among friends," Heck said happily.

"I want a do-over," Early said. "You held tighter to the longer straw."

"No time," Heck said with a nod of his head, and Early heard it before he saw it, the coach coming into view around a bend in the road. "Do your best to keep up without exhausting the horses."

***

The driver of the coach eyed Heck as he stepped toward the door into the passenger compartment.

"I thought you was going," he said to Early, holding the lines in one hand as he scratched at the underside of his round belly with the other.

"Huh," Early grunted. "You get my deputy. I'll be riding behind."

"I don't want no Mexican bandito in my coach," the driver said.

Early quickly forgot his agitation with Heck winning the straw drawing contest.

"He ain't no bandito. He's my deputy marshal, and you'll get him or you'll get a severe ass stomping from me," Early said. "Take your pick, I'm in the mood for either."

The driver moaned and complained some under his breath, but he didn't raise any further objection that Early could hear.

The shotgun rider struck Early as a mite nervous. He was young, younger than Early by some years. He had lively, clear eyes and a clenched jaw, and he held his shotgun instead of leaving it at his feet.

"What's your name, son?" Early said to him.

"Melvin Reiner."

"You ever been held up riding a stagecoach?"

"This is just my third time out," the boy said.

"All right, Mel. You be steady and don't do anything stupid. You follow my deputy's lead. Don't shoot unless he starts shooting."

Early stepped up on the side of the coach, pulling himself up with a hand through the window, and looked in the passenger compartment. Empty, except for mail bags, and now Heck.

"No other passengers?" Early asked.

"It ain't uncommon," the driver said. "I've run this route fifty times or more, and I bet half them times there warn't passengers."

Early nodded. He wasn't exactly satisfied with the situation Heck was walking into, but he didn't know what else to do.

"I'll see you at the San Francisco River trading post," Early said to Heck.

"Or you'll see me before," Heck said.

"Good luck, amigo."

Early jumped off the coach and the driver drew up his lines and called to his mules and in a moment the stagecoach disappeared behind a cloud of dust.

The buckskin stallion side-footed away from Early as he cinched the strap on the saddle.

"Come on, Tim," Early snapped at the horse. He slid a foot into the stirrup, and threw himself into the saddle. He took up the lead on Poco a Poco, Heck's pinto, and then started along the road behind the stagecoach.

Early kept the horses at a walk, but he stayed close enough to the stagecoach through first mile or so, that a layer of dust hung in the air in front of him. The coach, with its team of six mules, could only make so much time on the narrow and winding trail through the hills. In the saloons in Mogollon, the miners talked about the dust down in the mines as they coughed out brown grit even hours after coming up from the mines, and Early figured these mountains just consisted of fine dust all the way through.

Heck and Early had come in from the east on this same road, but this was all new terrain to him, and he caught himself absentmindedly admiring the rocky peaks and ledges bursting out among the tall pines along the hillsides. The beauty of the mountains was undeniable.

Autumn had surely arrived. The narrow gulch and the tall pines and the canopy of the hardwoods growing along the creek bed prevented the sun from being able to beat down on him, but even so, Early felt the coolness in the air. The leaves were beginning to change colors, too. The cottonwoods were coming bright yellow, others looked like they might turn a pretty red or orange, but a lot of them had gone from green to brown, and a few limbs and branches were already turning skeletal. In a week or ten days, this entire valley would be as pretty as a painting.

As the dust in front of him settled, and Early realized the stagecoach was distancing out in front of him, he got the horses into a lope. He wouldn't catch it, but he wanted to keep as close as possible. If bandits stopped to the coach, Early wanted to be close enough that they could begin an immediate pursuit. Even now, if something happened, Early might still come up on them before the bandits managed to start away. Opening a treasure box took time. The thing was mounted into the floor of the coach. They'd need an ax to bust it open, or they could try dynamite if they were in a hurry and had a stick available to them.

After some time, the sunlight glinted against the dust in the air again, and Early slowed the horses to a walk. He figured at most, the stagecoach was probably half a mile ahead now. If he could stay within a couple of miles of it, he'd be able to get to the coach quickly if there was trouble.

When Early first talked about his plan – one of them riding on the stagecoach and the other one following behind with horses – Heck had insisted on the need for secrecy. That led them to decide to meet the stagecoach below town where no one would see either the marshal or deputy marshal boarding the coach. And they'd told no one of their plan, stealing away from town about half an hour before the stagecoach. The only person Early talked to was the driver, giving him just enough information to arrange for him to stop for his additional passenger.

On this twisting road, it would take the coach a couple of hours to get along the first dozen miles, and according to the driver, that would be about the time they'd drop down off the mountain trail into a wide, north-south valley. That's where they would hit the road to Silver City, the driver had said.

"If anything is going to happen, it'll happen before we drop down into that valley. There's too much traffic on that road, too many trading posts and stagecoach stops and little ranches."

They came to a spot where the banks of the creek were not so high, and Poco a Poco, always the slower of the two horses, tugged at his lead and stopped to drink some water. Early let Tim Buck Too step over to the creek, as well, and he took a drink from his canteen.

The morning couldn't be nicer for a ride. The dust in front of him had settled enough that Early had dropped the bandanna he'd used to cover his face. Probably the stagecoach was a mile or so ahead of him.

And it was there, with the horses drinking from the pool and Early daydreaming about the cooler weather and the solitude of the trail, that he heard a pop in the distance. He cocked his head, pointing his ear to the west, and heard another pop, and another.

Gunshots! Probably about a mile-and-a-half farther up the road.

"Dadgumit!" Early said, and he gave a jerk to Poco's lead and touched Tim's side with his knee.

Both horses seemed to sense the urgency, and even Poco a Poco started to make a good run.

Over the noise of the horses bounding forward, Early heard more pops, some of them louder than before, suggesting they were probably rifle or shotgun blasts. And they weren't all in one volley and then over, there were several shots, some spaced out, and that sounded to Early Bascomb like folks trading shots in a gunfight.

"Get up!" Early called to Tim, though the stallion needed no encouragement to make a run.

The road ahead twisted to the left, cutting a narrow trench between two steep and rocky walls. Trees obscured anything farther than a hundred yards, and just beyond that the road curved to the right.

Early heard more pops, now – and these were much louder and echoed off the canyon walls.

Now there was dust hanging in the air, not so thick as to obscure his vision, but Early could definitely feel the grit in his teeth.

The horses had made a good run, galloping as hard

as they would go, but Early felt tension in the lead rope and knew that Poco was starting to slow. The pinto gelding never had quite as much in him as the buckskin.

"A little farther, Poco," Early encouraged the horse. "Heck's in trouble up here!"

And then they came down a slope, both horses still at the gallop, and up ahead, dust filled the air and through it, Early could see the bright red and yellow stagecoach, stopped in the middle of the road. He saw the driver kneeling close to the ground, his fat belly blocking what he was kneeling next to, but from fifty yards, Early could see boots and legs on the ground beside the driver. Someone was down.

And now Early was pulling back on the reins, and dropping from the saddle and running the last fifteen yards or so to where the driver was kneeling over a body that made no movement. The driver looked up at Early and shook his head.

"He ain't going to make it," he said as Early ran up to him and dropped to his knees beside the body.

Melvin Reiner was shot more times than Early could count, and though his eyes were open, he made no expression of recognition.

"Where's my partner?" Early said to the stagecoach driver.

***

Under the best circumstances – a well-maintained, flat road and good springs on the coach – Hector Espinoza despised riding on a stagecoach.

The drivers whipped the teams into a frenzy, threw the stagecoach like a careening boulder at the road, and drove with complete disregard of tight curves or steep slopes. And this particular journey was not in the best of conditions. Silver Creek ran right along the side of the road, inches from the coach's wheels. A slight breeze pushing in the wrong direction, and the damn thing would skid into the embankment and topple over like a drunk at midnight. The road was also full of ruts and holes, and he bounced around inside the coach. The only grace about the entire trip was that they so often came to inclines that made it hard on the animals to pull at speed, and so they never could get going too terribly fast.

Heck kept the short-barrel scattergun across his lap and his Winchester rifle on the floor of the coach beside his feet. He did not have a good plan for what he would do if they encountered bandits on this run. He and Early both agreed it was best not to get into a shooting fight, especially if only one of them was there. But if Suttles' suspicions were right and the outlaws who'd been holding up the stagecoach were based in Mogollon, they'd know that Heck was the deputy marshal, and they might start shooting the moment they recognized him. Then he'd be left with no choice but to shoot back.

Still, he reasoned, in spite of the rough ride, it was better that he was here than Early.

Early didn't have discretion in him. They could agree between them that a shooting fight was the wrong way to handle this if the stagecoach was held up, and if the roles were reversed and Early was here, he'd come out of the coach with hammers cocked and looking for his first shot.

What Heck really wanted was to let the outlaws take the treasure box and then trail them. They'd have a hideout somewhere, and like as not, he and Early could arrest the entire gang in one go. And if they were outnumbered to such an extent that they needed to ride for help, they could raise up a posse and go back. With a little luck, they might not just recover the gold from this holdup but maybe some gold and silver from previous holdups.

What they did know was that for all the holdups on this road, the fewest number of them involved any bloodshed. Only one bandit had ever been killed – and that was long before the present crop of them ever appeared – and only a few guards had been shot. No passengers had ever been killed on a holdup through this stretch of the mountains.

Heck felt the sickening drop in his stomach as the stagecoach lurched down a slope, and then it leveled out. And then he thought maybe they were on a straightaway because he couldn't see any bend in the road up ahead, and he hoped they were coming out of the mountains to the valley road.

But up ahead, now, Heck could see the mountain walls narrow again and the road would make a bend, and just then the jehu let out a string of curses as he jerked back the lines to slow the mules, and the stagecoach lurched at the sudden shift in motion, and Heck felt himself nearly tumble forward.

"Road's blocked!" the driver shouted.

As the coach rolled to a stop, Heck heard a man shout at the driver and the shotgun rider, "Don't do anything foolish, all we want is the gold."

Heck slid toward the window where he could get a look. Up ahead a half dozen men or so were coming out from behind the trees and the undergrowth. They'd chopped a pine down so that it blocked the road, and they had horses waiting for them on the other side of the felled tree. All of the men had bandannas pulled up over their faces. Some of them had rifles and a couple of them had shotguns.

"Passengers out!" someone shouted, and Heck now had to make a decision. He'd seen at least six men, and maybe there were seven or eight. He looked at the shotgun across his lap and decided to leave it on the seat. He unholstered his Colt and left it on the seat with the shotgun. Then he threw open the door and stuck his hands out first.

"Just me inside," Heck called. "I'm coming unarmed."

As best he could, Heck watched for reactions from the men as he stepped out of the stagecoach. It was hard to say, their faces largely covered by bandannas, but he thought he saw recognition in the eyes of one of the closest ones to him when he stepped out.

"What are you doing in there?" the man with the covered face asked.

"Protecting the stagecoach," Heck said.

"Doing a piss poor job at it," the man laughed.

Heck eyed the man, trying to remember all the details. He had a red bandanna stretched over his face, his eyes were light – hazel or a light brown – he wore a dark shirt, damp with sweat and gray with trail dust, but nothing particularly memorable about it. But his gunbelt was memorable. The thing was dark with white stitching and swirling patterns cut into the leather. The white stitching followed the swirls, decorative. The holster matched the belt. The leather was hard, too, like the gunbelt was new. The brass buckle was polished and clean, no dings or wear that would suggest he'd had it for long.

Heck was unarmed. His Colt Peacemaker sat on the bench inside the coach alongside the short-barrel scattergun, and his Winchester was on the floor.

Maybe if he'd come out with a gun in his hand, or at least with the Peacemaker in his holster, things would have been different. But maybe if he'd not left the guns inside the coach, the outlaws would have shot him, too.

It was Melvin Reiner's fault. The boy's inexperience got him killed.

Heck saw it, the same as Reiner did. A couple of the outlaws were helping the driver down from the box. Three of them were watching Heck to make sure he didn't try anything. One of them was checking to see that the brake on the stagecoach was fully set. A couple of them stayed back, on the other side of the felled tree, where they held the horses.

Nobody had eyes on the shotgun rider.

Except Heck. He saw the boy, his profile stark against the cloudless blue of the sky.

The boy had put his gun down beside him and raised his hands, but with no one watching him, he dropped his hands into his lap as he sat on the roof of the stagecoach just above the driver's box. Nobody noticed the movement. Heck saw it from the corner of his eye. Reiner reached down and swung the shotgun around. Reiner fired with one barrel and struck one of the men who had his eyes on Heck, blasting the man in the face and chest with buckshot.

Reiner didn't get off a shot with the second barrel. Every man there in the vicinity of the stagecoach had a gun in his hand, even the two helping down the driver, and Reiner stood like a beacon atop the coach. He was an easy target standing over them with nothing but the sky to give him cover.

Heck reached into the stagecoach and grabbed the first thing his hand touched – the Winchester rifles, still snug in its scabbard.

He didn't wait to watch the bullets smash into the shotgun rider, nor did he see the driver fall headlong to the ground as one of the men helping him down gave him a sharp jerk.

Heck dashed for the cover of the river bank back the way they'd come. The bank was steep and deep and narrow, and the thick growth of scrub oak and tall grass there along the bank meant that Heck could have cover to get behind – not protection from the bullets, but a place to hide, at least.

He sensed that he was now the target of the shooting behind him as the bandits turned their guns against him, and he knew that meant it was all over for Melvin Reiner. A bullet tore past him and into the leaves of the scrub oak, and Heck heard it tearing through the leaves. He jumped now, and his boots landed into the rocky bottom of Silver Creek. A couple more bullets passed overhead, but Heck squatted down so that the bank gave him some protection, and he slid the rifle from its scabbard.

His first shot smacked one of the bandits in the hip.

Two of them were down now – one shot all to hell by Reiner's shotgun, and the other one with a hip wound that would probably be fatal. A wound like that would shatter the bone and bleed for days without stopping.

The outlaws gathered up their wounded sending a couple of fleeting shots in Heck's direction, and then they were gone.

Heck sent one last shot with the rifle, a long shot that he didn't think hit anything useful. He stepped up out of the creek and started to push his way through the undergrowth, and before he cleared it, Early Bascomb charged past him on the back of the buckskin, trailing Poco a Poco behind.

Early never saw him, instead riding directly for Melvin Reiner's body and the driver who kneeled over him.

"Where's my partner?" Heck heard Early demand.

"Back here, hombre," Heck called. "Get back in that saddle, they can't be more than a minute in front of us."

Heck and Early had been friends long enough. When Early spun around and saw his partner, Heck could see the relief wash over him.

- 14 -

The trail cut between enormous boulders and followed closely to a small creek. Small hardwood saplings and cottonwoods spread out along the bank, though nowhere interfering with their ability to follow the worn path. Large rock walls rose up on both sides of the narrow canyon. Ferns here and there clung to the walls, but they were mostly bare and loomed in ominous fashion over the two riders. The trail cut through the creek in places, and in other spots rose high on a ridge that dropped steeply down to the creek.

Heck and Early kept a watch on the rock walls as much as they watched the trail in front of them.

Assuming that up ahead somewhere their prey could find a way to mount one of the walls and get up to the cliffs above, the canyon was the perfect place for an ambush.

"They won't be expecting pursuit," Heck said. "They only saw me and the driver."

Still, he watched the cliffs above.

"Did you recognize any of the men?" Early said.

"They had their faces covered."

"What about voices?"

"All you gringos sound just alike to me."

Early laughed.

"I suppose we do."

"There!" Heck said, pointing to a flash mark on a rock. It was bright and white and clearly fresh – a shod horse had dropped a hoof down on that rock and the metal shoe had gashed the rock. "We're still on the right trail."

"We knew that, though," Early said. "There ain't no way to get out of this canyon. At least not that we've come across yet."

"It must open up ahead somewhere," Heck said. "Or else they've got a hideout here."

"That's what worries me," Early said. "If they've got a hideout, they'll have a lookout. They might well know we're coming up behind them before we catch them."

"Keep your eyes on the cliffs," Heck said.

They walked their horses. The path through the canyon was too rocky for anything faster than a walk, but even if they could go at a lope, they wouldn't for fear of missing some sign or losing the trail.

After helping to load Melvin Menier's body into the back of the stagecoach, they'd told the driver of the stagecoach to turn around and head back to Mogollon. They didn't have time to chop up the pine tree blocking the road, and there wasn't space here for him to maneuver around it. Someone needed to alert the folks back in town about what had happened.

They came across evidence that men had worked this creek for gold – empty cans of beans and fruit, long-ago burned out campfires, discarded cradles and other tools, left behind either in glory or frustration. A couple of times they found abandoned campsites with makeshift huts.

Up ahead, the canyon narrowed even more so that the two riders were forced down into the creek. It was a shallow thing, but fast moving in its narrow banks. Early had to squeeze the stallion between his knees and keep up a steady stream of encouragement to keep Tim Buck Too confident about moving upstream in the water. Poco a Poco moved forward without a problem, and Heck took the lead as they had to walk through the stream.

"Whoever we're following knows these mountains," Heck decided.

"Huh," Early grunted, giving Tim a pat on the neck to keep him moving. "You just stay behind old Poco, there, and we'll be all right. He can pick his way up through a creek."

Now there were no banks to the creek, just rocky ledges jutting up forty or fifty feet overhead. The walls of the narrow canyon so close here that Early could almost reach both arms out and drag his fingertips along the walls.

"It gives a man a closed-in feeling, don't it?" Early said.

"It gets better up ahead," Heck said.

Early craned his neck to see, and sure enough, as they moved through a bend in the creek, going around a bulge in the right wall, Early could see that up ahead the canyon opened to wide daylight, and for the first time he took an easy breath.

"Almost there, partner," Early promised the horse.

They reached the place where the canyon opened and found themselves in a much wider valley here, and there were four or five little streams pouring into the valley to form the creek they'd been through. Two of them were completely dry here, and the other weren't much more than a trickle. The valley was covered with pines and juniper, and the slopes here were gentler. The problem, though, was that the trail broke apart into several other trails, following each of the streams. Farther up ahead, something blowing in the wind caught Early's attention.

"Hell, Heck, there's a tent up there!" Early hissed, reaching for his rifle and dropping down out of the saddle.

Heck, too, grabbed his Winchester and quickly swung a leg.

Both men on their feet now, they crouched down and ran up to a stand of pines, leaving the horses where they stood.

Heck hugged one of the big pine trunks while Early stood against another, both of them eyeing the tent up ahead.

Now they could see that in addition to the tent there were a couple of lean-tos and some livestock, chickens and mules. A man squatted down beside a campfire, another man was taking a drink from a canteen. Neither of them had noticed the riders come up.

"Is that them?" Early asked.

"I don't hardly think so," Heck said, squinting at the men. They weren't but maybe sixty or seventy yards away. Heck didn't recognize any of their clothes, but the men also didn't look like they'd just tried to hold up a stagecoach. They were unconcerned about pursuit, and neither Heck nor Early could see a gun on either of them. Also, they had no horses.

"What do you think, amigo?" Early asked.

"I think we should walk up there and ask them if they've seen any banditos ride through this way."

Heck held the Winchester casually across his arms as he picked his way up the slope, following along a worn path. Early toted the Henry rifle low, but kept it pointed generally in the direction of the men up by the tent.

A third man they'd not yet seen came out of the tent, and he was the first to see the two men approaching.

"Afternoon!" he called with a raised hand. "If you're here to rob us, you're going to be disappointed. We ain't had no success all summer."

"We're not here to rob you," Heck responded. "This is Marshal Bascomb from Muggyown, and I'm Deputy Marshal Espinoza. We're trailing some men who tried to hold up the Silver City stagecoach a while back."

The three men looked at each other, confusion evident on their faces.

"When was this?" the man from the tent asked.

"Earlier today," Heck said. "They can't be too far in front of us."

He shook his head.

"Deputy, if you're thinking the men you're looking for came up this way, you're on the wrong trail. Ain't no outlaws come this way."

"We're following their tracks," Early said.

The men all looked at each other, and the one squatting down by the campfire started to chuckle.

"You've got your tracks mixed up, marshal," he said.

"What makes you think so?" Early asked.

"Only folks come through here in the last week are some of the men from the Three Sweethearts Mine. They came up through here maybe an hour ago. But ain't nobody else come this way. If they had done, we'd have seen 'em. We ain't left the camp all day."

Early narrowed his eyes at the men, wondering if they were really that dim.

"The Three Sweethearts?" Early said. "Which way did they go?"

The man from the tent indicated a switchback trail that went up the northern slope.

"That trail yonder cuts up the side of the mountain and leads through a pass. It meets the Muggyown Road up there and leads down to a little timber camp. Then beyond that is the Three Sweethearts Mine. They come this way pretty often, though marshal. I can tell you, they ain't your stagecoach robbers."

"No," Early agreed with the man. "Of course they

wouldn't be. Obviously, we've gotten our dadburn tracks crossed all to hell. Haven't we, Hector?"

Heck nodded.

"I reckon we have."

"You say this trail leads to the Muggyown Road?"

"You can't miss it," the man from the tent said. "Cuts right through a timber camp."

"Sure, we know the one," Early said.

Through the course of the conversation, Heck and Early had continued to move up to the camp so that now they were standing just a few feet from the men. Both of them, Heck and Early, surveyed the campsite for any evidence, but it was pretty plain that these men hadn't been holding up stagecoaches or done much of anything else.

"How long you boys been prospecting here?" Early asked.

"Been up at this camp all summer long."

"Had no luck?" Early said.

"Not the least bit."

"You ought to get them pans wet," Early advised. "You won't find any gold settin' here drinkin' coffee."

The man from the tent chuckled.

"Ain't that the truth, though."

Heck had already turned to go and fetch the horses and was halfway there now, moving at a quick pace.

"Well, I reckon we're going to head on back to Muggyown and these banditos we're after will live to fight another day. You boys keep your eyes open, and if you see anyone suspicious, you come on up and give us a holler up in Muggyown and let us know."

"We'll do it."

Heck and Early mounted and made their way quickly up the switchback trail, and in no time, they'd mounted the tall northern slope to a ridge where they could see the deep canyon through which they'd come carving its way through the mountains back to the west. At the top of the slope, with an excellent vantage behind them, they stopped to examine the terrain around. The mountain continued to rise high above them, covered in tall ponderosa pines and big rocky outcroppings. But the trail followed the ridge out across the face of the mountain.

"You're thinking what I'm thinking?" Heck said.

"Only if you're thinking it's the Three Sweethearts outfit that held up that stagecoach this morning."

"That's what I'm thinking," Heck said.

***

"Some boys from the Three Sweethearts outfit rode through here a little bit ago, said they were coming in with supplies from Silver City," Stan Davis said when Heck and Early arrived in his timber camp.

He seemed genuinely surprised to see Heck and Early again, and even more surprised to learn that they'd hired on as the new marshal and deputy.

"Did they have supplies?" Early asked.

"They didn't stop for a chat," Davis said. "They just rode past, waved, said they'd been down in Silver City.

There was four of them, and they had two horses toting bundles that was wrapped up in blankets. I suppose they were supplies."

Davis didn't seem fully convinced, though.

"You don't think the bundles were supplies?" Heck asked.

Davis shrugged his shoulders and leaned against the side of a wagon he was standing next to. While he talked, some of his men continued to load fresh boards into the back of the wagon.

"I don't want to speak out of turn, you understand. But both those horses was saddled, like for riders, and the bundles was laid over the saddles. And one of those bundles was wearing boots sticking out of the blanket."

"That don't sound much like supplies," Early said.

"I didn't reckon so, neither, but it ain't my business."

"How long ago did they pass through here?" Heck asked.

Davis gave another shrug.

"Maybe an hour."

But he said it like a question, doubtfully.

The road to Mogollon cut to the left, but another trail went up through a canyon directly ahead of them.

"That's the trail they followed, straight ahead?" Heck asked, pointing.

"That trail leads right up to the Three Sweethearts Mine. But if you're looking to follow them up there, you boys had best be careful. They's a pile of folks working for the Three Sweethearts, and they might not be happy to see you coming."

Early nodded his thanks for the information, and they continued to follow the trail.

The ride up to the Three Sweethearts Mine took another hour or so up a narrow canyon, but there was no question when they arrived. The timber had been cut heavily from the hillside, leaving it almost completely bare. They'd blasted tons of rock from the hillside as well, and there were dozens of log buildings – everything from small huts that were obviously cabins for the men to much larger buildings like a dining hall and an office building. All of it was rough-cut timber construction, clearly made from the logs they'd taken right there off the hillside.

Caleb Rathbone came down from one of the larger buildings and met Heck and Early on the trail. He seemed to be expecting them, or at least wasn't surprised at their appearance.

"Either they knew they were being trailed, or a lookout rode ahead and told them we were coming," Early muttered to Heck.

"Afternoon, marshal," Caleb Rathbone said, though there was no pleasant greeting in his tone. "You're a long way outside of your jurisdiction, ain't you?"

"Trailing some outlaws that tried to hold up the stagecoach to Silver City this morning," Early said.

Caleb looked around.

"Nothing of that sort around here. I'm afraid you've trailed the wrong trail."

"Could be," Early said. "I ain't much of a tracker, if the truth is known."

"How much did they get from the stagecoach?"

"Just a murder charge, as soon as we catch them," Early said.

"Who got killed?"

"The shotgun rider."

Caleb Rathbone nodded his head and frowned.

"Well, that happens in that line of work, I suppose."

"You haven't had anybody ride into your camp this afternoon?" Early asked. "We think those men are about an hour ahead of us, give or take a few minutes."

"Nope. Nobody's come through this way," Caleb Rathbone said. "I'll tell you, marshal, these hills are full of trails and cutbacks and little passes. The Apache have been moving through these mountains for generations. If you know where you're going, there's a thousand different ways to go. If you ain't so familiar, it's easy to get turned around and lost. Or to miss some little trail where the men you're tracking might have veered off."

Early nodded thoughtfully.

"I reckon it is," he said. "All the same, would you mind if we got down and had a look around your camp? I'd hate it if we tracked some bandits right up here and they were lurking nearby and y'all didn't even know it. Why, if something happened up here because we didn't do our due diligence, I'd never forgive myself."

"Like hell," Caleb Rathbone said. "You stay in your saddle, marshal."

Now Jubal Rathbone came down from the office building, and he had a couple of men with him. Early immediately recognized the two men as those who'd tried to steal the drummer's case of laudanum bottles at the hotel on Saturday.

"What's going on here?" Jubal Rathbone asked, looking from Heck and Early to his brother.

"Marshal says somebody tried to hold up the stagecoach earlier today," Caleb said. "Says they shot and killed the messenger rider."

Jubal frowned.

"What's that got to do with us?" he demanded, looking squarely at Early.

Even as they spoke, Early noticed that the men from the Three Sweethearts outfit were fanning out among the trees and buildings around their camp. Several of them were toting rifles.

"We tracked the men here," Early said.

Jubal Rathbone started to chuckle.

"You tracked the wrong men, marshal. Now, we did have some men come up with supplies today from Silver City. Maybe their trail crossed with the men who tried to hold up the stagecoach. You must have gotten confused."

Early twisted around to look at Heck, and he noticed his partner staring intently at one of the men with Jubal Rathbone. Early looked back at the man and saw where Heck's eyes had lit.

The man wore a dark shirt, stained with sweat, and gray with trail dust. Around his waist he wore a fancy new gunbelt, dark leather with ornamental white stitching that followed the path of swirls cut into the belt. He had a fancy, brass buckle that was shiny. Early couldn't say for sure, but he thought Heck was looking hard at that gunbelt.

"All the same, we'd like to take a look around," Early said. "Like I told your brother, if those boys that tried to hold up the stagecoach are up here somewhere, I'd be distraught if my partner and I failed to find them and then something happened here."

Jubal shrugged his shoulders and smiled happily.

"Surely, marshal. Step on down and have a look around. You're welcome to."

Early nodded and took a breath. He glanced back at Heck, whose face was tight.

"Whyn't you stay here with the horses," Early said. "I'll make a quick look around and make sure those boys that tried to hold up the stagecoach aren't hiding somewhere in the woods."

Heck started to argue, but then stopped. He understood. If something happened, Early wanted Heck away from him and ready to ride out in a hurry.

Jubal Rathbone nodded his head at the two men who'd walked down to meet Heck and Early.

"This is Haven and Ballew," Rathbone said. "They'll show you around."

***

Early walked into the trees over the camp and started looking around there. Haven and Ballew followed him. All through the woods, men from the Three Sweethearts outfit leaned casually against trees, but they watched Early as he passed by them.

"You boys haven't seen any stagecoach robbers up around here?" Early would ask as he passed by the men. They grunted their responses or ignored him out-right.

Everywhere he walked, Haven and Ballew followed close behind.

They didn't say anything, either of them, as they walked through the woods.

The camp had a decent sized corral with numerous horses. There were a half dozen or so mules, but far more horses than one would expect to find in a gold mining camp. The horses looked bred for travel and speed. Early would happily throw a saddle on any of these horses if he was planning to make a journey. A gold and silver camp should be more concerned with hauling loads, either in wagons or on the backs of mules. Early walked toward the corral. He wanted to get a look at the horses, see if any of them were lathered like they'd just made an escape after a stagecoach holdup.

"Where're you going?" Haven asked.

"Just thought I'd look at your livestock," Early said.

"There's no need for you to bother the horses. You can see there's no stage robbers in the corral."

"Fair enough," Early said.

He started toward one of the big buildings, but Haven stopped him again.

"I can promise you, nobody's gone into the dining hall. I was just in there fifteen minutes before you arrived."

Early didn't want to push his luck. He wanted to find something that would be definitive – absolute proof of his suspicions – but he needed to find it without making trouble. If the Rathbones decided to, they could throw him out of here, and Early didn't have any authority to prevent them.

He rounded the dining hall and noticed a couple of men with shovels in a meadow down below the camp. The meadow wasn't particularly wide, though it stretched a long way through the valley, and there were a few pretty hardwoods down that way. It was an idyllic sort of spot, and Early could see building a little house down below the tree where the men stood.

As he looked, though, Early noticed that there was some sort of marker, like a tombstone, standing up by the two men.

"What's going on down there?" Early asked.

"We had an accident in the mine yesterday," Haven said. "A couple of our men were killed."

"Is that right?" Early said. "I'm sorry to hear that. They're burying the dead?"

"They are."

"Y'all already got the graves marked?" he asked. "I see what looks like a tombstone standing up."

"That's someone else's marker is what that is," Haven said. "You got any more foolish questions?"

Early grinned at him.

"I reckon I probably do, but I can tell you're getting irritated, so I'll keep them to myself."

Early didn't have proof by the time he'd finished his tour of the place, but he'd reinforced his suspicions.

As he made his way back down to Heck and the horses, Jubal Rathbone came down from one of the buildings again.

"I invited your deputy to come sit in the office with me, but he chose to stay in his saddle," Rathbone said.

Early nodded.

"Well, he's rude like that," Early said, within Heck's earshot. "Señor Espinoza, there, he doesn't possess the benefit of any sort of proper home training. A good Southerner, such as myself, who was raised right at the end of his mama's wooden spoon wouldn't be so uncouth as to turn down an invitation like that. Isn't that right, Hector?"

Heck frowned and shook his head.

"I appreciate your hospitality, Mr. Rathbone," Heck said. "I certainly didn't intend to offend you."

Rathbone waved him off.

"No apologies necessary," Rathbone said. "Marshal, I trust there's no stagecoach robbers threatening our camp?"

Early stepped into his saddle and let Tim Buck Too make a little dance.

"No, sir. I think if anyone is safe from them robbers, it's you folks up here at this camp. I reckon you're right, we just got crisscrossed on the tracks we were trailing and followed your boys coming back from Silver City."

Now he wheeled the horse back down the trail, and Heck followed him.

When they got twenty or so yards below Rathbone, Early muttered to Heck, "If they don't get a sharpshooter to shoot both of us in the back as we ride away, we can consider ourselves mighty fortunate."

"They did it," Heck said. "I know it was them."

"Me, too," Early said. "I can't prove it, but they were burying two bodies."

"I recognized the gunbelt on that one, Ballew, who went with you on your tour."

Early nodded.

"What do we do?" he asked.

Heck shrugged his shoulders.

"I don't know. They've got an army up here."

"Why would a successful mining camp be holding up a stagecoach?" Early said. "From everything I hear, these folks are getting plenty of their own gold."

"Now that's a damn good question, hombre," Heck said. "Why would they?"

"You know, Heck, we saw a bunch of boys toting rifles, and a burial party, and a bunch of standing around up there. But you know what we didn't see?"

"What's that?" Heck asked.

"We didn't see a single man swing a pick or light a stick of dynamite. Hell, Heck, they don't even have a stamp mill up here. How do you have a gold mine without a stamp mill?"

"What's your point?"

Early shrugged.

"Maybe they're not digging as much gold as they want folks to think."

Heck nodded his head.

"I've got the feeling that there's more going on here than we know about, hombre."

"More going on here they we know, and less going on than they want anyone to know," Early said.

- 15 -

"Tell me about the Rathbones," Early said.

Maybe O'Malley sniffed and looked away.

"Early, love, I've said I don't want to talk about them. Haven't I, now?"

They were sitting outside Maybe's tent, watching the folks down below in gulch. A man driving a two-mule wagon up to the butcher's shop had a couple of slaughtered pigs in the back. A group of men were down in front of Admiral Moe's arguing about something, and Early was watching them particularly close to see if he was going to have to break up a fight.

The stagecoach was parked down by the livery, and Early could just see one of the brightly painted yellow wheels and the boot on the coach.

There'd been no time, yesterday morning, when they'd gone in pursuit of the robbers to cut that felled tree out of the way, and so they'd told the driver to get back up to the town. The coach would be at least a day late arriving in Silver City. While Heck and Early followed the trail to the Three Sweethearts camp and after the coach had arrived back in Mogollon with the news of what had happened, Captain Beaumont had sent Suttles with some men to remove the tree from the road. But now the stagecoach sat motionless by the livery. Everson's men had toted the gold back up to the Little Fannie mine to keep it safe. They'd already buried poor Melvin Menier's body by the time Heck and Early rode back into Mogollon after dark.

They'd not yet mentioned to anyone in town what they'd found when they'd gone in pursuit of the stagecoach robbers, that the trail had led them directly to the Three Sweethearts Mine and that Heck recognized the gunbelt on one of the men there as belonging to the robbers.

"I know you don't want to talk about it, but I need to know about them," Early said. "Heck and I think that the folks in town haven't been on the up and up with us. You mentioned to me about another marshal – the first town marshal – and you said he was killed. Tell me about that."

Maybe shook her head.

"I'll not talk about it."

"Sure you will," Early said, and his confidence went against her resolve. "There's something I need to know – some history between the Three Sweethearts outfit and the town."

"Gettin' on my nerves is what you're doing, Early. I'll ask you again to leave it."

Early had an ace in the hole, a name that Heck had given him. Heck had gotten it from Admiral Moe.

"Tell me about Jeremiah," Early said.

"Oh, you know about Jeremiah, do you? Well, then you should understand the trouble between the Three Sweethearts and the town."

"I don't know about Jeremiah, that's why I'm asking."

Maybe cast a sideways glance at him. She was a rare beauty.

"Why do you think it's called the Three Sweethearts?"

Early shrugged his shoulders.

"I reckon because the Rathbones named it for three women."

"Right," Maybe said.

Early thought about it for a moment.

"But there's only two Rathbones," he said. "So was there a third woman?"

"Try again."

"A third Rathbone?" Early asked, narrowing his eyes at her. "Jeremiah – was he a Rathbone?"

"The youngest brother," she said. "There was Jubal, Caleb, and Jeremiah. The three of them came prospecting together and discovered gold up at the Three Sweethearts Mine. They named it for their girls back home."

"What happened to Jeremiah?"

Maybe sighed. Her resolve surrendered.

"I don't remember any of the Rathbones before they hit gold. I know they'd come to town some for supplies and to drink, but I don't even remember seeing them. I'd only been here a few weeks when they hit it big. I'd come here because it was a booming town with recent silver and gold strikes, and I knew there'd be opportunity for me. So maybe they never came to town while I was here, but nobody much remembered them. You know what I mean? They were just an outfit of prospectors like any other. Well, when they hit big, people started to notice them right away. They threw their gold around like they were big shots – and I suppose they were. And that was fine when it was just the three of them. But then their outfit started to grow, and when it's ten or twenty men causing trouble in town, it's not so easy to ignore, no matter how much gold dust is in their bags. They were a thieving bunch, the men in their outfit. They were rowdy. I remember one night a group of them beat some gambler half to death. Another time, one of them got drunk and stabbed one of the girls at Captain Beaumont's place and killed a man who tried to stop him.

"Of the three brothers, Jeremiah was the worst. The meanest of them. He used to beat on the soiled doves. You expect a man to hit you from time to time – most of them do. But he was cruel about it."

"He ever lay a hand on you?" Early asked.

"Caleb would've killed him if he did," Maybe said. "He never came to see me, and I can tell you I met that with some relief."

"So what happened to him?"

"Captain Beaumont and Beatty at the hotel and some of the shopkeepers, they met with Everson at the Little Fannie Mine, and between them agreed the town needed a marshal. They hired one of Captain Beaumont's men for the job, and everyone knew that his only job was to get the men of the Three Sweethearts under control. Drunken revelry and fights and card cheats, none of that now was within his purview. Just the Three Sweethearts men, with Captain Beaumont's other men backing him up."

"One man against fifty?" Early said.

"It wasn't so many back then. But you have the right idea. It was that marshal against an entire outfit, maybe twenty-five or thirty men, and the Three Sweethearts men always traveled in packs."

"What about the stagecoach robberies?" Early asked. "Didn't they want the marshal to deal with those?"

Maybe shrugged her shoulders.

"They weren't so common back then. They were a problem, to be sure, but nothing like they are now. The real problem then, as it is now, is that the Three Sweethearts men were bad for business. They ran off the paying customers, they stole what they wanted.

"So one night, right after the new marshal was hired, Jeremiah gets himself a little drunk in a card game. He accuses a man of cheating and goes for his gun – kills the man right there in the Two Forks Saloon. Shot him in the head with the first shot, and then stood over him and shot him two or three more times.

"The new marshal comes running, and he knocks Jeremiah to the ground and throws him in the newly constructed jail – christens it with a Rathbone, if you like.

Jubal and Caleb threatened the marshal, demanded he release their brother. About half the men of the town turn up armed to support the marshal, and the Three Sweethearts men ride out of town back up to their camp.

"This was in July, so the days were blazing and when the marshal went to check on Jeremiah, he found the man dead inside the jail. He'd cooked in there."

"Huh," Early grunted, immediately understanding the implications. "I imagine that didn't go over well with Jubal and Caleb."

"No, it did not, indeed," Maybe said. "They killed that marshal and dragged him behind their horses up and down the thoroughfare, promising to burn the town and kill every living man in the gulch. They didn't, of course, but if it was bad before Jeremiah died in the jail, it was plenty worse after. I entertain Caleb because he protects me, I'm safe from them. But anyone else in town needs to fear for his life on Saturdays when the men from the Three Sweethearts turn up."

Early took a heavy breath. He understood better the situation between the town and the Three Sweethearts men, at least why there was such deep-seeded hatred. Now, while Maybe was feeling talkative, he tried one more question. He knew that it was possible she didn't even know the answer, but he was confident that if she did know, she would tell him now.

"They're all outlaws, not miners, aren't they?"

Maybe twisted her lips.

"They've got the mine," she said.

"But they're not digging their gold out of any mine. Are they?"

179

"They have plenty of gold up in their camp, marshal. But they don't use pans or shovels or picks to get at it."

"Their guns are their tools, aren't they?"

Maybe sighed heavily.

"Are you tryin' to get me killed, now?" she asked. "I've said all I want to say about it."

"All these stagecoach robberies – it's the men from the Three Sweethearts, isn't it?"

"If you want to rob gold and silver off a stagecoach but you don't want anyone to question where you get your gold and silver from, then the best story is to tell folks you've got a mine that's producing gold and silver."

***

At dusk, Early walked Maybe down the trail from her tent toward Captain Beaumont's theater.

"Will you be coming to hear me sing, then?" she asked.

"I reckon I will," Early said. "At least for a bit. Wednesday is the big night in Muggyown, ain't it?"

"It is, since the Three Sweethearts men have ruined Saturdays."

"Then I'll probably be working all night," Early said. "But I'll stop in from time to time to hear you."

He deposited Maybe down at the theater and then walked back up to the hotel where he found Heck Espinoza in the dining room. Heck had a table against the far wall, and though there were a few others in the dining room, it wasn't crowded at all. Early went to the buffet table and fetched himself two beefsteaks, some green beans, and a pile of mashed potatoes. He drowned every bit of it in gravy. He loaded up the plate. A few days had taught him that Beatty had a knack for turning up just as he was thinking about returning to the buffet table for a second round.

"She tell you anything worth knowing?" Heck asked.

"She did at that, partner," Early said. Keeping his voice low and talking between mouthfuls of his supper, Early related to Heck what he'd learned about the history of the town. He finished up with Maybe's acknowledgment that the Rathbones were leading a gang of outlaws and not a company of miners.

"That confirms everything we suspected," Heck said, and he leaned back in his chair with his eyes on the ceiling and shook his head in bewilderment. "What do we do now, hombre?"

Early shrugged.

"I reckon we're going to have to arrest those fellers up there, and kill off the ones that won't come quietly."

Heck groaned.

"I don't expect any of them will come quietly," he said.

"Then it's going to be a heap o' boys we have to kill," Early chuckled.

Heck sighed and watched Early scoop in another mouthful of potatoes that he followed immediately with a bite-and-a-half of steak. It was a wonder the man didn't choke on every mouthful, but Heck had confidence in his partner, having seen him eat with such gusto a thousand times.

"I don't like our chances," Heck said. "Let's come up with a different plan."

"Heck Pinoza," Early said, squinting at the man. "I'm disappointed at you. Since when are we the sorts who back down from a fight? These folks here in this town hired us on to do a job, and it surprises me to hear you balk."

Heck frowned.

"Come on, Early. This is too much for just the two of us. We need to meet with Beaumont and Everson and whoever else and let them know what we've found out. I think we should tell them to send for the cavalry."

"Or the Pinkertons," Early said.

Heck shrugged.

"Or the Pinkertons."

"Maybe we could gather up a posse here in town," Early said. "We could take seventy men up there and deal with the Three Sweethearts outfit."

"Those are bad men up there," Heck said. "Those are gunfighters and outlaws, and they know their business. If we round up a posse of miners and drifters and gamblers and take them up there to face those men, every one of them who gets killed will be our fault – and you'd better believe most of them will get killed. Can you live with that?"

Early shrugged.

"Then let's you and me deal with them on our own, in our own way. We could do it."

Heck shook his head.

"I can't believe we're even talking about it, hombre. Everson needs to send for the cavalry, and that's all there is to it."

Early frowned, but he didn't make any further argument about it.

"Well, whatever we do about the Three Sweethearts outfit, we've got to keep order tonight. I'll tell Beaumont we want to meet with the town fathers, and he can decide who should be there and who shouldn't."

"And when we meet with them, what are we going to tell them?" Heck asked.

"We'll tell them what we suspect about the Three Sweethearts outfit," Early said.

"And suggest that they send for the cavalry?" Heck prompted him.

"Sure," Early said. "We can suggest that they send for the cavalry."

Heck nodded, but he didn't care at all for Early's dismissive tone.

"Anyway, if we have to arrest someone tonight, we won't put them in the jail," Early said.

"Ha!" Heck scoffed. "I can't believe they cooked a man inside their jail."

"That's a rough way to die," Early agreed.

Through the course of the evening, Early several times suggested plans to Heck of how the two of them might deal with the Three Sweethearts outfit in spite of its advantage of numbers. Heck showed no more interest in one plan than he did in another, and he was more than a little perturbed that Early kept coming up with suggestions.

- 16 -

As Early Bascomb finished his story, Captain Beaumont drew a heavy breath.

"Can you prove it?" he asked.

"I reckon if Mr. Everson took a look inside their mine, he could prove it," Early said, glancing at Heck who sat across the table from him.

A cool breeze came through the window inside the office of the Little Fannie Mine. Everson sat at the head of the long table.

"I'm not sneaking inside their mine," Everson said. "What do you propose? We ride up there and ask to have a look around? They'd have every right to kill us on the spot, even if what you're saying isn't true. But if it is true, my Lord, they wouldn't even hesitate to cut us down."

Captain Beaumont nodded his head.

"They're just a gang of outlaws," Beaumont said.

"An army of outlaws," Suttles corrected him. "They've got fifty-odd men up there."

"It changes things here for us," Heck said. Up to now, he'd let Early tell the story and do all the talking, but he wanted to make this point clear.

"Are you quitting?" Beaumont asked, clearly getting riled at the suggestion.

"No, sir," Early cut in quickly. "We're not quitting. We hired on to do a job, and we'll do the job."

"What we're saying is that this changes things," Heck interrupted. "We're two men with a legal authority that is questionable at best. We're not in a position to deal with this problem."

Beaumont looked from Heck to Early and frowned.

Beatty, the hotelier, cleared his throat.

"You're the law in this town. Who else is going to deal with it?"

"There's a cavalry fort over near Silver City," Heck said.

"Fort Bayard," the man standing behind Everson said. Everson had introduced him as Jack Webb and said he was head of security for the Little Fannie Mine, charged with dealing with high graders and thieves, and Everson had requested that Webb sit in on the meeting. So far, he'd only uttered those two words, preferring to listen rather than speak. Webb looked to be in his late thirties. He kept his face clean shaven. His skin was brown with the sun and weather beaten, but he was a handsome man and looked to be about as tough as they come.

Heck nodded.

"Early and I think y'all should send for the cavalry at the fort. Let them sort it out."

"It's an idea," Beaumont said. "Or we could provide you with men enough to deal with them."

"Where do those men come from?" Everson asked.

"You have more men on your payroll than there are at the Three Sweethearts Mine," Beaumont said.

Early got the distinct feeling that this was a conversation these men had already had around this table.

"My men are miners, not soldiers," Everson said.

"We proved in the war that with the right man leading them, farmers and shopkeepers can be made into soldiers," Beaumont said.

"Are you the right man?" Everson asked. "Because I'm not going to entertain this idea again – not even now that the situation has changed. I'm not asking my employees to take up arms against another mining outfit."

"They're not a mining outfit," Suttles said. "It's a camp of outlaws."

"Whatever they are," Everson said, dismissing the suggestion. "I'm not doing it. The cavalry is our quickest option. Or I could contact my employers. In a few months, they could have Pinkertons here, and I'd wager they would know how to deal with this."

At this last bit, Everson gave Early a meaningful glare, and Early bristled at the look.

Beaumont noticed the marshal's reaction.

"Marshal, is your deputy speaking for you?"

"We're partners," Early said with a glance at Heck.

"Is he speaking for you?" Beaumont pressed. "Because you don't look like a man who's happy to be standing down."

"I think there's another way," Early said. "I think Heck and I could probably deal with this if we had a dozen good men we could trust to back us up."

Heck sighed loudly and leaned back in his chair, his frustration evident. Early, who was looking at the table, glanced up at Heck and grinned.

"Enlighten us," Everson said, casting a glance over his shoulder at Jack Webb.

"I think on Monday morning, you should send that gold shipment on to Silver City, Mr. Everson," Early said. "Load it back on the stagecoach and send it on. In fact, if you've got more you could send, I think you should add to it. Make it the biggest shipment of the year, if you can."

Heck Espinoza glared. He chewed his lip and rolled his eyes. But he didn't raise an objection, not at the table in front of the others. All the same, Early caught the look on Heck's face and knew what Heck was thinking.

"But we'd need a score of men," Early said. "Not miners and gamblers and volunteers, but men who know how to use a gun and can ride."

Early looked past Everson at Webb.

"I have fifteen men up at the mine who are guards," Webb said. "Mostly, we just watch to make sure the miners aren't stealing too much. But I think all of them are former cavalry. They're solid, dependable men. I'd be willing to bring them and ride along, if Mr. Everson approves."

Everson raised his hands in a gesture of surrender. He didn't appear to like the idea, but with Webb offering, Everson didn't seem inclined to oppose.

"Fifteen would be enough," Early said. He looked at Suttles. "You would make sixteen if you'd ride along."

Suttles didn't have a chance to answer.

"Mr. Suttles and I will both join your posse, marshal," Beaumont declared. "That gets you to seventeen, and if you have seventeen then you might as well have twenty."

Early didn't want Beaumont. Not that he doubted the man's resolve, or even his ability, but he didn't think Beaumont was the sort of man who would follow directions. Still, they would need all the help they could get.

"All right," Early said. "Then we'll send a letter to the cavalry, ask them to come up here and help out. But in the meantime, if Mr. Everson can give me his men and get that gold on the stagecoach Monday morning, then we'll see if we can't deal with the Three Sweethearts outfit ourselves and when the cavalry shows up, they can just clean up the mess."

***

Heck had little to say after the Thursday afternoon

meeting up at Everson's office, even as the pair patrolled the town through the evening. When they retired to their room and took up their separate spots on opposite sides of the hotel's bundling board, Heck didn't engage in Early's attempts at conversation.

Friday morning broke crisp, the first truly chilly morning that seemed to announce the coming of autumn.

Early was reluctant to leave the warmth of the bed, but Heck rose and poured water into the basin and washed his face.

"Ain't that water cold?" Early asked.

"It is," Heck confirmed.

"You're a braver man than me," Early said. "Why don't you get dressed and go down to the kitchen and get some hot water for me."

Heck sighed heavily.

"I don't know if I'm a braver man, Early, but I'm smarter than you, hombre."

Early's face broke into a wide grin. He knew once Heck started tossing insults at him then it wouldn't be long before the man's anger subsided and they could get on with the business at hand.

"How do you figure you're smarter?" Early challenged.

"Because I know that fifty is more than two."

Early nodded and sat up in the bed now, ignoring the chill in the air.

"Tomorrow is Saturday," Early said. "We're going to push the situation a little tomorrow."

"Push in what way?" Heck asked.

He'd heard Early's suggestions Wednesday night about possible plans, but if Early had settled on some specific idea of how to handle the Three Sweethearts outfit, he had not yet laid it out for Heck – or anyone, for that matter. All he'd said to Everson and the others was that they should send gold on the stagecoach on Monday, and then he'd asked them to send a rider to Fort Bayard and ask for the cavalry's help in chasing down some stagecoach robbers.

In Silver City they would know that the stagecoach never arrived, but they wouldn't know anything more than that.

Everson sent a team of riders from his company, four men to notify the stage stations that there'd been a holdup attempt and that the stagecoach was going to make the run this coming Monday. The riders were to go through Silver City, spreading the word the entire way, and then to go on to Fort Bayard and deliver a letter asking for a company of cavalry to help with a roost of robbers that the local marshal had discovered – that was the message. Everson wrote the request on his company's letterhead, hoping that would carry enough weight to convince the army to move quickly.

"They tested us last Saturday," Early said. "This Saturday, we'll test them."

Heck grunted.

"I don't like the sound of that, Early."

"It'll be fine," Early said. "Trust me."

For Heck Espinoza, trust wasn't the issue. He did, as he'd proved many times before, trust Early Bascomb with his life. Heck never worried about his back because he always knew that Early would be there. But he also knew that Early's Southern roots gave him a bit of a wild streak, a recklessness, and that's what worried Heck. Early saw fifty guns pointed at him and reveled in having so many targets.

"When those boys from the Three Sweethearts find out that a jury exonerated that gambler and he's lit out of town, they're going to be a mite riled," Early said.

"You think?"

"If any of them start trouble like they did last Saturday, we'll lock them up. I figure we'll lock them up in twos and threes, and by the end of the evening we should have ten or fifteen of them in custody. And we'll hold them for trial, and set all the trials for Wednesday. That reduces their numbers a little bit."

Heck narrowed his eyes but held his argument.

"Some of them will try to holdup the stagecoach on Monday," Early continued.

"Because they'll hear while they're in town that the coach is going for Silver City on Monday morning."

"That's right," Early said. "Only this time, we'll let them take the gold. And we'll trail them, just like you and I did the other day. But we'll have Everson's security and Suttles and Beaumont with us. And we'll ride up there and arrest everyone."

"On what charges?"

"Stagecoach robbery," Early said.

"How do you prove that they've all been involved in a stagecoach robbery?" Heck asked.

"The gold is the proof," Early said confidently. "That, and the fact that they don't have a mine up there."

"We think they don't have a mine up there, partner. We don't know that."

"We'll know it on Monday," Early said. "If we let them take that gold up to their camp, then we can get everyone – not just the ones who hold up the stagecoach, but all of them who're up there in possession of the stolen gold. And when the cavalry shows up, we'll turn them all over to the cavalry and let them cart the Three Sweethearts outfit off to the territorial prison. It's a simple plan."

Heck scratched at his hair and squeezed his eyes closed as if trying to fight off a headache.

"You don't like my plan?" Early asked.

Heck sighed loudly and kept his eyes shut.

"Hombre, I don't think that's your plan at all. I think your plan is to start some trouble with those boys from the Three Sweethearts Mine and hope that one of them goes for a gun. And I think your plan then is to just shoot all of them and be done with it."

Early grinned.

"Well, the town of Muggyown is paying for our bullets, so if it comes to that then it won't cost us nothing."

- 17 -

Heck and Early had taken up a position at the bar in the Two Forks Saloon, each of them with a mug of coffee and a short-barrel shotgun on the bar in front of them, when they heard the single shot, muffled by distance and canvas walls.

"Was that a gunshot?" Heck said.

Suttles stood nearby, behind the bar.

"That's what it sounded like to me," he said.

"Dadgumit," Early swore. "This was not part of my plan."

It was still Friday afternoon. The men from the Three Sweethearts wouldn't be in town for another day, and the last thing Early wanted was some new trouble to interfere with him dealing with the Three Sweethearts outfit.

The marshal and his deputy each grabbed their shotguns and made their way outside of the Two Forks. Already people on the street were starting to move up the thoroughfare, some of them at a run and some moseying along, figuring they'd find out what the excitement was all about soon enough. The Little Fannie miners were up the mine, most of them anyhow, and it was laborers and gamblers and penniless drifters now crowding their way up the thoroughfare toward Admiral Moe's saloon.

Heck and Early hurried past the moseyers and caught up to the stragglers among the joggers and had to push their way across a foot bridge and past the hanging door.

Inside the saloon the moment seemed to be frozen in time, as if waiting for the law to arrive.

One of the working girls stood there near the center of the saloon, wrapped up in Maybe O'Malley's arms. Maybe was shushing the woman, patting her on her back like she would a baby, and telling her that everything would be fine.

In front of the woman, a chair was turned over on its side, and Early caught a glimpse of a man's legs. A table obscured his view, and it wasn't until he walked around a few steps that he saw who it was, shot through the chest and bleeding profusely on the ground.

"Everson?" Early said in surprise. "What the hell?"

There were some glasses on the floor, a couple of them were broken but the rest appeared to be intact. Maybe five or six glasses on the floor. Early presumed that Everson had knocked them from the table when he'd gone down.

Maybe looked up sharply at Early.

"Now, you just hold on there, Early Bascomb," Maybe said. "He hit her, right in front of all of us. He had this comin' to him."

The girl – Early didn't know her name, but he'd noticed her before inside Admiral Moe's – picked her head up from Maybe's shoulder and looked at Early. Her eyes were red, her cheeks wet, and her breathing came in short, rapid gasps.

"I told him not to hit me no more!" the woman sobbed.

Heck bent down beside Everson's body. There wasn't much life left in him. No one seemed to have done anything to offer the man any help, and Heck didn't know what to do, either. Everson was coughing some, but it was all blood and foam, and the pool of blood collecting on the plank floors and seeping down between the boards suggested he'd bled extensively in the short time from when they'd heard the shot to when they arrived in Admiral Moe's. There wasn't anything to ask – they needed no deathbed accusation to find the killer, she was sobbing right here in front of them. And unquestionably, if Everson made any statement now it would be from his deathbed. In front of them, the man's life was rapidly seeping out.

"Did anyone see Everson hit the woman?" Early asked, a general question directed to the room at-large.

"Everyone saw it," Admiral Moe said, standing from a table at the side of the room.

Though the Admiral had indicated to Heck that he wanted to meet the new marshal, Early hadn't yet met the man who earned his title riding a door down a flooding creek. Each time he'd come into the saloon to see Maybe O'Malley, the Admiral wasn't present.

"Who're you?" Early asked.

Admiral Moe gave a friendly nod and a grin to Heck Espinoza, and he stepped forward now, past the two women, and toward Early with his hand outstretched.

"They call me Admiral Moe," he said. "You must be our new marshal. I'm sorry to have to meet you like this, marshal. Particularly when I've been wanting to make your acquaintance. But this is the sort of thing we expect to have happen in a place like this. Too bad about it being Everson."

"Huh," Early said, a noncommittal response as he still hadn't sorted out what had happened.

"You saw what happened?" Early said.

"I did. Everson was here having some drinks with Alice. He started getting louder, to the point that he drew my attention. I was just about to say something to him when they both stood up abruptly, and Everson smacked her across the face. That's when she came out with the gun."

Early looked around, on the floor and on the table. He'd only been in the room for a few moments, but he realized now he should have already secured the murder weapon.

"Where's the gun?" Early asked.

Admiral Moe shrugged his shoulders as he looked around.

"Where did it go?" he asked.

Now, the girl Alice, still sobbing in Maybe's embrace, stepped away from Maybe and held out her hand, in it was a little pocket gun, and though she didn't appear to have any intent, she was carelessly pointing it directly at Early.

"Whoa!" Heck shouted, and he reached out and snatched the gun by the barrel, twisting it out of the woman's hands.

Early, frustrated with himself that he'd not dealt with the gun the moment he walked into the saloon, walked over to the woman and grabbed her by the wrist.

"You're coming with me," he said to her.

"Where are you taking her?" Maybe asked, and she struck a defiant pose, shifting her way in between Early and Alice.

"I'm going to ask her some questions," Early said.

"Then I'm coming, too."

Early kept a grip on Alice's wrist.

He turned to Heck. "Figure out who saw what in here. Don't let anyone leave until you've talked to them. I'll be back in a minute or two."

"What do you want me to do about him?" Heck said, nodding his head at Everson.

The coughing had stopped. There wasn't any pink foam escaping his mouth now. His eyes were open but blank.

"Is he still alive?" Early said.

Heck bent down, his shotgun in one hand and Alice's little pocket gun in the other. He set the pocket gun on the floor away from the body and held his hand over Everson's mouth.

"I don't feel any breath," he said. He pinched the man's wrist and squeezed. "I don't think there's a pulse."

Early shrugged.

"I guess send someone for the undertaker."

Dealing with bodies wasn't the sort of thing either Heck or Early knew much about. Typically, they either left a body for someone else to deal with or they tied it to the back of a horse and toted it to a lawman to collect a bounty. But here, they had to assume some sort of authority, and Early thought it was best to just make it someone else's problem as fast as possible.

***

"He's beat on me before," Alice said. "I told him if he got drunk and hit me again, I'd kill him."

"You can see her face," Maybe said.

They'd walked outside, out behind Admiral Moe's saloon, and there in the sunlight, Early could see the bruises on the woman's face – faded now, suggesting they were a week or so old, but definite bruises. She also had a small, fresh cut under her eye.

"Been beatin' on her for months, he has been," Maybe griped. "And when you ask a man to do a thing about it, he can't be arsed. Forced to do something herself, she has been."

Early looked at the girl, Alice. She had brown hair and dark eyes and a nice figure. Early, who never had a type of woman that he preferred, might as easily have latched on to Alice as he did to Maybe if he'd seen her first.

"Everson left those bruises on your face?" Early asked.

"Them, and plenty more just like them," Maybe said.

He frowned at her.

"Let the girl answer for herself," Early said, and it came off as more of a snarl than he'd intended.

"It's like she says," Alice said. "He's hit me before."

"Why did he hit you?" Early asked.

Maybe flushed red and turned on Early.

"Now tell me what that matters," she demanded. "It's enough that he hit her, isn't it, now?"

Early tried to give her a stern look to keep her quiet, but Maybe O'Malley wasn't the sort of woman who kept quiet – not from a stern look or much of anything else.

Alice sobbed, tears streaming from red eyes.

"Why did he hit you?" Early asked again.

"Who knows?" Alice asked, her eyes rolling toward the sky. "He always gets like that when he drinks too much."

Early remembered the broken glasses, the glasses on the table. If most of those had been Everson's, it would be tough to argue that he'd not had too much to drink.

"I told Moe not to let him get so drunk," Alice moaned, the sobs coming again. "I told him if he hit me again, I was going to kill him."

Early glanced at Maybe, he realized she'd gone white as a sheet. The change had come over her quickly, and he wasn't sure what was wrong with her.

This right here was why Early Bascomb never wanted to be a lawman. He kicked the dirt and rubbed the back of his neck and looked at the big pine trees reaching skyward from the slope of the gulch wall overlooking Moe's saloon. Up through the trees he could see the dirty white tent where Maybe lived. There were other tents up the slope, scattered in places where ledges of reasonable size would permit, but none were as high up or prominent on the hillside as Maybe O'Malley's.

Everson had been beating on this woman for no better reason than he was drunk. She had every right to defend herself, and she was as justified in shooting him as she was justified to sell herself in order to feed and shelter herself. Yet here he was, wearing a badge that forced him to arrest her and make her sit in front of a jury of men who would judge whether she had the right to not get beat on.

"I'm going to have to hold you for a trial," Early said.

"Oh!" Alice cried out. "You can't put me in that jail!"

Maybe immediately agreed.

"You can't do that to her, Early!"

Early sighed and clenched his jaw.

"I'll see what arrangements I can make," he said. "Maybe there's an empty room in the hotel where we can hold her."

"He's got a wife and children back in Denver," Alice sobbed.

"Who has?"

"Everson. He talked about her all the time. He loathed her. She complained at him about everything. But he loved his children. Someone's going to have to write to her."

"I'm sure his company will take care of that," Early said.

"Do you think they'll tell her that he was shot by a whore?" Alice asked.

Early shook his head. The woman had bigger problems than Everson's wife in Denver and how she would receive the news of her husband's death. No jury of men in a boomtown was going to look favorably upon a whore who shot a drunk man in a saloon just for giving her a smack across the face. The trouble with these miner's courts was they didn't have much real authority. They couldn't send someone off to a prison, and they typically only convened for the worst sorts of offenses, murder being one of those. Their ability to mete out justice usually fell to proclaiming innocence or condemning the defendant to a hanging.

Early had to wonder if the woman wasn't already condemned.

- 18 -

Captain Beaumont scratched at his chin and squinted up the hillside where they were digging a grave for Everson. The town's cemetery sat in the wide space where the two canyons met, beyond a cluster of tents. It was the only reasonable place to put a cemetery in the entire gulch where they could be relatively certain that floods wouldn't wash up the bodies.

Beaumont wore grave look on his face.

"Without Everson's support, we can't expect the Little Fannie Mine to back us up," Beaumont said. "If the Three Sweethearts men ride in here and start trouble tomorrow, it'll just be you and whoever you can muster to help you from the town. And you can forget about gathering enough men for a posse to go up to the Three Sweethearts Mine."

Early shrugged.

Beaumont and Beatty were there, standing down below the Two Forks Saloon. They'd asked Heck and Early to join them.

"Who's in charge now up at the Little Fannie?" Early asked.

"A man named Stuart Collier. He's a numbers man, not really what you would think of as a manager, but he'll be in charge temporarily. The thing about Collier is that he's not going to risk anything. He's got no nerve, no backbone. Not what you would call a hard bit man," Beaumont said. "He's just going to make marks in his ledger and send his books to his employers and be happy he has a job."

"Is he going to stick to our plan? Will he loan us the security and risk that gold on the Monday stagecoach?" Early asked.

Beaumont took a deep breath through his nose, the air rustling the whiskers in his mustache.

"That's an interesting question," he said. "My gut tells me no, he will not. But if Everson had it set up already, then maybe Collier will see the risk in not doing what Everson planned. It's hard to say."

Early shrugged his shoulders.

"We need to get it settled before tomorrow," Early said. "I'm counting on those men from the Little Sweethearts. Otherwise, we're going to be in for some trouble that we might not be able to handle."

Beatty looked nervous.

"He won't go for it," Beatty said. "I know Collier. He orders all the supplies for the mine. I've seen how he quibbles over every cost, how he worries over every delivery. He's not the sort who is going to turn over the company's security detail for extracurricular duties."

"Only way to know is to go up there and ask the man," Heck said.

"Then let's get to it," Early said.

Beatty shook his head.

"Let me know how it turns out. I'm going back to my hotel. We've started something in motion here that we're going to regret," Beatty said before walking away.

Heck and Early followed Beaumont up to the Little Fannie mine and found Stuart Collier in the mine's office.

"I'm just writing a letter to my employer to let them know that the mine manager has been murdered," Collier said, and his tone made it sound like an accusation directed at the three men who'd just entered his office.

"Stuart, this Early Bascomb, Muggyown's new marshal, and his deputy Señor Espinoza."

"I'm aware of who they are," Collier said, hardly bothering to look up from his desk.

"Good. We're sorry about Everson," Beaumont said. "He was a good man."

"He was a good manager for the mine, but he was a terrible man," Collier counted. "Married, yet cavorting with that whore. He got what he deserved."

"Was he a good manager?" Early asked. It gnawed on him that Everson was so drunk so early in the day. In his short association with the man, Everson didn't strike Early as the kind of man who would leave his responsibilities to go drinking in the middle of the day."

"He was an extremely good manager of the mine," Collier said. "He had experience at other mines, and he was thorough. He knew how to get work out of the men, and the mine produces well because of it. He'll be difficult to replace."

"Did he go drinking in the middle of the day very often?" Early asked.

Collier sniffed.

"Certainly not."

"What prompted him to go down there today?" Early asked.

He was more making conversation than really trying to get into Everson's affairs. The fact was, Early didn't care much about it. What's done was done, and there was no great mystery. They'd put the whore Alice in a vacant room on the second floor of the hotel, and to Beatty's objections, nailed the window shut. They'd affixed a lock to the outside of the door to prevent her from getting out and left her in there without any kind of guard. If she somehow managed to break out, she'd still have to get out of the hotel without being seen, and that wasn't likely. But in truth, Alice was hardly a concern for Early. More than anything, he regretted what he expected a miner's court would do to her.

"That man, Moe, who owns the saloon. He's the one that summoned him. Everson told me he was taking the rest of the day off, that Moe was buying his drinks."

Captain Beaumont chuckled at that.

"That's how a saloon owner goes broke," he said.

"If he'd stayed at the job like he should have, he'd still be alive right now," Collier noted.

No one could argue the truth of the statement.

"We're not here about Everson," Early said. "Mr. Collier, we've got a problem that we hope you can help us with. Mr. Everson promised to lend us the men who make up the mine's security detail."

Collier shook his head and gave Early a stern look.

"I'm aware, Marshal Bascomb. Randy Everson and I discussed all matters related to the operation of the mine, and he told me about your meeting and your plan."

"Good," Beaumont said. "That makes this easier. So we can still count on the Little Fannie's cooperation? We'll need help from your security both on Saturday and on Monday. And the gold on the stagecoach."

"I can tell you right now that none of that will be happening. We won't be lending out the use of our guards. Those men have a job, and it's not to start a war with another mining operation. And our job certainly is not to use our employer's gold and silver as bait for a trap for thieves. Our job is to insure the safe and timely delivery of the metals from this mine."

"Everson offered us the men as help," Early said. "He agreed to ship the gold on Monday's stagecoach."

"And the responsibility for that would have rested on Mr. Everson's shoulders should that gold shipment be lost. But now the responsibility falls to me, and I'll not be a party to it. I am already making arrangements for the shipment to go to Silver City, but I can assure you it won't be on Monday's stagecoach."

Beaumont sniffed.

"If you'll excuse me, I have a letter to finish writing," Collier said.

The delegation from the town stepped out of the Little Fannie office. Early squinted against the wash of sunlight as he looked around the mining camp at the activity all around.

"That's it then," Beaumont said. "That's an end to your plan."

"It seems so," Early said. "We'll have to come up with some other way to prove that the Three Sweethearts Mine is behind these holdups."

- 19 -

Heck Espinoza liked a stable. He liked the smell of the wood and the straw and horses, he even liked the unpleasant smells that came as part of the bargain.

He liked the peaceful way of the horses in the corral. He liked the way Poco a Poco came to the edge of the corral to greet him and stood to get scratched behind his ears. The pinto gelding knew even before Heck produced the carrot from his pocket that this visit bore a treat.

"I've got one for you, too," he called to Tim, who was eyeing the two of them from the center of the corral. Tim Buck Too seemed to have made himself dominant among the other horses.

The hostler saw Heck standing over between the stable and the corral, and he made his way over there now. He scratched his thick beard and his large chest rose and fell with a heavy breath.

"You're going to have a rough time of it today," he said.

"How do you figure?" Heck said, though he didn't need to ask the question.

Already, all up and down the thoroughfare, it felt like the people of Mogollon had made the same prediction. The town felt buttoned up, and there seemed to be an unspoken acknowledgment among the populace that today would prove to be a dire day, a day of a showdown. No one was out on the street. Since the rush at breakfast, most everyone had gone to their campsites to hole up for the remainder of the day. As he walked down to livery stable, Heck caught a glimpse of people up at their camps, their eyes on the deputy marshal like they were watching a condemned man headed for the gallows. Nobody doubted what sort of reaction the men from the Three Sweethearts Mine would have when they arrived in the camp and discovered that the sporting man who'd shot and killed one of their men had been turned loose by a jury.

"The Rathbones and their outfit will be coming to town today," the hostler said.

"And that means a rough time of it for me?" Heck said.

"I expect so."

"We want to rent three or four of your stalls," Heck said.

The hostler frowned at him.

"No need to stall them horses," he said. "They're fine in the corral."

Heck glanced at the horses.

"Not the horses," he said. "We're thinking you might be right – about the rough day – and we need somewhere to house prisoners."

The hostler started to laugh, a big belly laugh.

"New marshal decided he didn't want to cook prisoners in that little jail, huh?"

The incident with the third Rathbone brother had taken place long before Heck and Early showed up in Mogollon, but still, for some inexplicable reason, he bristled at the jest, as if he owned some of the responsibility for what happened in the jail.

"We're just worried we're going to have more prisoners than space in that jail," Heck said. "The best place we could figure to house folks was here in your stalls."

"It'll cost you," the hostler said. "A dollar a day."

"We can pay that," Heck said.

"For each stall," the hostler added.

Heck shrugged.

"That's fair."

"And I ain't gonna feed them the oats and hay meant for my horses. If you want them fed and watered, you'll have to take care of that yourself."

Heck nodded.

"We'll bring our own oats and hay," he said.

He spent the next hour with the hostler, helping to

muck out four stalls and lay down a bed of straw. Then Heck devised a way to secure the stalls. The outer shell of the livery was made of stacked logs. There was no chinking, and the logs gapped in enough places that it didn't take much for Heck to work chains around the logs. Temporarily, they could shackle prisoners to the chains and secure them in the shelter of the livery without much worry of escape.

While Heck secured a jail, Early was out looking for some of jailers.

With Everson killed, Beatty and Beaumont had become the heads of the community. Though some of the shopkeepers also had a hand in the running of the town, they'd largely given up any decision making, consenting to Beatty and Beaumont. They'd agreed between the two of them to foot the bill for renting stalls and hiring men to watch the makeshift jail, but they'd not agreed to exorbitant sums for either.

"Fifty cent a day to get myself killed? That won't even pay the undertaker to bury me. No, thank you."

That from a gambler staying at the hotel who had a reputation for being quick enough with his gun that he hadn't had to use it in Mogollon yet, but Early's offer of a job was met with some variation on the theme each time he extended it.

Finally, Early found a drifter at a campsite a little ways from the forks who was far enough down on his luck that he could be tempted.

"Fifty cents a day, and a meal at the hotel," Early said. "I just need you to stand guard at the livery."

Early didn't know the man's given name, but everyone called him Frog because of his bulging eyes, and

Frog embraced the name and introduced himself as such. The eyes were gray and spaced too far apart. He was thin, too thin, with long arms and legs and a narrow face, but he wore an earnest smile. Fifty cents a day was all Beaumont and Beatty had agreed to, but Early thought the man could use a meal or two.

"I don't have a gun," Frog said.

"Are you sober?" Early asked, unable to hide the doubt from his voice. He didn't think Frog was necessarily tangle-legged, but Early could smell the cheap liquor on his breath.

"Mostly," Frog said.

"We'll give you a gun," Early told him. "Probably be best if you don't use it for anything more than a shot in the air to send a warning. You fire one off into the air, and I'll come and deal with whatever trouble you're having."

Frog accepted the job, and Early sent him straight to the hotel's dining room to collect the first of his wages.

Early allowed Frog to get a good head start toward the hotel, and then he strolled that way himself.

He'd gone from the promise of fifteen gunmen to lend a hand to now just Frog, and just now he didn't have much confidence in the plan he'd concocted. That was his thought when he looked up the road toward Admiral Moe's place and saw the first of the riders coming into town. They came in a long line, walking their horses, just as they had come the previous week.

Early let out a heavy breath as he stood still for a moment and watched them approach.

"It starts now," he said to himself.

- 20 -

Jubal Rathbone swung himself down from his saddle outside of Admiral Moe's and handed his reins to one of the men riding behind him. His brother Caleb was the next to drop down from his saddle, followed by the two men, Haven and Ballew. The four of them walked over the foot bridge and up the incline toward Admiral Moe's Saloon, and the rest of the men then continued to walk their horses down toward the livery.

Early stood like a statue, watching them approach. He felt a pit in his stomach as each rider rounded the bend in the road, appearing from behind the wall of the mountain out beyond Admiral Moe's place. He expected to see fifty or so men, like he'd seen the week before. But after about twenty men rode through, a gap appeared. At first it meant nothing, but the gap widened as the front men left that bend behind them and no new riders appeared from beyond the rock wall of the gulch. Early didn't allow himself to get too excited, but then the riders were well within the town, passing by the hotel now, and still no new rider appeared.

Early started to count them in two, muttering aloud to himself. "Two, four, six, eight –" he trailed off. "Fifteen."

Including the four who'd walked into Admiral Moe's, they'd ridden into town with just nineteen men.

Even as the line of riders drew even with where Early was standing, he continued to watch the bend in the road, waiting for more riders to appear.

Nineteen men were plenty to deal with, but that number was a damn sight better than fifty.

The men from the Three Sweethearts outfit caught sight of Early. He was standing back from the thoroughfare, over by a lean-to built up near the edge of the slope where Frog made his camp. Once they saw him, several of the men started jawing to each other, grinning at the marshal and laughing among themselves.

Early grinned back and waited for them to pass, keeping a good hold on his shotgun. When the last of them had ridden up to the livery to put their horses in the corral, Early walked up to the Two Forks Saloon where Heck was standing outside.

"Looks like we caught a break, amigo," Early said.

"How do you figure?"

"They only rode into town with nineteen," Early said.

"Huh," Heck grunted. "Doesn't seem like much of a break."

"You don't think so? I reckon handling nineteen men will be a heap easier than trying to deal with fifty or so."

Heck nodded.

"I don't doubt that. But while we're catching a break here, thirty men are off somewhere that we don't know about doing things we're not aware of, and that hardly seems like a break to me."

"That's a fair point," Early conceded.

"There's a reason they didn't bring the whole outfit to town on a Saturday," Heck said. "That reason may not be good for us."

Heck and Early kept to the front of the Two Forks Saloon, even as some of the Three Sweethearts men began to come into the saloon in small groups. A few others headed for stores, and a couple of them walked back up the thoroughfare to Admiral Moe's.

It wasn't long, though, before the Rathbone brothers came out of Admiral Moe's with Haven and Ballew behind them. From their perch in front of the Two Forks, Heck and Early could see the two clearly, and in a moment, the four of them were walking with a purpose toward the Two Forks, their eyes clearly locked on the marshal and his deputy.

"What's this about that gambler being turned loose?" Jubal Rathbone demanded, squaring up in front of Early.

Heck had already taken a few steps back and off to the side, creating distance between him and Early. It would force the other men to split their attention if they had some trouble in mind, but it also gave Heck a clearer view of the door of Captain Beaumont's saloon. There wasn't much he could do about it if the ten or so Three Sweethearts men who were inside decided to come out and pitch in with the Rathbones and the other two. But at least he would see them coming and maybe not have to take a bullet in the back.

"Jury found him not guilty," Early said in an off-hand way. "All the evidence indicated that your man drew first and that gambler was just defending himself."

Jubal Rathbone was running hot. His face was red and his breathing seemed labored, like he'd just run down from Admiral Moe's – or ridden a door in a flood.

"That ain't justice," Rathbone said.

"It's the law," Early said. "A man has a right to defend himself."

"Say I draw on you right now," Rathbone fumed. "Say I go for my gun. Ain't no jury in Muggyown dumb enough to convict me."

Heck saw the corner of Early's mouth curl, almost imperceptibly, into a grin.

"That sounds less like a legal argument and more like a threat, Mr. Rathbone," Early said.

"You take it how you like," Rathbone said. "Now, last Saturday and when the two of you came up to my camp, I had a lot of patience for you, marshal. But my patience is done run out. You make a wide berth around me and my men, or you're going to find yourself in a heap more trouble than you can handle."

Early glanced at Heck. He stood up now, moving close to Rathbone.

"The rules ain't changed since last week. You and your men behave yourselves while you're in town, and there won't be any trouble. It's that easy. Don't go reaching for your guns or doing any damn foolish thing like that."

Jubal's face had turned beet red. His fists were clenched into balls as tight as boulders. Early had been in plenty of scraps in his time, and everything about Jubal's tensed body suggested he wanted to throw down right now. He rubbed his hand across his face, and Early thought sure the punch was coming now. But then Caleb Rathbone reached out and put a hand on his brother's shoulder.

"This ain't the time," Caleb said. "There'll be plenty of time later."

Jubal clenched his jaw and stood staring at Early for several moments. Early kept himself loose, ready to move fast if he had to, either to throw a punch or grab his gun, whatever Jubal's next move dictated. But then Rathbone took a step back, almost stepping into his younger brother.

"Another time," he muttered.

***

With so few men from the Three Sweethearts outfit in Mogollon, more than a few of the locals ventured out from their tents in the late afternoon to take up seats at the gaming tables or in front of the bars. Clearly, they felt the odds were in their favor tonight. At first, the evening seemed to hold the promise of being a quiet one. Outside of the brief exchange of pleasantries between Early and

Jubal Rathbone outside of the Two Forks, the Three Sweethearts men had behaved themselves. There'd been no thefts from the stores – at least none worth calling the law for. There'd been no altercations at the gaming tables. There'd been no drunken fighting.

Even Heck was beginning to believe that Early's prediction that they'd caught a break might have come to pass.

But some time close to ten o'clock, the trouble came.

Heck and Early made their rounds, walking up to Admiral Moe's for a cup of coffee, then heading down to the hotel to sit for a while on the front porch. Then they stopped by the door of the theater where they could hear the entertainment. Then they had another cup of coffee down at the Two Forks and watched the gaming tables before walking back up to the theater, this time stepping inside.

Maybe O'Malley was on the stage, now. She was singing a raucous Irish ditty and had the crowd fully engaged. Pumping her raised index finger she got the crowd singing along.

"One, two, three, four, five!" she called out in rapid succession, and as one her audience let loose with a clamorous shout, "Hunt!"

Maybe took up the rest of the chorus, with a few men in the crowd lamely trying to keep pace: "The hare and turn her down the rocky road all the way to Dublin. Whack fol-la-de-da!"

The audience made an atrocious mess of it, unable to keep pace with Maybe's Irish tongue. But they were having fun, laughing and carrying on.

A big brawler type from the Three Sweethearts had a

beer in his hand. Though the seats were not all occupied, the floor space was crowded, and the brawler from the Three Sweethearts stepped in too close to a miner who was enjoying himself overmuch.

Heck Espinoza saw it happen, and decided immediately that it was a setup.

The brawler stepped into the back of the miner. The miner, too far into his drink, jigged backwards like he'd tripped along the rocky road to Dublin, and splashed the brawler's beer all down the front of the Three Sweethearts man.

Several people standing nearby saw it, or saw some of it, and they immediately backed away, creating a circle around the two men. The miner continued his jig as Maybe and the players in the band continued the song, all equally unaware of the sodden brawler from the Three Sweethearts mine.

And then the brawler gave a heavy, two-handed push that sent the miner sprawling into a couple of other men. More drinks turned over, someone hit the floor, and the miner came around with his fists balled. In the space of a heartbeat, the back of the theater turned into bedlam. Two men from the Three Sweethearts outfit grabbed up an innocent man who was just enjoying the show and began to pummel him. The miner who started the incident with his dancing threw in to the brawler, and the combatants went after each other with spirit.

The audience forgot the song. Maybe gave up singing, though the band bravely continued to play. The shouting that arose from the back of the theater carried forward, until soon even those who were seated had come up and turned around.

Early went for the brawler, pushing his way through

the crowd.

By the time he arrived, the fight had already turned sour for the miner. He'd taken two heavy jabs to the face, and already a little tipsy from the drink, he was now wobbling on his legs. The brawler cocked back his arm just as Early stepped into the circle created by the crowd. Early held his shortened scattergun in his left hand. He reached the brawler from behind, and Early grabbed the man by the forearm and gave him a yank backwards, at the same time, Early swiftly kicked the backs of the brawler's legs, dropping the man onto the ground.

Some of the shouting died down.

With the brawler at his feet, Early turned quickly, grabbed the wobbly miner by the shirt collar and gave him a heave so that he fell over onto the ground.

"Do not get up," Early said to the two men, his voice sounding strong and clear.

Early turned now to the two men from the Rathbone's outfit who were beating the hell out of the innocent man. One of them held the man upright while the other continued to throw punches. Early threw himself bodily into the one throwing punches, shouldering him off the man, and then raised up the shotgun into the face of the man holding their victim.

"Enough of that!" Early shouted.

When his partner moved forward to break up the fight, Heck stood his ground. The whole thing seemed staged to him, planned out. The brawler started the fight on purpose. So Heck waited and watched, and when the ambush came, he was in a position to see it coming.

Two men who Heck recognized as being from the Three Sweethearts mine stepped away from the crowd, one came from behind Early, and the other came at him from the side. They moved fast, closing the distance to the marshal in just a couple of steps.

Heck ran forward, charging the man who was coming at Early's back. He shouldered a couple of people out of his way, and just as he saw the flash of the knife as the man drew back, Heck smashed the butt of his shotgun into the man's face.

The other man from the Three Sweethearts outfit, the one closing in on Early from the side, he wasn't as fortunate.

Early hadn't seen him at first, though he was aware of the movement in the corner of his eye. As he turned to look, the man was already there, and Early saw something in the man's hand.

Early didn't aim or think or anything – he saw a weapon in the man's hand, saw the man coming nearer to him, and he squeezed the trigger on the scattergun. It was all instinct, a drive for survival. Only one barrel fired, but they were so close that the man caught the full of it in his abdomen and chest, and it knocked him down with such force that he seemed to have disappeared – one moment there, right beside Early with an object in his hand, the next moment just empty space where a man had been.

"Dadgumit!" Early cursed.

The blast of the shotgun finally brought the band to a full stop.

The entire theater went silent, except for the sound of the gun that seemed to hang in the air, fill everyone's ears even though it had died away.

The brawler was the only one in the place who

moved. He started to get to his feet, though no one could say what his intention might be. Heck swung the butt of his shotgun around and rapped the man in the head with such force that it laid him out. The brawler went over on his side, awkwardly poised on his side with his head and shoulder on the ground and his legs crisscrossed unnaturally.

Heck spun the shotgun around so that he gripped it ready to shoot, and he waved it back and forth at the entire audience in the theater.

"I'm going to kill the next man who moves," Heck said.

***

The man Early shot died instantly. There was no moaning or crying for his mama, no time to regret his decisions that night. He died with the knife still clutched in his fist. No one stepped forward to examine the body, there was no need for a closer look.

"That's two of my men killed in this town in a week!" Jubal Rathbone shouted from the bar, though he did not make a move.

Heck released his grip on the forestock of the scattergun and dragged to his feet the man who'd tried to stab Early in the back. He saw the knife on the ground, and he bent over and picked that up, tucking it into his own belt for safekeeping. He took off the man's gunbelt and then checked him for any hidden weapons. Finding none, Heck took him by the collar and marched him out of the crowd.

Early stood still, keeping his eyes on the crowd. He was shaken a little, not because he'd killed a man, but because he'd come so close to getting stabbed. Early didn't mind taking chances, but he always did so with a naive confidence that he'd come through unscathed. That knife on the ground was as close as he'd come in a while to a scathe.

But after a couple of breaths and a moment to collect himself, Early took control of the situation again.

With a man dead and leaking on the floor, the crowd had now backed away even farther. Early opened the top of the shotgun and tossed away the empty shell, replacing it with a fresh one from his pocket.

"Drop your gunbelts," Early said to the two men from the Three Sweethearts outfit who'd been beating on the one. Both men did as they were told, almost without hesitation. Early nodded at the brawler who'd started the whole thing, now half-conscious on the ground. "Pick him up, and move over there with my deputy."

As they raised him up from the ground, Early slid the man's gun from its holster and dropped it on the ground beside the body of the man who'd tried to gut him.

"Heck, you take those men down to the jail. If any of them cause you any trouble, you shoot the hell out of them, and I'll send the undertaker to you when he's done here."

Heck motioned with his shotgun toward the door and marched his four prisoners in that direction. Meanwhile, Early stood over the body of the man he'd killed. Mostly he watched Jubal Rathbone, but he also kept his eyes open for any more threats to emerge from the crowd. As he did, he noticed for the first time that Curtis Suttles was standing in a corner at the back of the bar, a shotgun in his grip, ready to back Early up if there was more trouble.

"We're going to let my deputy get situated before we empty this place," Early said. "But I think the night's just about over."

"You can't put those men in your jail," Jubal Rathbone said. "I won't allow it."

"What you need to worry about, Mr. Rathbone, is keeping the rest of your men under control. It's going to be a slow week at the diggings if I have to keep arresting men from your outfit. You round your boys up, and you take them on out of town to camp for the night. Then you head back up to your mine in the morning."

"You can't force me out of town," Rathbone snapped back.

"Your choice is to go on your own or I'll arrange to keep you here in shackles," Early said. "That's the size of it. I've already had two men come at me tonight with knives, and had to kill one of them, and I'm not in a mood to get particular with you about what I can and cannot do."

Suttles came out from behind the bar now and walked part-way across the room so that he was standing nearer to Early.

"Y'all heard the marshal," Suttles called out. "Theater's closing early tonight."

The band started to leave the stage. The bartenders behind the bar started to put away the bottles and collect the glasses. No one from the audience made a move yet, most of them worried because Early had not yet told anyone to leave. He let several more moments slide by, in part because he wanted to give Maybe time to leave through a back door just in case this thing turned into a battle.

"What are you going to do with my men? The ones you're taking to your jail?" Jubal Rathbone asked.

"They'll be held for trial," Early said. "They're all charged with disturbing the peace. I expect trials to be on Wednesday, Mr. Rathbone."

"What about him?" Jubal Rathbone nodded at the body on the floor.

"You can pay the undertaker to bury him in the cemetery," Early said.

"We've got a place where my brother is buried up at our camp," Rathbone said. "If it's all the same to you, we'll take the body."

"It's all the same," Early said. "But that knife stays where it is."

Now, slowly, people started to drift out. Most of the men who were from the Three Sweethearts outfit lingered. Rathbone instructed a couple of them to tote the body outside, and he came over and stood near Early while they did that.

"Marshal, I thought you was all right when I first met you, but I've got a deeper and deeper feeling that you and me is gonna come to a conclusion together."

Early grinned at him and gave a little nod to of his head.

"I expect that's so, Mr. Rathbone," Early said. "And it may come sooner than you think."

When the place was empty of everyone except those in Captain Beaumont's employ, Suttles finally had a word with Early.

"That fight was all just a setup so those two could come after you," Suttles said.

Early nodded.

"That's how I read it, too."

"You'd better keep both eyes open when you walk home tonight."

"I intend to," Early said. "Rathbone's cooking something."

"You didn't get confused following that trail back to his camp the other day, and Jubal Rathbone knows that you know it," Suttles said. "He wants you out of his way."

"That's probably right," Early said.

"He's made sure to get rid of the other marshals we've hired. He's planning to get rid of you, too. You keep arresting his men, he'll do it sooner rather than later."

Early shrugged his shoulders.

"He may find I'm harder to get shed of than those others were," Early said. "I'm going down to the livery to check on my partner."

"I'll walk with you," Suttles said.

Together, the two men made the trek out across the town. It seemed that word had spread quickly that there'd been trouble in the theater. Captain Beaumont had shut down the Two Forks Saloon, and it was quiet and dark. The bartenders from the Two Forks sat outside the place, both of them with scatterguns draped across their laps. In fact, as he looked around, Early could see that several of Mogollon's residents had taken up arms and were sitting up keeping vigil around campfires. The place looked like an armed encampment, so many people sat on rocks or logs or on chairs, long guns and pistols at the ready.

Most of the men from the Three Sweethearts outfit had already cleared out of town. The hostler was down at the corral helping those who remained to fetch their horses.

Heck stood in the doorway of livery stable, his shotgun casually held across his chest in his crossed arms.

"Everything all right?" Early asked him.

"Four prisoners shackled in one stall," Heck said. "I figured I'd keep the other stalls empty in case we need them."

"It looks like we won't need them tonight," Early said. "The Rathbones and their men are leaving out peacefully."

"Huh," Heck grunted. "We'll see what you say at sunup."

"Frog standing guard over the prisoners?" Early asked, craning his neck to look inside the livery.

"He's in there, but I don't think we should leave him alone tonight."

Early nodded.

"You want first watch or second watch?" Early asked.

"I'll take first watch," Heck said. "I'll come wake you up in three or four hours."

"I'll sleep light," Suttles said. "If I hear anything, you can count on me."

- 21 -

The night clerk from the hotel was asleep on the sofa inside the lobby. He hardly stirred when Early came in. Otherwise, the lobby was completely vacant, which was no great surprise at this time of night.

Early got his own key and noticed that Heck's key was missing from its hook. Maybe Heck still had it? Or maybe not. Suddenly, Early was filled with trepidation.

Early took the stairs slowly. The confined space up the stairs made him a mite nervous. If a man was to swing around the door at the top of the stairs with a scattergun, Early wouldn't be able to do anything except catch the shot. So he went slow, his finger on the trigger of his shotgun.

The hallway leading to the rooms was empty, and it was dead silent, and Early caught himself wishing that Heck was here with him so they could make this walk together.

An assassin could be in any one of these rooms, just waiting to burst through the door at the sound of footsteps. So Early tread lightly, though his boots on the blank boards seemed like drums, beating to the same tempo as his heart.

Had it not been for the two men who'd tried to stab him earlier, and the sense he had that the Rathbones intended to do something more, he'd have laughed at himself for his sudden nervousness. Early wasn't a nervous sort of man, typically, and he did not at all care for the feeling he had now. He wanted to break and run for his hotel room, but he didn't do it.

He passed by Alice's room and just confirmed that it was still locked shut. Beatty had the key and had promised to make sure she got supper and anything else she needed.

At the door to his hotel room, Early knew something was wrong.

He'd left the door pulled-to and locked, but now he could see it was slightly ajar.

Someone had come into the room since he'd last been here. He could see light coming from around the door, too, and that could easily mean there was still someone inside.

Early stood for several moments, debating whether to walk into his hotel room. Was it an assassin in there? Or multiple assassins? With the shotgun in his hand, he could probably get one. With some luck, he might be able to get a second one. But if there were three men inside his room, one man would walk out when it was all finished, and it wouldn't be Early Bascomb.

At last, Early decided he might be a lot of things, but he wasn't yellow.

With the toe of his boot, he gave the door a slight push, enough to swing it open, and then he stepped aside, waiting to hear the shot intended for him. When none came, Early swung himself around the side of the door. There was one figure there, standing at the foot of his bed, and Early damn near pulled the trigger.

"Dadgumit, Maybe!" Early hissed, seeing her red hair before fully grasping who was in front of him. "You just about got yourself shot. What in hell are you doing in here?"

Maybe was white as a sheet, staring at the twin barrels of the shotgun. She watched it as Early lowered the gun.

"Caleb'll be looking for me," Maybe said. "I didn't want to go back up to my tent."

"How'd you get in here?" Early asked.

"The night clerk gave me a key," Maybe said.

Early shut the door behind him.

"They let just anybody into a person's room?" Early grumbled.

"I'm not 'just anybody,'" Maybe said. "Caleb and his brother are up to something."

"I think so," Early said.

"It has to do with that man, Everson that was killed

in Moe's saloon."

Early frowned at her.

"What do you mean?" Early asked. "You told me you saw what happened. You told me Everson slapped her and she shot him."

"She did shoot him," Maybe said. "But I think Moe set it up. That entire thing with Alice, it was just a charade."

"Explain it to me," Early said. "Moe didn't force Everson to hit her."

"Everyone knows that when Everson gets drunk, he gets too mean," Maybe said. "This wasn't the first time he smacked Alice, or other girls, for that matter. He's a mean drunk, Early. Everson and Moe were tighter than people know. Everson used to come into the saloon regularly, and he and Moe would sit and talk, friendly like."

"So why did Moe set it up?"

"Don't you see, Early? Moe was givin' him them drinks. I've never seen Everson in there in the middle of the day like that, and Moe was givin' away drinks like there was no tomorrow. When Alice said that she 'told him,' she wasn't talkin' about poor Mr. Everson. She was sayin' that she told Moe. She told Moe not to give him them drinks because if Everson got drunk and hit her again, she'd shoot Everson. She meant it, too. And Moe knew that she meant it. And Moe just kept on feedin' them bloody drinks right to him anyway."

Early took a heavy breath and dropped down into a chair. Maybe started to take off her dress, just like they were a married couple. It struck Early as funny the way she felt so carefree in his room.

"So you're saying that Moe knew Everson would hit

Alice, and that he knew that Alice was threatening to shoot Everson if he hit her again. And Moe got Everson drunk on purpose because he knew Everson would hit Alice and that she'd shoot him."

"Precisely what I'm sayin'," Maybe said, now taking off her bustle.

"That's a helluva way to kill a man," Early said. "And to what purpose? Why would the Admiral want Everson dead?"

"Oh, Early, love. Don't be so naive. Admiral Moe is thick as thieves with the Rathbones. Don't you see that? Why do you think the Three Sweethearts men never cause any trouble down at Moe's saloon? He gives the Rathbones information, and their men don't destroy his place and run off the customers like they do everywhere else. Oh, they drink for free, but they don't bust up the faro tables and bloody the customers the way they do everywhere else."

"But why kill Everson?" Early asked.

"Well, I don't know that, now do I? That's for you to be figurin' out as the marshal. All I'm sayin' is what I know to be true."

- 22 -

Early Bascomb watched the wagon in the blue light just before dawn. The driver worked his way down through the gulch with little consideration for those still abed in their tents.

"C'mon there!" he called to his mules. "Get up, now!"

The wagon creaked with every twist of the unlevel ground. Gear strapped to the side clanged and banged and knocked. During daylight hours, the wagon didn't make enough noise for a person to notice, but in the wee hours, it was like a symphony of out-of-tune instruments performed by a band of deaf men. A fair number of folks would wake up on the wrong side of the bed this morning.

A shotgun rider sat beside the driver, and Early thought he caught a shadow of movement inside the canvas-covered back of the wagon. Another three men rode horses behind the wagon, all of them looking like they were riding into a private war with six-guns holstered on their hips and rifles strapped to their scabbards and one of them riding with a short-barrel scattergun laid across his lap.

"Mornin', marshal," one of the mounted men said with a nod of his head as he rode past.

"Where y'all headin' so early?" Early asked him.

The man chuckled.

"Ridin' for Silver City."

Early didn't recognize the men, though that didn't mean anything. They might all have been introduced to him, for all he could remember. He'd met a lot of folks over the past several days.

"You see that, Frog?" Early asked, looking over his shoulder at the hired jailer who was dozing in a chair with his back against the wall of the livery stable.

"Wagon?" Frog said with a yawn.

"Wagon and three riders," Early said.

"I saw 'em, marshal."

"Is that a common thing?"

"How do you mean?"

"I mean, is it common for those men to drive that wagon out of town before sunup like this?"

Frog stood up and walked a few feet toward the

thoroughfare, past where Early was standing. He watched after the riders. They were still near enough that a good throw with a rock might hit one of them.

"Those men work for the Little Fannie Mine," Frog said.

"Miners?" Early asked, though he thought he knew the answer to that question.

"No, sir. They're guards up at the mine, keep the men from thieving."

Early took a deep breath, the air almost cold as it hit his lungs.

"Yeah, that's what I figured."

"I don't recall them ever riding out like that before," Frog said. "But I ain't been here more than a few months, so I can't say they've never done it before."

"Collier," Early said.

"Beg your pardon?" Frog asked.

"Just thinking out loud," Early said.

Not long after sunup, Early sent Frog to the hotel to get himself some breakfast.

"Drink plenty of coffee," Early advised him. "When you get back, you'll be on your own guarding these men, but hopefully by then, the threat will have passed."

It was Sunday morning, and Early hoped that it wouldn't be long before the men of the Three Sweethearts Mine headed back up to their camp. Their proximity to the town made Early nervous. As long as those men were still camped beyond Admiral Moe's, Early had to worry that they might come and try to take his prisoners by force. Once they rode out, Early thought it was less likely that the Rathbones would try to break their men from the makeshift jail.

Admiral Moe.

Since Heck had turned up at the hotel to wake him for his turn at watch, Early had continuously turned over in his mind what Maybe O'Malley had told him. What was Admiral Moe's involvement? Early knew Heck had spent some time with the man, and he wanted to ask Heck's thoughts about him. But the time for that wasn't the middle of the night when Early needed to join Frog in his vigil, and Heck had already been irked to find Maybe sleeping in the bed.

"Where am I supposed to sleep, hombre?" Heck complained.

"Put the bundling board back on there, and you can sleep in the bed," Early had whispered at him. Probably, though, Heck had slept in the chair and had a miserable night of it.

Randy Everson.

At first, Early dismissed Maybe's accusation. It seemed preposterous to him that Admiral Moe could have arranged to kill Everson by getting him drunk enough to slap that woman. But Collier – Everson's number two at the Little Fannie – he'd said it was uncommon for Everson to go and drink during the day. He'd claimed that Moe was buying the drinks, something Maybe also said. But to what purpose? Even if Maybe was right that Moe set up the whole thing, plotted the murder and it unfolded just as he intended, what was the possible point of it?

Early was eager to talk to Heck about it, get his thoughts. He also wanted to pay a visit to Collier up at the

Little Fannie Mine. Collier, uncooperative as he seemed to be, might have some answers that would be worth hearing.

***

When Frog returned from his breakfast, Heck came with him.

"I left your guest still asleep in our room when I went for breakfast," Heck said. "She's probably awake now."

"You might find this hard to believe, amigo, but this morning, you're the one I want to see."

"She's a sight prettier than I am," Heck said.

"She is at that," Early agreed. "But I was thinking about walking up the thoroughfare a ways to see if the Three Sweethearts outfit is getting ready to move on yet, and if those boys start shooting at us, I'd rather hide behind you than her."

Before going up the road, they went back to the hotel to trade their shotguns for rifles. Both men believed in having the right tool for the job. In the close confines of a saloon or on the thoroughfare of Mogollon, a shotgun would almost surely prove to be the right tool. But walking up through the gulch, the threat most likely would come from distance – an ambush from the hills, a sharpshooter behind a tree.

Maybe was still in their room at the hotel when Heck and Early went in to get their rifles.

"If you don't mind, I'd like to stay here until I know for sure that Caleb is gone back up to his camp," she said.

"I don't want him to figure out that I've been talking to you."

"You can stay here," Early said, without bothering to ask Heck's opinion.

A quarter of an hour later, Heck and Early walked up a little slope into a stand of pines where they had a perfect view of the camp where the Three Sweethearts men were still rousing from bed and cooking their breakfasts over campfires.

"Looks like they'll be gone soon," Heck said.

"I'll be glad when they are," Early said. "We should be close to the livery when they go to get their horses, just in case they decide to bust those men loose. And when they're gone, we need to go and see Stuart Collier up at the Little Fannie again."

"Why Collier?" Heck asked.

"When Miss O'Malley turned up at the hotel last night, she had a story with her."

"What was her story?" Heck asked.

"She claims that Admiral Moe set up Everson's shooting on Friday. She says that the girl Alice, the one who shot Everson, told Moe that if Everson hit her again, she would kill him."

"She said that to Moe?" Heck asked.

"That's what Miss O'Malley says. And she says that Moe was buying Everson's drinks on Friday. Didn't Collier tell us that Everson said Moe invited him down there?"

"I think he did," Heck said.

"And Maybe – Miss O'Malley – she also told me that

Moe is in pretty tight with the Rathbones."

"Huh," Heck muttered. "Now that's something we didn't know. It would explain why the Admiral is indifferent toward the Rathbones and every other shopkeeper and saloon owner in town hates them."

Early nodded.

"One other thing you don't know."

"What's that?"

"A wagon left out of the Little Fannie this morning just at first light. Three riders trailing the wagon, at least one and maybe two gunmen riding inside the wagon."

Heck nodded his head thoughtfully.

"Collier sent the gold on to Silver City."

"He told us that he'd make his own arrangements," Early said. "It's no surprise. But it seems like a damn fool thing to do when the best suspect for the holdups is camped just outside of town."

Heck and Early were not long in the woods before they saw the Three Sweethearts men start to douse their fires and pack up their gear. Most of them had just slept on the ground, using whatever liquor they'd had that night to keep them warm in lieu of tents or blankets. So Heck and Early did not linger. As soon as it looked like they were packing up for the night, they hurried back down the road toward town.

In another hour or so, all of the men from the Three Sweethearts outfit had collected their horses and started out of town.

Once they were gone, Early went to find something to eat at the hotel, having missed breakfast, and then he and Heck walked up to the Little Fannie Mine.

As the manager of the mine, Everson had a small cabin near the office that he called home. It wasn't much, but it had a stove and a bed and a sofa. When Heck and Early arrived at the mine, they found Stuart Collier packing Everson's personal belongings so that he could move in that afternoon.

"If you're here to ask me to change my mind about the shipment to Silver City, marshal, I'll not waste your time," Collier said.

He met them at the door to the cabin, leaving Heck and Early to stand outside in the sunshine.

"No, sir," Early said. "My guess is the gold is already on its way to Silver City on that wagon that came out of here just before sunup."

Collier flinched.

"You saw the wagon?"

"I did."

"Well then, you know that even if I wanted to participate in your scheme, I cannot do it now."

"That's not what we're here for," Early said. "I want to know about your last conversations with Mr. Everson."

Collier narrowed his eyes.

"In what respect?"

"You knew about my plan to send the gold on the stagecoach," Early said.

"Everson told me about it."

"You told him you didn't approve of it?"

"That's right," Collier said. "I made my objections known to him."

"What were those objections?" Early said.

"The same as what I told you Friday. Our job is to deliver gold and silver to Silver City, not to risk our employer's wealth for a scheme to catch thieves."

"Everson knew if anything happened to him that you would take over up here, right?"

"Of course," Collier said. "Everyone knows that. Of course, for now this is only a temporary assignment. The mine's owners will have to decide if I'm to take over the position permanently. But, of course, I'll seek the appointment."

"Did you suggest your plan to Everson?" Heck asked. "Did you tell him it would be better to send the shipment in a wagon today instead of on the stagecoach tomorrow?"

"I did," Collier said.

Early stood for a moment, wondering if he had any other questions to ask the man. Collier's indifference bordered on hostility, and Early wanted to press him with further questions. But Heck reached up and touched his partner's arm and swung his head back toward town.

"I think that answers our questions," Heck said abruptly, and Early glanced at him. He could read it on Heck's face that he had something in mind.

"I would tell you to feel free to come back if you have any more questions, but I get the impression you will with or without the invitation," Collier said. "I do apologize if my responsibility to my employer has disrupted your plan, marshal."

They started back down through the gulch leading to Mogollon. The Two Forks Saloon was in front of them, about two hundred yards below the Little Fannie Mine.

When they'd walked out of earshot from Collier, Early said, "What you're thinking, amigo?"

"I think we need to figure out why Admiral Moe is helping the Rathbones," Heck said. "We met with Everson on Thursday afternoon. Friday, he's down at Admiral Moe's place. I'm reaching here, but I think Everson told Moe about your plan for the stagecoach. I think he told Moe that Collier opposed it. Maybe he was looking for advice. Maybe he was just talking."

"Maybe said they're friends, Everson and Admiral Moe," Early interjected.

Heck nodded. "She also told you that Moe is friendly with the men from the Three Sweethearts outfit."

"She did."

"I think for some reason that we don't understand, the Admiral didn't want that stagecoach plan of yours to come off. And I think Moe figured out that if Everson was out of the way, Collier would kill the idea of using the Little Fannie's gold as bait to trap the Rathbones. When I talked to Admiral Moe about the Three Sweethearts outfit, he told me that they don't bother him the way they bother the other merchants in town, the way they bother Captain Beaumont at the Two Forks and Suttles at the theater."

Early nodded his head.

"That's what Maybe said. She told me as much last night, that Moe gives them information about what's going on in town."

"She thinks Moe set up Everson to get killed, and from all we know, that seems like a good bet. Maybe Moe got word to Jubal Rathbone about your plan, and Rathbone told Moe to make sure it didn't happen."

"When would he have had time?"

Heck shrugged.

"That's a good question. He wouldn't have had time. So did Moe make the decision himself, take it upon himself to kill Everson?"

"That's a big decision to make just to keep the Three Sweethearts outfit from causing trouble in the saloon," Early said. "But it does seem like it's a good bet that the Admiral is working for the Rathbones."

"He told me he prospected that entire area where the Three Sweethearts Mine is located," Heck said. "He told me he didn't find anything up there. Said the Rathbones were lucky."

"We don't think the Rathbones have found any gold up there, either," Early said.

They were nearing the Two Forks now, close enough that they could see both ways up and down the main thoroughfare running through the Silver Creek Gulch. So Heck and Early saw the rider coming at a full gallop before anyone else in town did. He was coming up from the west, the way to Silver City. He sat odd in the saddle.

"That man don't look all right," Heck said.

Early squinted down the road at him, craning his neck a touch for a clear view.

"No. Something's wrong with him," Early said. He held the reins in one hand, and his other arm hugged his torso. He had a funny lean, almost like he was about to fall out of the saddle. The horse, a black-maned bay, ran almost out of control, and white foam frothed on his sides like he'd been run too hard.

"Hell," Early said, now recognizing the rider and the horse. "That there is one of the guards I saw ride out this morning with the Little Fannie's gold."

- 23 -

It being Sunday and all the miners having the day off, word spread quickly through the little town, and it wasn't long before Collier and the head of the Little Fannie's guards turned up.

The rider was shouting when he pulled up on the reins out front of the Two Forks Saloon, and it was Captain Beaumont and Curtis Suttles who fetched him down from the horse. The man was shot twice, once through the back, with the wound coming out his front just below his ribs, and the other shot had got him in the neck. Though the neck wound was just a graze, it was bleeding ferociously.

They laid him out on the ground there in front of the saloon. Someone went to fetch some water and some rags. Suttles opened the man's shirt to check the chest wound. Neither Heck nor Early knew much about doctoring, but the wound looked bad enough to them. It was the sort of wound that they knew could bleed on the inside for days until the man died.

"They're all killed," he said. His breathing was labored, and he winced in pain as Suttles slid his shirt away and then rolled him to look at his back. "Ambushed us. Must've been ten guns."

"The other guards are all dead?" Early asked.

"I think they must be. They got us on a slope. The wagon was going slow. All of sudden, I hear shots coming from every which way. I felt one hit me in the neck, and I turned and just started riding. That's when they shot me in the back. But I saw Mark fall, he was shot in the head. And Kenny, driving the wagon, he got shot and hollered and stood up, and then he was shot twice more. I saw that before I ever got turned around. They was all over us."

A crowd gathered quickly, and Early saw when a couple of miners started up the hill toward the Little Fannie, and he thought with some satisfaction that Collier would soon know he'd made an error in making his own arrangements. He'd managed to get his security detail killed.

"How bad am I shot?" the guard asked. "It hurts like the blazes."

"You're shot," Suttles said. "No disputing that. But you hang on there, and we'll get you doctored up."

By now someone had turned up with a pail of water

and some rags, and Suttles was cleaning the blood away from the chest wound.

"Maybe it's a good thing we didn't go through with your plan," Heck muttered to Early. "That might be one of us laying there."

"Huh," Early grunted, and he raised his eyebrows at his partner. "You can say that again."

Now Early stepped over to the injured man and squatted down next to him.

"Did you get a look at any of the men? Can you tell us who they were?"

"I didn't know any of them," the guard said before letting out a long groan of pain. "They all had their faces covered, at least the ones I saw. I don't know how many there were. They were all over the place. Both sides of the roadway, and in front of us."

"How long ago did it happen?" Early said.

The man closed his eyes, and for a moment, Early thought he was going to die right there in front of them.

"I don't know," he said. "An hour ago? Maybe longer than that. I ran my damn horse as fast as he would go to get back here."

Collier was coming down the slope at a run, and right behind him was a man in a black suit coat with a black hat. This was Jack Webb the head of the guards up at the mine who'd sat in on the meeting with Everson on Thursday and offered to join in with Early's posse when he first proposed the plan of using the Little Fannie's gold as bait.

Collier and Webb ran directly up to where the wounded man was on the ground, and it was the man in the black hat who questioned the guard, getting the same story out of him a second time. The man in the black hat also nudged his way in, gently pushing Suttles out of the way, and took over examining the wound.

"You're a lucky boy, Carlton," he said, his voice deep and confident. "You were shot all the way through, and I don't believe anything vital was hit. You're going to be sore for a few days, but you'll be all right."

Collier bent over, looking at the guard square in the face.

"Did they get the gold?"

"I don't know, Mr. Collier," Carlton said. "I didn't see. But I reckon they did."

Collier walked away muttering a string of epithets, and Webb got up now and stepped away from the man.

"Get those rags bandaged onto his wounds good and tight, pressing down on it," Webb said, though it wasn't clear exactly who he was talking to. "Once it quits bleeding, pack both the hole in his back and front with honey. Honey will draw out any infection. Change the bandages every couple of hours, and give him some whiskey to help with the pain."

Webb looked around now for someone in the crowd from the Little Fannie Mine, and he had plenty to choose from. Maybe on purpose, maybe by chance, but he nodded to the youngest, fittest man among the onlookers.

"You run up to the mine and find George Butler. Tell him to gather up the rest of my men and to saddle their horses. Tell him to grab my gear and my horse, too. Don't let him forget my gear and my horse. Tell him I want him down here in a quarter of an hour, ready to ride. Now repeat that back to me."

The young man blinked a couple of times at Webb.

"You want me to find George Butler. He's to get your gear and your horse and your men and be back down here ready to ride in a quarter of an hour."

"That's right," Webb said. "Go!"

The man set off at a run up the slope toward the Little Fannie Mine, and Webb now stepped away from Carlton as others bent over him to keep pressing the rags against his wound.

"Walk with me, marshal," Webb said to Early.

Heck and Early both followed Webb away from the crowd outside of the Two Forks Saloon, and when the three men were well away from everyone else, Webb stopped walking.

"What's your plan?" Webb said to Early.

Early shrugged and looked at Heck.

"Our plan for what?" Heck asked.

Webb twisted his lips in frustration. He was a confident man, and he didn't seem to be the type to waste much time on indecision. He had little patience for anyone who wasn't identical.

"That was a significant shipment of gold on that wagon," Webb said. "As the law here, you're going to have to do something about it. My guess is that you're either going to ride to the scene where my men were ambushed and try to trail the men who did it, or you're going to go directly to the place where you think the thieves are taking the gold."

"The Three Sweethearts Mine?" Early said, but he said it like he was asking a question, and that irritated Webb even more.

"Of course, the Three Sweethearts Mine," Webb snapped. "What have we been talking about for the last three days?"

Early looked at Heck, and Heck looked at Early, giving him a shrug.

"It's six of one, half a dozen of the other, hombre," Heck said. "Whether we go to where the ambush happened or not, we know we'll end up in the same place."

Early nodded.

"Then I reckon we'll ride for the Three Sweethearts Mine," he said.

Webb nodded.

"I think that's the smart thing to do," he said. "I'll ride with you. We should try to enlist Suttles, too. He's a good man. I'll divide what's left of my men, send some down to see if there's any survivors from the wagon, and we'll take the rest with us. It's important that we catch them with the gold. And when we do, we'll kill every man up there – send a message to any other thieves who want to come into these mountains."

Early's mouth fell open. Not that he would balk at a good shooting match, but the cool, callous way that Webb talked about killing fifty men caught him aback.

"When we've got proof – when we find gold that we can prove came from the Little Fannie – we'll arrest them," Early said. "Only with proof, you understand? And we won't kill anyone. Not without provocation."

Webb raised his eyebrows.

"Don't you boys want to go and saddle your horses?"

- 24 -

"Mr. Butler was a sharpshooter in the war," Webb said with a nod of his head toward George Butler, who rode out ahead of them about thirty yards.

Jack Webb rode his horse the same way he did everything else, with straight-backed confidence. He sat tall in the saddle of a big buckskin, not dissimilar from Early's stallion, But the horse, like the man, made every step look like an exact art.

"He's got eyes that are frightening," Webb continued. "I never have known another man who could see so well. He's also smart as a whip. He won't lead us into trouble."

"All the same, we should move off this trail before too long," Heck advised. "If these men from the Three Sweethearts Mine are who we think they are, they'll have lookouts. Considering the difference in numbers, it would probably be best if they don't know we're coming."

"I won't argue with that," Webb said. "But we're traveling through a canyon, there's not many places to hide through here."

"Just before we get to the Three Sweethearts Mine, it opens up and is pretty wooded along the slopes," Early said. He typically rode Tim Buck Too with the reins loose in his hand, giving the stallion the freedom to go as he pleased. But something about Jack Webb made Early feel like a kid again, and he didn't want to do anything that would embarrass himself in front of the man. So he kept the reins tight in his grip and his hand close to the horse's mane. "We'll be able to walk the horses up through the woods and get pretty close to their camp without being seen."

"Unless their lookouts are posted in the cliffs over the canyon here," Webb said. "They might see us before we ever reach the cover of the trees."

"I suppose so," Early said, feeling foolish.

Suttles rode just behind Early. Heck was even with him. Webb rode slightly ahead, with his man Butler far up in the lead. Trailing them, Webb had three more men. Everyone in the group was armed with rifles and six-shooters, and Webb's men turned up with enough boxes of cartridges that they could shoot for days.

"What's your background, Mr. Webb?" Heck asked.

Already, Heck and Early had answered a series of similar questions put to them by Webb. He was sizing them up, trying to figure out who he was riding with, and probably trying to decide if they were trustworthy. Heck decided it was his turn now to do the sizing.

"My background is that I work at the Little Fannie Mine, mostly watching out for high graders among the miners."

"You've done that all your adult life?" Heck asked.

"Nope," Webb said with a chuckle. "I've done enough other things that the owners of the mine trust me to do this now."

"Mr. Webb doesn't like to talk too much about himself," Suttles said, leaning forward some in his saddle as the horses climbed a slope. "I reckon his name ain't Webb, and I reckon – as private as he is – somewhere there's a wanted poster with his real name on it."

Early glanced at Webb, and he could see a small grin across the man's face. He didn't answer Heck's question, and he continued to evade any other questions that Heck or Early sent his way. He wasn't rude about it, but by the time the riders came down into Stan Davis's timber camp, they still didn't know anything about Jack Webb beyond that he was responsible for the guards at the Little Fannie Mine.

"The Three Sweethearts boys rode through here a little while ago, headed back up to camp," Stan Davis said when Early asked him if he'd seen any riders come through.

"About twenty of them?" Heck asked.

Davis shrugged.

"I don't stand here and count riders that come through this way," he said. "But it looked to be a lot less than we usually see. Now, maybe fourteen or fifteen of them rode through early this morning. Woke me up."

"Is that right?" Early asked. He'd been at the livery and he knew none of the Rathbones' outfit had come to the livery to fetch their horses early. "They were coming back from town?"

"Oh, no," Davis said. "They were leaving out of their camp. They came through here before the sun was even up. Maybe an hour before first light. That's how come they woke me up – it was well before dawn."

"Were the riding toward town?" Early asked.

"Nope. Took that same trail you came along the other day. The one that cuts south from here."

Early looked at Webb and Suttles who were sitting their horses just over his shoulder.

"That's the trail Heck and I were on when we trailed the outlaws who held up the stagecoach," Early said.

"That trail cuts around to the Silver City Road below Muggyown," Heck added. "If they rode out before first light, they'd have been just in time to meet the wagon and escort from the Little Fannie."

With Butler in the lead, the eight-man posse started out from the timber camp.

"I told my men who rode down to the site of the ambush to do their best to try to track the men who did it," Webb said. "If those men are coming back to the Three Sweethearts, then they should ride right in behind us."

If there were lookouts on the cliffs overlooking the canyon leading to the Three Sweethearts mine, George Butler never saw them. As the canyon walls widened and the slopes rounded, covered in ponderosa pine, the Three Sweethearts camp came into view up ahead. It was late in the afternoon, only four hours or so of daylight left in the day.

"Dismount," Webb called back to his men, keeping his voice low, though they were still well out of earshot of the camp.

Now the small group led their horses in among the trees. With all the others staying back with the horses, Early, Webb, and Butler made their way through the trees, going slowly so as to not draw any attention.

"What are we looking for when we get up here, marshal?" Webb asked.

"The stolen gold," Early said.

"The sacks we put the gold in are all stamped with 'Little Fannie Mining Company.' If these boys did that stagecoach holdup, I would bet they never changed out the sacks. That'll be your proof."

Webb sniffed the air.

"I smell smoke," he said.

Early pointed through the trees. "That's the dining hall over there. I see smoke coming from the chimney."

They were close enough, now, that they could see activity taking place around the camp. Mostly, it was men at their leisure – card games, a handful of men throwing horseshoes, another couple of men working a young colt.

"They don't look much like an outfit of bad men," Webb said.

"How many stamps does the Little Fannie have on its stamp mill?" Early asked.

"We've got four banks of five-stamp mills," Webb said.

"How many stamps do you see around here?" Early asked.

Webb looked across the camp.

"Yep. It's hard to run a gold mine that's producing as much gold as these boys claim without a stamp mill."

"They're stealing your gold off those stagecoaches, and they're using a mine that doesn't exist as the cover for their activities."

Early said it, and even as he spoke the words, he was uncomfortable with how much he sounded like a lawman.

They heard a whistle from behind them that sounded enough like a bird that Early almost ignored it. But then he looked back and saw that Heck and the others had pulled the horses back some, and the men were all squatting down low behind trees.

"Look here," Early said, crouching low himself. "Riders coming in."

***

The riders tied their horses in front of the dining hall. With Early and Jack Webb and Webb's man George Butler all watching, the men pulled away blankets that they had laid across their horses. He couldn't see well enough to say for sure, but they unloaded into the blankets what looked remarkably like heavy sacks, about the right size for being sacks of gold.

"Yep," Butler said, squinting his eyes. "I'd swear those are our bags."

"Huh," Webb said. "What do you say, marshal? Is that your proof? Sacks of gold from the Little Fannie seems like proof to me."

"It seems like proof," Early agreed.

Early counted the riders as they came up to the camp – fourteen of them. He'd also made a count of the men he could see. With the fourteen who just rode up, Early knew for a fact that there were at least thirty-eight men in the camp, and he'd not yet seen men he knew by name – Jubal and Caleb Rathbone, Haven and Ballew.

The men folded their blankets around the sacks of gold and hefted them up over their shoulders and then took them into the dining hall. Several of the men around camp who'd been killing time with cards or other activities now left what they were doing and started toward the dining hall.

"As far as I'm concerned, we can start shooting now," Webb said. "Butler here can probably kill a dozen men before the rest of them even come out of that building there."

"We can't just start shooting folks," Early said.

"So what do you propose we do?" Webb asked.

"Me and my partner will walk up to the dining hall," Early said. "We'll offer the Rathbones an opportunity to come with us. If they refuse, we'll tell them that we're going to bring the cavalry up."

Webb chuckled.

"You know all that's going to do is bring out the guns."

Early grinned at him.

"I reckon that's when we find out just how good of a shot Mr. Butler is," Early said.

Webb grunted.

"Just to be clear, you're telling me, marshal, that if we see guns come out, you want me and my men to intervene."

"That's what I'm saying."

"All right, then. Good luck to you."

- 25 -

"We're going to get killed," Heck muttered as he and Early walked up the roadway into the Three Sweethearts camp.

"Maybe not," Early said, his tone optimistic, a small grin on his face.

"You're enjoying this, aren't you?" Heck said.

Early could hear in Heck's tone how tense he was, and he couldn't blame Heck at all. Just walking into the camp, trying to appear casual, Early felt like his legs were weighted down with iron balls. With each step, it seemed tougher to take the next step. Outgunned and outnumbered, Early wasn't exactly sure how they could manage to get through this one unscathed.

As they approached the camp, the men who were still outside and engaged in whatever time-killing activities appealed to them all stopped what they were doing and watched the two men approaching. One of them ran toward the dining hall, presumably to alert the Rathbones.

"Won't be but a minute now," Early said. "If this thing turns into a shooting match, best thing to do is run like hell. Find a building or a tree or a rock to get behind."

"Oh, I'll run all right," Heck said. "Don't you worry about that."

"Webb and his men will give us some help, but it'll be up to us to finish this thing fast."

"How do you propose we do that?" Heck asked.

"Same way you kill a rattlesnake, Heck. Cut off the head. Once you're hunkered down somewhere, you shoot for Jubal and Caleb. I reckon about half these men will run like hell when the shooting starts. Outlaws, by their very nature, are not a trustworthy bunch. They'll cut and run to avoid getting their heads blowed off, and easily abandon their brethren in their time of need."

"And the other half will stand and fight? That's still twenty or twenty-five men, Early. Right about now, I'm wishing I was an outlaw so I could cut and run."

"Too late for that," Early said with a nod of his head. "Here comes Jubal."

Up ahead of them, coming out of the dining hall, Jubal Rathbone and about ten followers started toward Heck and Early. They were walking with pace, closing the distance rapidly, and Early was glad of it.

Curtis Suttles and Jack Webb and his men were spread out in the woods now, the horses all tied back behind them. Six guns worked quickly could make it seem like twice or even three times their number, and if Jubal Rathbone walked out here into the open, he was just giving Webb and Butler and the others an easier shot. Early wished that Rathbone had twenty men with him.

Early carried his Henry rifle in his hand, but he gripped it around the receiver and carried it casually down by his side in the least threatening way he could. Heck had his lever-action Winchester in similar fashion. They might have been hunters rather than lawmen looking to make arrests.

"I'm going to ask you to stop right there!" Jubal Rathbone shouted from forty yards away, continuing to walk at a quick pace even as he spoke. "This is twice you've come up here bothering us, marshal. You've got my men in your jail down yonder, you're up here bothering us again. You've no right to harass me and my employees like this."

Early stopped. Heck took two more steps and then felt foolish about backing up, so he took another couple of steps wide so that he and Early were more spread out.

They waited for Jubal Rathbone to get to them.

"Where's your brother, Jubal?" Early said.

Rathbone glanced over his own shoulder, back toward the dining hall.

"He's eating his supper, but that don't make a difference. I want you and your deputy to turn around now and walk right out of this camp. You've got no business here."

"That's not exactly right," Early said. "The Little Fannie sent a shipment of gold to Silver City today. Somebody held up the wagon and killed the men guarding it."

"Then you should be off looking for them, marshal, not wasting your time here," Rathbone said.

"We found 'em," Early said. "The men who held up that stagecoach just rode into your camp about a quarter of an hour ago and took the stolen gold into your dining hall. The same building you just came out of. I reckon you saw it, and I reckon that makes you – what's the word, Heck?"

"Culpable," Heck said.

Early grinned.

"I think that is the word. Anyway, it's the word I'm going to use when we get you in front of a jury."

He saw Ballew, standing a couple of feet behind Jubal Rathbone, drop his hand down to the grip of his gun. He didn't try to clear leather, but he was ready to pull the gun.

"Now, you and your men step aside while my partner and I go and fetch that gold out of your dining hall."

"You're a couple of hard bit men, ain't you," Jubal Rathbone said. "Walking up into this camp where we've got all these armed men, making accusations that you cannot prove, and demanding to see this and that we do that. Well, all right marshal, you want to go into the dining hall. Come on, then, be my guest."

Jubal Rathbone stepped aside and waved his hands

as if ushering Early toward the dining hall.

For a moment, no one moved except for Heck, who glanced at Early.

Neither of them expected this, an invitation to walk right into the dining hall where they knew the men had taken the gold.

Early raised his eyebrows at Heck, as if acknowledging that this hadn't come up in any of the scenarios he'd planned for.

"All right," Early said, and took a couple of tentative steps past Rathbone and through the cluster of men, walking toward the dining hall. Heck fell in beside him, though still keeping several feet of distance between the two of them. He didn't see any point in bunching up together and making an easy target for the Three Sweethearts crowd.

Early felt Rathbone's men close in behind him. Rathbone was trailing just behind him.

Heck and Early both felt their vulnerability. They'd put themselves completely at the mercy of their adversaries. They wouldn't even see it now if Ballew or Haven or Rathbone reached for a gun. Early could feel the eyes of the men behind him boring into his back, picking their target. Would they all draw and shoot with a wave of Rathbone's hand? Would he get eight or nine or ten bullets in the back before he ever hit the ground – before he ever even heard the shots? He had a sick feeling in his stomach, and if he'd thought his legs were heavy before, that was nothing to this.

The tension broke when the sharp report of a rifle broke the stillness of the afternoon. Every man within earshot recognized the sound, and they all knew instinctively what it did portend.

***

They'd made it maybe fifteen yards, and the tension pressed so heavy on Heck that he finally couldn't resist it. He knew, without looking, that these men behind him were planning to shoot him in the back. So he made up his mind to cast a glance over his shoulder. Just as he started to twist around, Heck heard the crack of the rifle. In that instant, Heck understood that the shot had come from the woods, and he knew it must have been Webb or one of his men – probably Butler, the sharpshooter.

He was already twisting around, so Heck saw it happen as Haven pitched forward, stumbling into Early. He had a gun in his hand, his arm hanging loosely by his side. His hat fell to the ground, and Haven had an odd look on his face.

Everyone seemed to freeze right there, except Haven.

Heck took in the scene as it appeared to him. He thought at first that the hat came off when Haven knocked into Early, but as the man rolled and dropped to the ground, Heck saw the massive opening in the back of his skull. Butler, presumably, had shot Haven in the back of the head, and that odd look on his face was instant death.

The body crumpled to the ground and still everyone remained frozen. Maybe it was a moment, maybe it was half a heartbeat. Everything registered quickly in Heck's mind.

Four or five of the men with Jubal Rathbone, maybe even more than that, had all drawn their weapons when Heck and Early had their backs to them. Nobody's gun was up yet, and Haven's death had caught them all by surprise so that no one had yet followed through with their intentions. And it was the space of that moment that gave Heck and Early an opportunity to get clear.

The volley from the trees is what broke the trance that everyone seemed to be in.

It came as an eruption of gunfire, five more rifle shots sounding like rolling thunder coming from the tree line.

Immediately behind the rifle shots, men at the back of the party began to crumple and jerk and pitch forward.

Rathbone and most of the others turned to see where the shots were coming from. That was instinct, a reflex. They turned.

"Run!" Heck shouted, but Early didn't need to be told twice. Early took off toward the right, running the way he was facing which was away from Rathbone's group of men, but also away from the modicum of safety that Webb and his men offered.

Heck followed him, even though his instinct was to run toward Webb, away from the camp.

That's when the entire mountainside seemed to come alive with bullets buzzing and zipping past and the booming reports of rifles.

Two enormous, brown-trunked pines stretched high up over the middle of the camp, right between the dining hall and the big log cabin office. Between the two pines there must have been a wall of two hundred split logs stacked chest-high, and that seemed to be the safety

Early sought.

The woodpile was maybe sixty yards from where they'd started their run, and Heck watched as Early reached the center of the pile and threw himself bodily at it, leaping high and rolling so that he landed on the top of the stack of logs on his back, and then he and probably a dozen logs just disappeared as his momentum carried him over the woodpile. Heck heard the snap of a couple of bullets as they came perilously close to him, and then he dove for the same spot in the woodpile. Where Early had landed and then dragged down the top of the woodpile with him, Heck cleared the thing and landed hard on the opposite side, knocking the wind out of himself.

If they thought they'd run for safety, both men now knew better.

From up the slope, four or five men were shooting at them and had them pinned against the woodpile. If anything, they'd run into a more dangerous situation.

Heck tried to catch his breath from the ground, his chest heaving though he could get no air.

Early Bascomb grew up on a fine Mississippi cotton plantation in the middle of the War of Northern Aggression, and he'd talked about times when he and his mama couldn't eat if he didn't shoot a squirrel or a deer. He'd been a young boy then, nine- or ten-years old hunting for his family's supper, and a nine-year-old hunting for survival becomes a twenty-something-year-old who's a helluva shot. Early proved the point now.

He had the Henry up against his shoulder and was sighting down the barrel.

He didn't care that the men up the slope had a clear

shot at him or that their bullets were ripping into the logs just behind him. Early took the moment he needed to get his aim, let out a breath, squeezed the trigger.

"Gotcha!" he shouted, a whoop of victory that Heck had heard before.

He dropped the lever on the Henry without ever moving it from his shoulder, without ever lifting his head or breaking his concentration. He squeezed the trigger a second time.

"Gotcha!" Early shouted gleefully. "Whoa now, son! C'mon Heck Pinoza, get in this fight!"

Early scrambled a couple of feet to his left, just in case one of them had a bead on him, and he worked the action on the Henry again. He squeezed the trigger and cursed that he'd missed.

"Carajo!" Heck said, finally catching his breath. He was flat on the ground, watching Early. He'd dropped his Winchester when he hit the ground, and he rolled now to lift it up. He took a couple of breaths to calm himself.

Heck could hear shots coming from the other side of the woodpile, back where Jubal Rathbone and those others were. He didn't know if those shots were all aimed back into the woods at Webb or if some of them were coming toward him and Early, but stacked firewood kept him from having to worry about it. He could hear shots coming from the other side of the big office building – over in the woods. That was Webb and his men. There were shots coming from the men up the slope, those were the immediate danger for Heck and Early. But what worried him more than anything, about thirty yards to his left was the front door of the dining hall. In a moment that door was going to open up, and the men still inside would have an easy shot at Early.

Without making himself too big of a target, Heck rolled onto his knees, raised his Winchester up to his shoulder, and took an aim on the door of that dining hall.

"Gotcha!" Early shouted again. "Hell, Heck, this ain't nothin' but a turkey shoot!"

The dining hall door crashed open and two men bolted through it, both of them toting rifles. The first one came through so fast, he caught Heck by surprise, even though he'd been anticipating it. He squeezed the trigger on the second man. The bullet caught the man in the side of his hip and knocked his legs out from under him. Heck worked the lever on the Winchester and got the third man coming through the door, and with his eye still trained along the barrel, he sought out the first man.

But seeing his two amigos shot down and finding himself exposed, that first man did the smartest thing Heck had seen anyone do all day. He turned away from the shooting and ran down to where the horses were still saddled and lashed to a post in front of the dining hall. The man undid one of the horses, took up its reins and hunkered down low in the saddle, beating the hell out of the horse's rump with the loose ends of the reins and galloping north, away from the camp.

The men up the slope were finished.

Early had dealt with them. Four or five men, and he'd either shot all of them or one or two of them had run off. Whatever happened to them, Early was thrilled with the results.

"And I thought we wouldn't have any fun if we started wearing badges," Early said, giving Heck a slap on the shoulder.

"This isn't fun," Heck said.

Another man started to come through the door of the dining hall, but Heck nailed him through the ear – or close enough – and the man dropped dead right there in the doorway. The man he'd shot in the hip was lying four or five feet in front of the door, and he was howling for his mama. A shot to the hip bone, if it hits right, can shatter the bone, sending shards all through the lower extremities. It's a mortal wound, and usually it takes a man days to die from it. Those days are filled with agony. Heck wished right now that he'd shot that man in the head, too. His screams sounded over all the shooting, and it made Heck sick to hear the man.

Movement at the back corner of the dining hall caught Heck's attention, and he swung the rifle to his right just in time to let off a shot that backed someone back around the corner.

"They're coming from behind the dining hall," Heck said to Early.

"Yep! I see 'em!"

Early jumped to his feet, crouching low, and made a run to an outbuilding, some sort of storage shed, that would give him a position on the entire back wall of the dining hall. As he ran toward the shed, Heck heard several rifles explode to life from beyond the corner of the dining hall, and Early dove for cover on the far side of that shed.

Heck rose up onto his feet and chanced a look behind him, over the breastwork of the woodpile.

Jubal Rathbone and the men with him were in a bad spot. There were five men down in the middle of the road where Haven had fallen. They weren't all dead, but they were all in bad shape. The others had scattered, taking up positions where they could find cover. For most of them, that meant low spots along the side of the road. Heck scanned the area and found Jubal Rathbone hunkered down in the bed of a creek with Ballew and another man nearby. All those men had taken cover that protected them from Webb and the others up by the trees. But Heck had a clear shot at some of them. He set his hat on top of the woodpile and rested his left elbow down on his hat, crushing it. But the hat was of little concern just now.

With his left arm acting like a fulcrum, supported by the woodpile, Heck took close aim on the prone men fighting with Webb. The first two never even knew he was a threat to them, and they both died without even knowing where the shot came from. When two of them were dead, the others spread out in front of him broke cover and ran for some new point of safety, exposing them to Webb and his men.

The killing came easy, now. Except for Rathbone, Ballew, and the other one, all still hunkered down in the creek bed, these men were all easy targets. The men up in the trees weren't missing their shots.

Behind him, Heck could hear a resumption of shooting, and he knew that Early must've come around the side of that shed, exposing himself but also putting him in a position to throw some shots at the men against the back wall of the dining hall.

A shot hit a log two inches from where Heck had set his hat, and he spun back toward the dining hall doorway now. Just as he did, someone inside there jerked away from the opening and out of view. Heck fired off a couple of harmless shots at the entrance to the dining hall. He knew he wouldn't hit anything – there wasn't even a target there now – but he hoped a well-placed shot or two might give whoever was there something to think about before they tried another shot.

That moment that his attention was redirected must've been the moment Jubal Rathbone was waiting for. He leapt up out of the creek bed and started running off through a wide meadow. It was down in that meadow where Early had seen the burial party under a big acorn tree, and Jubal was making toward it now with Ballew and the third man.

Several rifle shots came from the woods, but none of the men went down.

And then, in a moment, Heck saw a rider coming from the direction of the camp's corral. He was trailing three saddled horses, and he was making for the same acorn tree as the three men running.

As fast as it had started, the shooting stopped.

All around, men scrambled to get away. Some ran up the slope to the north. Others took off up the slope to the east. And Jubal Rathbone mounted a horse under the acorn tree, and he and three other riders tore off to the west through the meadow.

- 26 -

"Thirteen dead, twenty-one wounded," Butler said after making a count of the shot men around the camp. "Of those twenty-one, I count another six who likely won't survive the next few days."

Webb grunted.

"I'd have liked to have killed more than that, but it's a good start."

"I'm guessing fifteen or so made off into the trees and escaped," Heck said.

"We need to be out of here before dark," Webb advised. "If the Rathbones collect enough of those men, they might come back here and try to retake the camp. And if they come at us after dark, when they know this place better than we do, they might be successful."

Butler and Webb's other men became responsible for collecting the dead and wounded. They treated those men who they thought might recover from their wounds, and found some liquor for those who seemed doubtful. Heck and Early, along with Suttles and Webb, made an extensive search of the property, though probably not a thorough search. They didn't cut open mattresses or look through the hay in the stable or search for loose boards in the buildings that might reveal hidden chambers. All the same, they found enough that if they ever caught the Rathbones, they could hang them.

"The evidence is pretty damning," Early said as they gathered in front of the Three Sweethearts office.

Early squinted into the late afternoon sun. He had a burlap sack in each hand, taken from a table in the dining hall. One was stamped "Little Fannie Mining Company" and the other was stamped "Three Sweethearts Mine." The battle that raged had caught the men in the middle of transferring gold from Little Fannie sacks into Three Sweethearts sacks. In addition, during a search of the camp, they'd found boxes taken from previous stagecoach holdups and other sacks, some of them burned out, with Little Fannie markings or stamps from other mines in the area. They found a couple of crates loaded with these sacks.

"Including what they took from our freight wagon today, I'm guessing they've probably got about thirty thousand dollars' worth of gold up here," Webb said.

What they did not find anywhere around the camp was evidence of a mining operation.

"It's all a sham," Webb said. "No stamps. No cradles. Certainly they've not sunk a shaft anywhere around here. I did find some evidence that at some point someone dug holes down along the creek and in that meadow, but nobody has ever worked this area for gold. My guess is that's because nobody ever found evidence of gold up here."

"Admiral Moe told me that he prospected this area and never found any gold," Heck said.

In part because they had so many wounded men who were going to have to be transported back to town and because they'd recovered so much gold, the men decided not to try to chase after those from the Three Sweethearts outfit who fled.

"They're scattered, and they'll know their days of robbing stagecoaches from here are done," Webb said. "I ain't suggesting they'll walk a straight line from here on out, but I don't believe any of those boys will be a problem for me up at the Little Fannie or for you down in Muggyown. In a couple of days, I'll reinforce with some of the men from our camp and come back out here and burn or knockdown every building up here. The cold weather will be along in a few weeks, and we'll guarantee that the Rathbones and whatever remains of their men will have to leave these mountains because they won't have any shelter here."

Heck and Early were satisfied with that.

After a while, Webb's other men turned up, having trailed the robbers who ambushed the wagon to the Three Sweethearts camp.

When they were all there, Webb had his men round up the horses and mules. They hitched teams four wagons. His men went around collecting rifles and boxes of cartridges and cans of food. Those wounded men who couldn't be tied to a saddled horse were loaded into three of the wagons. Supplies were loaded into the other one, and the gold they'd recovered.

"It'll be dark in an hour," Webb said. "It's slow going on that trail at nighttime, but it's better than sitting here waiting for them to come back."

Heck and Early drove the horses along the trail out in front of the wagons, but they tried to stay close. It was a nervous ride – dark and with the constant threat that the Rathbones might rally their men and try to get at the gold. Nobody talked much, either – everyone straining their ears into the darkness, waiting for any sound that might alert them to attack.

But no sound came, and the farther they got from the Three Sweethearts camp, the more secure they started to feel.

Only four of the men from the outfit had escaped on horseback – Jubal and Caleb Rathbone, Ballew, and one other man. Everyone else was on foot, and by the time they passed through Stan Davis's timber camp, there was small chance that the Three Sweethearts men could catch them, even though they were moving at a slow pace through the night.

Sometime around midnight, they arrived at the Little Fannie Mine.

It was Jack Webb's suggestion that they house the prisoners, the horses, and the gold up at the Little Fannie where someone other than Frog could keep a watch.

Finally, Heck and Early and Suttles returned to Mogollon sometime around two o'clock in the morning. Suttles went to tell Captain Beaumont what had happened, and Heck and Early went to the livery to leave Tim Buck Too and Poco a Poco in the corral.

Frog still had charge of his prisoners.

"They've been fed twice today, but they're all complaining about the shackles cutting into their wrists," he reported.

"Let them complain," Early told him. "After what we found up at their camp, they'll have a lot more complaining to do when they get to the territorial prison."

- 27 -

Ronald Beatty was in the lobby of the hotel, still awake despite the hour. The night clerk sat on a sofa, and Beatty was in one of the armchairs. A couple of other people were in there, also – men who Early recognized as guests of the hotel who were also staying on the second floor. He'd passed them in the hall or seen them in the dining room. One man was leaning in the doorway of the hall leading back to the dining room. Another man stood beside the stairs, using the point of a small pocket knife to clean under his fingernails in the light cast by the lamp. Another man sat on the third step up the stairway, his elbows on his knees. All but one of these men were in some state between underclothes or nightclothes and fully clothed. Only the one cleaning his fingernails was fully clothed, and he looked as if he'd just returned from a night out at the card tables.

The silence in the lobby hung like a heavy fog.

Beatty wore a nightshirt tucked into a pair of britches, and he looked something like what someone might expect if there'd been a midnight fire in the hotel and he'd had to flee for his life. Disheveled, certainly, but also pale and worried. He did not wear his glasses. When Heck and Early came through the door of the hotel, exhausted, dirty and ready for sleep, Beatty stood up. He wrung his hands and his mouth fell open as if he wanted to speak but didn't know what words to use.

Heck and Early stopped at the front door and looked at all the men in the lobby.

"What's wrong in here?" Early asked, wearing a confused grin.

Beatty finally found his words.

"We heard you ride through town and then up to the Little Fannie Mine," Beatty said. "We almost came to get you."

"Why?" Early asked, the grin fading, but the confusion still evident in his expression.

"They came a little before midnight. Maybe around eleven o'clock. Not long before you came through town with those horses and wagons. We didn't realize that was you, of course."

"Who came here?" Early said. "Tell me what happened."

"The Rathbone brothers – Jubal and Caleb – and two

others. They went straight upstairs to your room."

"Maybe!" Early said, and he did not wait to hear any more. He took the steps two at a time, running up the stairs and down the hall.

The door hung loosely from just the top hinge. They'd kicked it in and tore hell out of the frame when they did. A table was overturned, but there was nothing else in the room to see. Nothing, including Maybe O'Malley. They'd come and taken her.

Early felt his heart pounding in his chest, and the exhaustion that had overcome him while they brushed down the horses was gone now. He felt suddenly wide awake.

Down in the lobby, they could hear Early's footsteps returning.

Heck's voice was almost a shout.

"The worst part is that you've given them hours of time, when we could have been trailing them from the get-go," Heck was saying. "Why the hell wouldn't you send someone immediately up to the Little Fannie to get us?"

"At first, we didn't even know it was you who came through with the wagons and the horses," Beatty protested. "We didn't know what was going on. We've only just realized when Mr. Reed here returned from the Two Forks and told us you were down at the livery and on your way here."

The man cleaning his fingernails looked up from his work at the mention of his name.

"I was down at Captain Beaumont's saloon when Mr. Suttles came in, and I heard the story of what happened up at the Three Sweethearts camp," Reed said. "Of course, I didn't know then that they'd come into the hotel and snatched the woman."

"So you see," Beatty said, but he left it at that, adding only a helpless shrug of his shoulders.

"Where did they go?" Early asked, pushing back past the man on the stairs.

"Well, we don't know that, do we?" Beatty said.

"We tried to stop them, marshal," the man leaning in the doorway to the back hall said. "But – well, they're rough men. You see what they did to my face."

Early gave the man a closer look and did see a small cut above his eye.

"I feel like we did all that we could reasonably be expected to do," Beatty said.

Heck sighed and shook his head. He did not have patience for men who could so easily be bullied out of the way when a woman was being abducted.

"Where could they have gone?" Early said.

"They're friendless and on the run," Beatty said.

"Not exactly friendless," Heck said.

Early read his thoughts.

"Admiral Moe."

***

In the chest of drawers inside their hotel room, Heck and Early found their short-barrel scatterguns along with a couple of boxes of shells. They left their rifles standing up inside the wardrobe and got the shotguns. Both men stuffed some extra shells into their pockets.

"Moe's got a number of guns up at his place," Heck said. "He told me about them – bartenders and faro dealers and whatnot."

"They do not matter to me," Early said. "Any man who protects men who go after a woman like that deserves to get cut down."

Heck grunted.

"I'm just saying, when we get up here, you need to be prepared for it. I don't think we'll just be facing the Rathbones. That's all I'm saying."

Heck hadn't seen Early like this before. It wasn't like him to get riled. But just now, Early was fuming. It worried Heck a little. Early was always a little reckless, but he was never careless. An angry man, though, a man bent on revenge, that could be a careless man.

The hour was so late that even Admiral Moe's was quiet. No musicians played an impromptu concert in the side yard. Only a few lights appeared to be burning inside.

"Do we have a plan?" Heck asked.

"Not unless you do," Early said.

"I figured we'd just go on inside and hopefully the Rathbones will be in there with Maybe, and we can just settle it right now."

"That's sort of what I was hoping for, too," Early said.

"If it doesn't shake out like that?" Heck asked.

"Then I'll wrap by hands around Moe's throat and I'll

throttle that sonuvabitch until he tells us where they are. You prevent anyone from pulling me off of him."

"There you go, hombre," Heck said. "Now we've got a plan."

A couple of Moe's faro dealers stood down by the footbridge that was the only way to access the tavern and keep your feet dry. Heck and Early saw them in the moonlight, but they went directly for the footbridge anyway.

"Sorry, boys, we're closed," one of the men said, holding up a hand.

"I'm the marshal," Early said.

"We're closed to the marshal, too."

"Come morning, you boys are going to be looking for a new job," Early said. "Nothing is going to change that. Whatever Moe is paying you isn't worth your life. Walk away now."

One of the faro dealers started to chuckle, clearly intending to come back with some wise ass retort.

They were faro dealers, not hardened gunmen or callous fighters.

Their mistake had been crossing the bridge and leaning against the rails on this side of Silver Creek. If they'd stayed on the saloon side of the creek, they'd have had ten feet of warning that the marshal and his deputy were coming through them, and maybe they'd have been able to get their guns up and gotten off a couple of shots, or at least they'd have been able to set their jaws and square their shoulders and put up their fists. But as it was, the two men had crossed the bridge to start their guard duty, and Heck and Early had both walked right up to within striking distance of the two faro dealers.

Early swung with the shortened barrel of the shotgun, using it like a club. He hit the faro dealer standing in front of him so hard in the head, that the barrel of the shotgun rang like a gong, or maybe it was the hollow echo inside the man's head.

Heck was a heartbeat behind Early, but he kicked out with his foot, getting it square between the man's legs. It was a cheap shot, but effective all the same. The faro dealer doubled over, and Heck bashed his exposed head with the butt of the shotgun.

Both men were rendered unconscious by the blows to the head, and they slumped into the dirt in front of the bridge. They disarmed the men, sliding their six-shooters from their holsters and emptying the cylinders. Heck tossed both guns into the creek.

Heck walked softly over the bridge, not making any sound as his boots lit on the blank boards. Early followed behind him. They didn't see anyone else out, neither in the yard or in front of the saloon. The moon cast a silvery light in the thoroughfare, but it was pitch black under every tree, and more gunmen could easily be hidden among the shadows. So they kept their shotguns ready in front of them, and stepped slowly as they made their way up the slope to Admiral Moe's saloon.

As they reached the door, Early put a hand on Heck's shoulder and leaned in close to whisper to him.

"There's a back door," Early said. "Go around to the back, and right where the trail is that leads up to Maybe's tent, you'll find that door. Why don't you go in the back so we aren't both standing here together and making it easy on anyone who's inside there with a gun."

Heck nodded his head.

"Give me a minute to get around," Heck said. "Don't go in yet."

"Sure," Early whispered.

As soon as Heck stepped away, Early pulled open the door and stepped inside.

- 28 -

Early slid in so quietly that no one even saw him enter the saloon. Only a couple of lamps were burning in the place, and the front door was completely cast in shadow.

Five men sat around a table right in the center of Moe's saloon.

The two Rathbones were there, and Ballew, and Moe was sitting with them. The other man was also one of Moe's faro dealers.

A bottle of whiskey sat on the table, with a short glass in front of each man.

Ballew and Caleb Rathbone sat with their backs to the front door. The other three men at the table sat to where they would have at least some view of the front door, but still none of them noticed Early.

Several feet away at another table, Maybe O'Malley sat in a chair between two more men, one of Moe's bartenders and the fourth man who fled the Three Sweethearts camp with the Rathbones and Ballew. The bartender appeared indifferent. The man from the Three Sweethearts leaned forward, his elbows on the table and his head resting in his hands. He was all tuckered out from his big day of shooting it out up at the camp.

Everything from her body language to the way she clenched her jaw made Maybe come across as livid. The dim lighting inside the saloon cast an odd glow on her face, deforming her features in shadow so that she almost resembled some sort of redheaded demon of Hell, just about ready to jump atop the table and spit venom at everyone in the room.

All the attention of the men at the table focused on Moe. He was speaking and rapping on the table with his knuckles to drive home his points.

"Of course we'll have to abandon this place," he said. "But there's too much gold up there to just leave it."

"They probably brought it back with them," Jubal Rathbone said.

"Then it's up at the Little Fannie," Moe snapped. "I don't care where it is, you've got to go and get it. How do we start over somewhere else without it?"

"What about all the money you've made at this place?" Caleb Rathbone said. "Surely that's enough for us to start over."

"Half of it is on credit anyway," Moe said. "And I've got expenses here. It's not like I'm saving money here."

"There's no time to figure out what they did with the gold and try to get it," Jubal Rathbone said. "We've got to get the hell out of here. As soon as that marshal gets back and figures out that we grabbed the girl, he'll know we're in town and he'll be looking for us. We've got to get out before dawn."

Early tried to make himself small against the wall so that they wouldn't notice him.

Moe looked at Caleb Rathbone.

"What the hell were you thinking?" Moe demanded. "You should have left her."

Caleb glanced over to the table where Maybe sat between her two indifferent guards.

"When I got up to her tent and saw that she wasn't there, I ran hot. The stove was ice cold. I knew she'd been staying with that marshal."

Moe looked at Jubal Rathbone.

"You should've known better than to let him go up there."

Jubal just shrugged his shoulders.

Maybe, though, finding herself the subject of the conversation, spoke up.

"Just let me go, Moe," she said. "There's no reason for you to keep me here."

But Moe shook his head.

"I can't do that, Maybe. Not now. You've heard too much now and seen too much. If Jubal and Caleb hadn't brought you back here, then maybe I could just tell them to turn you loose. But you can testify now and tie me to them."

"I won't say anything to anyone," Maybe said. She didn't plead with him, though. Her voice was level, matter-of-fact. No panic or fear in her. She wasn't begging him. And Early didn't think she would.

"Sorry, honey," Moe said. "Whatever we do next, you'll have to come with us. At least for now."

"We could still make for the hills," Jubal said. "Me and Caleb and Ballew and Smitty. The four of us can take the girl and ride out of here. That leaves you to still try to get at the gold."

Moe shook his head.

"Who saw you bring Maybe back here?" he asked. "Who out on the road saw you? Who at the hotel followed you back up here?"

"Nobody from the hotel followed us," Caleb said.

"You think," Moe said. "You don't know. And I'm not about to risk my freedom and my life on you making a guess."

"I say we get out fast," Jubal said. "I say we forget that gold and move on. I done watched half our outfit get shot all to hell today, and the rest of the boys have scattered to the wind. I don't feel much like getting shot up, neither. Let's just pack up and get away tonight."

"Not without the gold," Moe said. "It makes everything we've done here worthless if we don't get it. That's too much gold just to give it up."

Jubal continued his argument.

"We can get gold somewhere else."

Now Admiral Moe slapped the table with his open palm, making a loud crack, and he raised himself up out of his chair.

"I'm in charge here," Moe said. "If it weren't for me, you would have never seen any gold except maybe for a gold watch you picked from someone's pocket. I make the decisions, and I say when we leave, and I say what we leave behind."

So that was it, Early realized. Admiral Moe was in charge the entire time. It wasn't Jubal or Caleb Rathbone. It was Moe who ran this outfit, Moe that Jubal and Caleb answered to. Once they'd concluded that the Three Sweethearts men were robbing stagecoaches and not sinking shafts, they'd figured that someone in town was feeding them information about the comings and goings of the Little Fannie gold. That was probably why Moe had gotten so close to Everson.

Early figured, too, that Everson must've told Moe about Collier's suggestion of sending the gold on Sunday instead of Monday, and he'd seen that as an easier target because they wouldn't be expecting an ambush, thinking they were shipping the gold out in secret. Moe wanted Everson out of the way because Collier's plan gave him a better shot at the gold. So Moe set Everson up, got him drunk, knowing that he would probably get violent with Alice because of his history.

Both barrels of the shotgun would clear the five men sitting around the table. They might not all be dead, but they wouldn't be in the fight for a few moments. Then it was just clear leather with the Colt on his hip, shoot Moe's bartender first and then the fourth man who escaped from the Three Sweethearts Mine with the Rathbones – Smitty, they said his name was.

The whole damn thing could be over right now, and Early was certain he could move fast enough that the risk to Maybe would be minuscule.

Slowly, desperately hoping to avoid making any more noise than possible, Early started to thumb back the first hammer on the shotgun.

And that's when there was shouting outside the saloon, and then two shots went off, one of them the clear, sharp bark of a six-shooter, the other sounded like the bigger thump of a shotgun. The reports sounded all that much louder because of the silence of the night, and echoed off the walls of the gulch.

"What the hell!" Moe said, and every man at the table joined him in getting to their feet. They were all turned toward the back door. Caleb and Jubal Rathbone both reached for their guns. But with the men standing, Caleb and Ballew took away Early's angle. He'd be less likely to hit all five of them with some portion of the two blasts from the shotgun.

A moment later, and the back door flung open. Two men dragged Heck through the doorway. Heck was slouched down, dark red liquid on his face, and for an instant, Early thought he'd been shot in the face.

***

Just as Heck Espinoza walked away, he realized that Early had slipped inside Moe's saloon through the front door.

"Carajo, hombre!" Heck hissed silently to himself. "Why not wait for me like I said?"

Heck rounded the corner of the saloon, and in the silver light saw that he was going to have trouble sneaking in the back way. Most of Moe's men were standing around out back, not exactly guarding the back door, but they were there all the same. They were talking and laughing among themselves, and they hadn't seen him. Heck pressed himself into the shadows against the side of the building and waited, hoping maybe they would wander off.

He had no idea what was happening inside the saloon, but he knew that no one had discovered Early yet. If they did catch him, there would be shooting.

He stood there, frozen in the darkness, for what seemed like an eternity, not knowing what to do. He could slide back around to the front and try to go in the front door to join Early. Or he could watch these men in the back, and if there was trouble inside, he could open up on these men and try to help Early by keeping them out. That would leave Early on his own inside, but Early could usually handle himself in a fight.

The moment of indecision stretched into a minute, and then another.

And then the decision was made for him.

One of the men from around back came to the side of the building and dropped the front of his trousers, relieving himself there beside the saloon. Heck recognized him as one of Moe's bartenders.

Heck held his breath. The man wasn't more than six feet from where Heck pressed himself into the shadows.

Suddenly, the man stumbled back, and Heck watched as he fumbled with the front of his pants and reached for his holster that he'd slung over his shoulder while he did his business.

"Carajo!" Heck said, and he twisted around just in time that the man lost him in the shadows, and when he fired the six-shooter, the shot went to where Heck had been standing instead of where he was standing.

Now Heck squeezed one of the triggers on the shotgun, the flash of the gun blinding him for a half a second.

Moe's bartender collapsed in a heap, and Heck was sure the shotgun blast from such a close range must have cut the life out of the man.

But before Heck could draw back the other hammer or turn and run or make any other move, a half dozen men set upon him. Fists and knees collided into him as they wrestled him out of the shadows, and all Heck could do was try to ball himself up to protect himself. He caught one punch to the nose and immediately felt blood flowing freely down his face. His arms and thighs took the brunt of most of the punishment. When they were satisfied that they'd subdued him, a couple of the men grabbed him roughly by the arms. Someone dropped his gunbelt from his waist. And then they dragged him around to the back door of the saloon.

"We found him outside," one of the men said. "He killed Mike."

Through swollen eyes, Heck took in the scene in front of him. He saw Moe and the Rathbones and Maybe and a couple of other men, but he didn't see Early – not at first. He couldn't make out the door clearly, but now he saw a dark shape in the dark shadows by the door, and Heck realized that dark shape was his partner.

"Dammit!" Moe shouted. "That means the marshal

must be out there somewhere! Get to looking for him!"

"What about this one?" one of the men holding Heck asked.

"Take him back outside and kill him," Moe said.

Heck saw the two barrels of the scattergun drop out of the darkness, and then came the thunder and the flash.

Caleb Rathbone was there, and an instant later he was gone. Heck didn't know if he'd been knocked across the table, or the blast dropped him to the ground, but one moment Caleb was standing there facing him, and the next moment the man was gone.

Ballew swung around, shouting, and Heck could see his arm hanging loose by his side like the bones inside had been shattered by the blast.

The second shotgun blast tore through the man standing beside Jubal Rathbone – Heck thought he recognized him as a bartender or one of the faro dealers from Moe's saloon. The man had been turned around at the table facing Heck, and he caught the shotgun blast in the back. The force of it pitched him over his chair, and he went ass over head onto the ground.

Jubal Rathbone might also have taken a couple of lead balls from the second shot, but he didn't go down. Instead, he started shouting a long string of epithets – and of course he did. He'd just seen his brother killed.

Moe swung around, a six-shooter already in his hand, but from the shadow, a short-barrel scattergun came spinning through the air as if hurled by the darkness itself. Moe raised up his arm to protect himself from the missile.

Heck had a man on each arm, both of them clutching

to him, but when he'd gone limp outside, he was mostly just playing possum. For all the punches and knees to the thighs he'd endured, not many of them had connected with good force. He ached, and he'd have some bruises, but he still had all his strength.

He used it now.

First, he feinted to his left to try to put both men off balance, and then he threw all his weight to his right in a sudden move. He was helped by a chair sitting up against the wall near the door. The man on his right tripped on the chair and plummeted over, dragging Heck and the other man down to the ground with him.

Now Heck's hands were free, and started throwing punches, quick jabs to ribs and stomachs. Then he was up over the men, and it was a flurry of fists raining down upon the two of them. He went for their faces, and he threw hard jabs. He leaned his weight on his left and got his right knee into it, connecting with the groin of one of the men.

He didn't know where it had come from, but Heck saw a loose six-shooter on the floor. He presumed it had come out of the holster of one of the men who'd been holding him. He snatched it up and pressed it into the stomach of one of the men below him.

The flash of the gun ignited a fire on the man's shirt.

The other one, who he'd kneed in the groin, scrambled to get away, twisting and going on hands and knees, but Heck fired another shot.

Heck wasn't alone in shooting. The saloon seemed to be filled with blazing guns. His ears seemed filled with cotton, and the tremendous racket of all the gunfire left a constant whistling in his head.

Jubal Rathbone emptied his six-shooter into the far wall where he'd had a momentary glimpse of Early. Moe was shooting, and the two men who'd been opposite sides of Maybe had both taken shots. And Early was shooting back, but from where, Heck didn't know.

He rolled now and scrambled back over the body of the man he'd just shot. When he backed into a table, Heck scrambled to his feet and turned the table over and used it for cover. One of the men who'd attacked him outside was coming through the back door now, and he fired a couple of shots that splintered into the overturned table. Heck came around on one side and shot back, hitting the man in the arm. That one fell back, only to be immediately replaced by another.

That was when Maybe O'Malley made her run, tripped, and fell headlong behind the table, sprawled out on the floor behind Heck.

Jubal Rathbone, his gun empty, now fell to his knees, searching his younger brother's body until he came out with his brother's six-shooter. He came up, facing away from Heck in the direction of the door where Early had been. Heck fired a shot that caught Jubal in the back of his left hip. Enraged, Jubal spun around and fired twice at the table as Heck dropped down behind it again.

The tabletop stopped every bullet, but Heck knew it was just a matter of time before Jubal Rathbone or one of the others managed to get an angle where the table would offer no safety.

"We've got to get out of here," he said to Maybe, but he didn't know if she even heard him through the cotton and the ringing.

The situation seemed hopeless, and that's when it got worse. From somewhere around the bar, a great blaze of fire seemed to spring up, lighting the entire room, and threatening to burn them all to death.

In the sudden light, Heck looked at the door, but he didn't see Early.

***

Early Bascomb ducked and ran when the shooting started his direction.

In the darkness, he was able to run behind tables and the posts that supported the canvas roof of the saloon, and he managed to slip in behind the bar with no one even knowing that he wasn't still over by the door. With some glee, Early raised up his head enough to see the hammer of Jubal Rathbone's six-shooter fall several times on empty rounds as he kept trying to shoot into the darkness by the doorway.

Early saved his shots, not wanting to expose himself, and he only squeezed his trigger when he was sure of his aim.

He didn't have a clear shot at Moe. A six-by-six post stood between the two of them. Jubal Rathbone was still trying to shoot an empty gun.

Heck was down on his hands and knees fighting with the two men who'd dragged him in through the back door.

Early saw Ballew spinning to get a shot at Heck, and he took his aim and fired, then ducked down behind the bar.

When he came back up, Ballew was sitting in a chair holding his stomach and trying to get a look at his injury, and Heck was scrambling to get behind a table.

Someone coming through the back door made a dash toward the center of the room, and Early saw the man was loaded with a shotgun.

Early shot and the man went over, but he squeezed the trigger on his scattergun and hit one of the hanging lamps. Oil and flame dropped down from the rafter, covering half of a table and the plank board floors.

Jubal Rathbone stumbled away from the flames and Early saw he'd been shot in the back of the leg. He fell forward, landing on a table, and when he did, he was staring directly at Early.

"You sonuvabitch!" Rathbone shouted, and he tried to swing his gun around.

Early shot first, and punched a hole right through Rathbone's cheek. Already collapsed on the table, Jubal Rathbone didn't move. He just laid there, his dead eyes locked on Early Bascomb.

Some of the oil must have splashed onto Admiral Moe, because the last Early saw of him, he was screaming and running through the front door of the saloon, his arm fully ablaze.

Nobody came through the back door of the saloon, the spreading fire enough to keep them back, and there was no one left alive inside who was worth shooting.

"Heck?" Early called. "You all right?"

Heck peeked up over the edge of the overturned table.

"I think so," he said.

"You're a mess, amigo," Early said. "Your face is bloody as hell. Have you seen Maybe?"

A mane of tousled red hair appeared behind Heck.

"I'm here," Maybe said.

"We should get out of here," Early said.

Already the fire was spreading, moving up tables and chairs and across the wooden plans of the floor, but it was moving from the center of the room out, and they still had plenty of time to leave.

Early came around the side of the bar and picked up his scattergun from the floor. He ejected the spent shells and replaced them, then he emptied the spent cartridges from his Colt and replaced those.

"You think they're waiting for us to come out?" Heck asked, loading the gun he'd picked up from the floor.

"We'd be foolish to walk out there thinking they're not," Early said.

He walked over to the door, Heck behind him and Maybe staying close behind Heck, using him as a sort of shield.

Early pushed the door open and stepped back, waiting for someone to start shooting. But no shots came, so he poked his head out and then recoiled quickly. Still no shots.

With the fire burning inside, his eyes weren't adjusted to the darkness outside, and Early couldn't see much of anything through the slightly ajar door.

"I'm going to go out and make for the bridge," Early said. "If they start shooting, I'm going for the riverbed. If they don't start shooting, you get Maybe out of here. Get across the bridge and take her on to safety."

Early went out, but there was no point in running, so he didn't bother.

At the sound of the first shots, Curtis Suttles had gathered up some men and come up to Admiral Moe's, all of them armed, and they were rounding up Moe's men outside as Early made his dash from the burning saloon.

Heck and Maybe followed him out.

They didn't find Admiral Moe until morning when the sun came up. The height of the banks of Silver Creek hid him from the light of the burning saloon.

The joke went around that the Admiral went down with his ship.

He had no bullet wound, though he had a gash in his head and his arm was badly burned. The best guess anyone had was that Moe fled the burning building, his arm on fire, and in the darkness, he tripped and went headlong into Silver Creek. They figured he knocked himself unconscious against a rock, and he drowned in the creek. Anyway, that's what it looked like.

- 29 -

When the buffalo soldiers arrived from Fort Bayard, Early turned over all of his prisoners to them.

The major in charge of the column of cavalry was none too happy about the situation. He'd come with the belief that he was going to clear out a nest of highwaymen, and instead he was given the task of transporting a town marshal's prisoners back to the U.S. Marshal in Silver City. A few weeks later, Curtis Suttles, Jack Webb, and Early Bascomb traveled to Silver City for several days to testify in a series of trials. The trials were mostly just a formality, and most of the men from the Three Sweethearts outfit were sentenced to five years in a territorial prison.

A handful of them who scattered during the fight up at the Three Sweethearts camp managed to evade prosecution, but most of the men from the outfit were either in prison or dead. Except for one. One of the men who came through the fight unscathed but in custody decided to turn against the rest.

He testified several times about Admiral Moe and how he'd traipsed the hills up around the Three Sweethearts camp, prospecting for gold without any luck. Then one day a group of three brothers – the Rathbones – tried to hold him up. He didn't have anything – no money, no supplies, hardly even any tools. But he had a plan, a plan formed in the bitter, lonely hours of failure. A plan to hold up gold shipments from prosperous, successful mines in the area, and a way to avoid detection. The Rathbones eagerly joined up, and over a couple of years, they brought in a slew of other outlaws. By posing as a successful mining company themselves, they avoided suspicion, and no one questioned where they got all the gold from.

Through the winter months, Heck and Early maintained peace and order in the little mining camp of Mogollon, mostly by doing not much anything at all.

Inexplicably, after the bloody events up at the Three Sweethearts camp and Admiral Moe's Saloon, the typical fights and drunkenness that one would expect to contend with in a mining town all calmed down, even though Saturday nights were now a bigger affair than they had been. On a Saturday night, even in the cold, the thoroughfare became cramped with people. A body couldn't pass through the Two Forks Saloon, or any of the other saloons, without jostling into folks. The gaming tables became standing-room only, and the theater was so crowded on a Saturday that Early missed the majority of Maybe O'Malley's performances through the winter.

Maybe stayed on, even though she'd intended to winter in Santa Fe.

What happened was that the town gave Heck and Early an increase in wages, of sorts. They still got their twenty dollars a month to be split between them as Early saw fit, but Beatty added to their benefits. It being winter now, and the traffic passing through the camp being lighter, Beatty found himself with spare rooms. So instead of having to share a room, now, Heck had his own and Early had his own – both at the back of the hotel on the second story, across the hall from each other. With Early having his own room, Maybe abandoned her tent and her plans for wintering in Santa Fe, and she moved in with Marshal Bascomb.

In December, a rider came into town having come across a prospector's camp that was disturbed. He said he didn't see a body, but he thought the Apache must've attacked.

Heck and Early rode up in the cold, following the directions the man had given, until they got about six miles from Mogollon where they found the camp. Sure enough, the tent was knocked down, the few personal belongings were scattered, and about twenty yards from the camp, in among the trees, Heck and Early found the bodies of two prospectors. The two men had been split open from navel to neck, their heads bashed in, and their innards strewn about. It was a mess.

The marshal and his deputy buried the bodies and searched for identifying papers so that letters might be sent home to anyone who cared.

Early suspected it wasn't Apache at all. He figured the man who claimed to find the camp had also murdered the men, abused the bodies to make it look like an Indian attack, and then stolen whatever valuables they had when he ransacked the camp. But Early had no way of proving that.

Early in January, right around the turn of the year and just after a good snowfall blanketed the hills around the Silver Creek Gulch, a prospector didn't turn up when his friends expected him. Heck and Early led a search over the course of a week, and they finally found where the man had apparently slipped from a ledge and plummeted thirty feet. He'd broken his legs in the fall and laid there for who knew how long before dying of exposure.

These events marked the highlights of an otherwise dull term as lawmen.

Mostly, Heck and Early patrolled the gaming tables and the saloon floors, and mostly they didn't have anything to do. Both of them gave up toting the shotguns around. Especially through the winter months, strangers weren't turning up in town on a regular basis, and there just didn't seem to be any need for heavy artillery now that the Three Sweethearts outfit was gone.

On one of the first days of spring, things in Mogollon started to change.

Maybe packed her bags and boarded the stagecoach for Silver City. She'd not said a word to him about it prior to packing, and if he'd not come back to the room after breakfast, he wasn't sure she'd have even said goodbye to him.

"If I don't leave now, I might never leave," she said, tears welling in her eyes. "I've dreamed this dream too long to give it up so that I can stay and be a marshal's wife in a mining camp."

Heck and Early carried her trunk and bags down to the stagecoach.

"She didn't want to be married to a marshal in a mining camp," Early told Heck as they watched the coach start down the road for Silver City.

"Huh," Heck said. "I didn't know you'd asked her to marry you."

"Well, that's the thing about it," Early chuckled. "I never did ask her."

Not long after Maybe left, Beatty said the warmer weather necessitated him taking back the room, and Heck and Early found themselves again with only half a bed and bumped up against a bundling board at night.

And then there was the shooting at the Two Forks Saloon.

It happened the same day they got their reward money from the Little Fannie Mine.

**

"Twenty dollars?" Early said, and Heck watched as his face went red.

Jack Webb offered to deliver the reward money authorized by the Little Fannie's ownership back east to save Collier the walk to town.

"I'm to deliver the reward money and the company's gratitude for what you did," Webb chuckled.

"We recovered thousands of dollars' worth of gold," Early said. "We locked up or killed – what was it, Heck? – fifty men. And they gave us twenty dollars as a reward?"

"With thanks," Webb grinned. "Look, marshal. Be glad you got anything. The way the company sees it, you were just doing a job you were hired to do, largely with money paid by the Little Fannie Mining Company. I think they'd make the argument that most of your wages have been the reward."

Early shook his head and sighed heavily.

"It ain't right," Early said.

"It is what it is," Webb said. "I'll leave you to decide how to divide it between the two of you."

Early counted out ten dollar bills and handed them to Heck. Jack Webb left them to complain to each other.

It was a Saturday, and the marshal and his deputy went to the hotel dining room early for their supper, and then they started making their rounds at the saloons. Since Admiral Moe's had burned to the ground, no one had built on the property, but when the weather started to warm up, two new saloons sprang up. Both of them offered faro and card tables.

A couple of hours after dark, Early stood alone at the bar inside the Two Forks Saloon. He was drinking a cup of coffee and watching one of the tables in particular.

Horace Cleveland hadn't been much of a problem through the winter months, but the man never did warm up to Early Bascomb. Whenever he could, he threw a jibe at Early or tried to instigate a drunk into fighting the marshal. Mostly, Early just considered him a nuisance.

But this night, Early watched the table where Ace Cleveland was playing cards, and he noticed that the soiled dove, Alice, was hanging around the table a lot and that Ace was watching her. Alice never did face any kind of jury over shooting Everson. They kept her locked up for a couple of weeks in a hotel room, but after all the bloodshed, no one much had the stomach to hang a whore, so they turned her loose.

Through the winter, Alice took up with Ace Cleveland. Everyone knew it, too.

Now, Early suspected they'd spent the cold weeks working on hand signals.

Early knew the routine – he'd earned his living on the Mississippi River helping a riverboat gambler from Georgia called Hooch Wooten. Hooch was a cheater of the finest quality, and he employed every trick available, from marked cards to hidden cards to stacked decks. Early used to catch a look at the hands dealt out to his opponents, and he and Hooch had an entire alphabet of signals they used to pass information back and forth. They'd come close, a time or two, to getting gutted or lynched for their troubles.

She was pretty woman, Alice, and that didn't change just because she'd shot and killed Everson. Even so, Ace Cleveland kept his eyes on the woman more than he should have. And when Early saw Alice brush her nose with her fingers and wink twice with her left eye, he knew what he was seeing.

A couple of hands later, when things got hot at the table and Ace won a victory with an unlikely bluff, one of the men at the table stood up angrily.

"You're a cheating bastard, Ace Cleveland!" Leighton Sterling shouted.

Early looked around the Two Forks, but Heck had left for one of the other saloons and had not yet returned. Whatever came next, he was going to have to deal with it himself.

"You'll prove it, or you'll take it back, Leighton!" Cleveland said, also standing. As soon as Cleveland stood up, Early saw the pocket gun that Ace had palmed in his hand.

"You boys simmer down," Early said, leaving his coffee at the bar and starting toward the table.

Leighton Sterling kicked his chair away and reached for the six-shooter holstered on his waist.

Early Bascomb cleared leather and thumbed back the hammer on his Colt just as Ace Cleveland flicked the pocket gun forward. The big Colt barked first, and the bullet smashed into Ace's hand. Everyone who witnessed the shooting thought it was both an act of restraint and incredible marksmanship. They all knew that Ace had been a thorn in Early's side, and no one could help but think the marshal would have been in his rights to kill the man. If he'd been honest about it, Early would have been forced to admit he was aiming for Ace Cleveland's chest and simply missed.

"Damnation!" Ace shouted, dropping the gun and grabbing the injured hand and toppling over like he'd been kicked in the gut by a mule.

Leighton Sterling saw his advantage and didn't hesitate to try to take it. He drew his gun and pointed it at Ace, bent over and exposing his back as a plenty big target.

Early rushed forward now, clearing ten feet in an instant, and he swung the barrel of his gun down on the side of Sterling's head, knocking the man senseless. Early snatched up both guns.

Ace lost two fingers at the knuckle, and for the next week told anyone who would listen that he intended to kill Early Bascomb.

But shooting Ace was the last act that Early could stand to commit as a lawman.

"Hector, I used to run that same swindle to support myself when I was a kid on the Mississippi. I've told you about Hooch Wooten?"

"Sure, you have," Heck said. He'd heard a thousand stories about Hooch Wooten and Early's days on the gaming boats on the Mississippi River.

"That was one of our tricks," Early said. "When Hooch was playing, I used to sneak a look at his opponents' cards. I'd walk around the table, stand behind them, and catch a look. Nobody ever knew we were together, and nobody ever suspected a kid. It was easy to do. We had all sorts of hand signals I would use to let him know what kinds of hands his opponents had."

"Well, it's a good swindle, I reckon, if you've got an accomplice," Heck said.

"And now here I am, wearing a badge and shooting a man for cheating at cards."

"You shot him because of that gun in his hand," Heck pointed out. "By the way, everyone I've talked to who saw it – including Captain Beaumont – says you meant to shoot him in the hand. Is that right?"

"Of course it's right," Early said. "I'm not going to kill a man for cheating at cards."

"Huh," Heck grunted.

"But that's not the point I'm driving at, Hector. This isn't the life I'm cut out for, hombre. Being a lawman just don't sit right with me."

"So what do you want to do?" Heck asked. "Quit and

go home? We're hardly better off than when we first came out here."

"We've got the reward money from the Little Fannie," Early said. "And we haven't hardly spent any of our wages. I figure we've probably got close to fifty dollars apiece."

"You do want to quit and go home," Heck said.

Early took a heavy breath.

"You know who'd make a good marshal of this town?" Early said.

"Curtis Suttles," Heck said.

"Yep. I think that's right. Better'n us, anyway."

"Let's go tell Captain Beaumont," Heck said. "We can start for home tomorrow."

Early grinned at him and nodded his head.

"I knew you'd jump at the chance to leave all of this," Early said.

"And how did you know that?"

"I know you, Heck Pinoza," Early said. "Ever since we come up here, you've been hot under the collar about me bein' the marshal and you bein' my deputy."

Heck chuckled at him and tugged on his hat.

"I reckon that's true," Heck said. "Anyway, it's truer than your claim that you shoot Ace Cleveland in the hand on purpose."

the end

309

ABOUT THE AUTHOR

Robert Peecher is the author of more than two score of Western novels. He is former journalist who spent 20 years working as a reporter and editor for daily and weekly newspapers in Georgia.

Together with his wife Jean, he's raised three fine boys and a mess of dogs. An avid outdoorsman who enjoys hiking trails and paddling rivers, Peecher's novels are inspired by a combination of his outdoor adventures, his fascination with American history, and his love of the one truly American genre of novel: The Western.

For more information and to keep up with his latest releases, we would encourage you to visit his website (mooncalfpress.com) and sign up for his twice-monthly e-newsletter.

OTHER NOVELS BY ROBERT PEECHER

THE LODERO WESTERNS: Two six-shooters and a black stallion. When Lodero makes a graveside vow to track down the mystery of his father's disappearance, it sends Lodero and Juan Carlos Baca on an epic quest through the American Southwest. Don't miss this great 4-book series!

THE MOSES CALHOUN MOUNTAIN WESTERNS: In the midst of America's Civil War, the fighting in the mountains of the Northwest is between the white soldiers and the Indian tribes. An independent man with bonds in both worlds, Moses Calhoun finds himself caught between the opposing sides. If he is going to survive, he must rely on his skill in the mountains..

W.F. & Co.: In a rough and lawless time of stagecoach holdups and bank robberies, when there are not enough lawmen to cover the land, Wells Fargo hires private lawmen to investigate crimes against the company and its clients. Calvin Hughes is a gunslinging investigator in Albuquerque, New Mexico Territory.

THROUGH A LAND ACCURST: A piebald horse and a land accurst. A rider sets out through hostile territory into the rough country. Perfect for readers who love gritty Westerns.

FIND THESE AND OTHER NOVELS BY
ROBERT PEECHER AT AMAZON.COM

Made in the USA
Las Vegas, NV
04 January 2025

15820647R00174